Baby Blues

by

Trish Finnegan

Book 3 in the Blue Bird Series

Burning Chair Limited, Trading as Burning Chair Publishing
61 Bridge Street, Kington HR5 3DJ
www.burningchairpublishing.com

By Trish Finnegan
Edited by Simon Finnie and Peter Oxley
Book cover design by Burning Chair Publishing

First published by Burning Chair Publishing, 2023
Copyright © Trish Finnegan, 2023
All rights reserved.

ISBN: 978-1-912946-38-9

Also by Trish Finnegan:

Blue Bird

Blue Sky

Prologue

The heavy curtains were still closed, which made the cluttered bedroom dark. The young policeman slid his hand around the door and flicked on the light before entering. He saw the woman lying still on the bed. No obvious wounds, no signs of a struggle, nor was there any evidence of forced entry anywhere, apart from the front door that he had forced to gain entry. It looked as if her passing had been peaceful.

He checked the bedside cabinet and found some tablets. He recognised them as heart medication because his grandfather took the same. He radioed in his findings and resigned himself to a long wait for the doctor to come to confirm death. He wondered how much the doctor would be paid to turn up and declare the obvious.

'Money for old rope,' the policeman murmured.

He went back onto the landing and looked over the banister down to the hovering neighbour who had called the job in. She had become concerned when she hadn't seen the woman for a few days. She looked up at him, silently asking the question.

'I'm sorry, love. She's up here.'

The neighbour started to cry and went into the front room. Not used to crying women, especially women older than his mother, he went downstairs after her and awkwardly patted her shoulder.

'There, there.' He looked around the dated décor, so like his grandparents' home. 'Do you know if she's been ill?' he asked the neighbour. It would mean that the coroner wouldn't have to bother with an inquest if the doctor had seen her in the last few days.

'Last time I saw her, she mentioned that she had been having bad heartburn, but that's all I know,' the neighbour said.

The policeman remembered being told, in first aid training, that heart attacks often got mistaken for heartburn, especially by older women. That tied in with the heart tablets upstairs. He was confident that this was a straightforward sudden death.

'She slipped away peacefully.'

'Can you be sure of that?'

He spun around and saw a woman with blonde hair. She had a tape recorder hanging from one shoulder and a camera dangling around her neck. She held out a microphone towards him.

'Who are you?' he demanded.

'Press,' she replied. 'Can you be sure this is a natural death? Will the coroner be informed?' Without missing a beat, she moved the mic to the shocked neighbour. 'How do you feel, knowing that your neighbour has been lying dead for days, just a few yards away? Does this make you feel unsafe?'

'Out!' The policeman ordered.

'Can I go upstairs to see the scene?' Without waiting for an answer, the journalist started upstairs, her camera now in her hand.

'Stop. Get down those stairs or I'll have to arrest you.'

The woman turned and photographed the policeman. 'I see the scene has been secured. So, this is a suspicious death.' She began talking into her microphone. 'I have entered the house where the dead woman lies and I have been threatened by the police officer here. It is evident that the police are taking this death very seriously, as I have been forbidden to go up the stairs. Luckily, I have photographs of the house.' She held out the mic as if it were a sword. 'The public have a right to know if there is a suspicious death, officer.'

'Which paper are you from?' the policeman demanded. He

intended to submit a strongly worded complaint about their methods.

'You said it was peaceful,' the distressed neighbour said.

'It was,' the policeman confirmed. He took hold of the blonde woman's arm and propelled her to the door.

'I'm being manhandled from the premises. Police brutality! I shall make a complaint about this,' she shouted into the microphone.

'Knock yourself out.' The policeman slammed the door behind her. 'And I do mean that literally.'

'How did she know about this?' the neighbour asked.

'Good question,' the policeman replied. There was only one way he could think of, and listening in to police communications was illegal. He peered out of the window to see if the woman had gone; instead, he saw her talking to another neighbour. 'What the hell is she doing?' he said to himself. He radioed in and requested another patrol to attend. This woman who claimed to be a journalist needed to be dealt with.

*

A few days later at the premises of *The Town Crier* newspaper, the journalist sat opposite the owner, the editor and a representative from human resources in the editor's office. They were not happy.

'Surely the duty of any investigative journalist is to monitor the police radio. They are not exactly forthcoming on these incidents. How else can we get the information we need? How else can we get to these places before the competition?' she argued.

The owner put his head in his hands. 'You just don't get it, do you?'

'I get that this paper was created to inform the public, to keep them abreast of events and news. The public have a right to know what is happening and I became a journalist to serve the public.' The journalist jutted her chin.

'This isn't the *National Enquirer* or the *News of the World*. You're not an investigative reporter. Your job isn't to speculate, or to try to cause alarm and drama where there is none. I need someone who will report on the facts of even the most mundane local incident,' The editor said. 'I suspect your motives are more about getting yourself known than to report truthfully.'

'This isn't the first complaint we've received about you,' the HR rep said. 'Some of the more memorable ones are the times you took photographs of a councillor inside his own house because you thought he was having an affair. You were lucky he didn't press charges. You tried to interview a mother whose child had been killed by a drunk driver, AT THE HOSPITAL! You then harassed the medical staff and suggested they had not tried hard enough to help the child. You later persuaded the mother to give an interview, which we published in good faith. This triggered an investigation at the hospital, which proved everything was handled as it should have been. We were criticised and circulation dropped.'

The journalist swished her hand. 'How is anyone going to break the big stories if nobody is prepared to dig a little and risk their neck from time to time?'

'There was no *"big story"*. This time, you barged in on an ordinary incident that the police were dealing with. You harassed neighbours. You took photographs of the house. You showed enormous disrespect and were generally unprofessional,' the owner replied.

'I am always professional,' the journalist snapped. 'I was manhandled by a bully, and my complaint about that was dismissed. They just look out for one another.'

'Look, the police are not happy with you and, by extension, the paper. That makes me very unhappy. I have spoken to them and they have agreed not to take further action for listening in to their transmissions,' the owner said.

'Quite right. The policeman overreacted. Calling another patrol like that. They took my camera, you know,' the journalist replied.

'You got it back,' the HR representative pointed out.

'Without the film,' the journalist muttered. 'That makes them thieves as well.'

'Enough of this,' the editor said. 'I can't trust you or anything you write. You're a liability, so we're letting you go.'

The journalist's jaw dropped. 'You're sacking me for doing my job?'

'We're sacking you for misconduct. Good luck for the future.'

The editor and the owner stood up.

'Just you wait until I'm reporting for the BBC,' said the journalist. 'One of the first things I'll do is an exposé of the corruption and unfairness in local media. Then I'm going to do the same about the police.'

'Goodbye,' the owner said. He and the editor left.

'You need to come with me,' the HR woman said, and led the still-protesting journalist out.

Chapter One

I liked sitting by the river. I took another drink from my can and watched a crane unload cargo from a ship on the opposite bank. Despite the industry and ships, it was peaceful, something I didn't experience much of these days.

In the two years since I had joined the Peninsula Police on intake two of 1976, I had experienced more drama than most experienced in a lifetime. Mum still worried about me, but since I had moved into Gary's, my fiancé's, flat, she had eased up a little. Just a little. Dad was working away on the rig so she didn't have him to distract her.

I liked my home station, Wyre Hall, and I considered myself fortunate to have been put on B Block. I had made good friends there, and now we had two new probationers: Charlotte Leader and Andy Broad. It would be interesting to watch them gain experience and become as cynical as the rest of us.

Gary had actually been our inspector when I had first arrived at Wyre Hall. He was on a three year posting in Hong Kong now, part of an anticorruption investigation. He asked me to go with him, but I was only just building my career and I didn't want to abandon that just yet. Time would tell if that was the right decision.

I had worked hard to get to where I was. I had overcome trauma from my teenage years and had just about come to terms with the guilt I felt from surviving that. I had a new bundle of guilt to replace it. I thought that we had managed a recent case badly, which resulted in two unnecessary deaths. On paper, we did everything by the book, but it felt wrong. I hadn't had a say in it but I still felt guilty. I needed cheering up, and who better to do that than my little cousins. I stood up and walked back to my car.

*

They were well hidden, but I could hear them whispering behind the hedge. I pretended I wasn't aware of them and continued walking to the house. Suddenly, a black shape flew towards me and landed at my feet. It was a huge black spider, obviously plastic. Okay then. I played along and threw my hands up in mock horror.

'A spider!' I shouted.

My little cousin, Christopher came out of hiding along with his younger sister, Carly. Both were laughing hard. To an eight and a five year old, this had to be the ultimate prank.

'Were you really scared?' Christopher asked.

'Terrified,' I lied. Actually, even real spiders didn't bother me. A source of frustration among my colleagues, who loved to try to wind me up.

'I told you it would work,' he said to Carly, who nodded in awe of her brother.

I fished two sherbet dips from my bag and handed them out.

'Thanks, Sam,' the children said and rushed into the house.

'Great! Thanks for filling them with sugar,' Beverley, their mother and my first cousin, laughed from the front door.

'Get the kettle on then.' I followed her into the house. We went into the kitchen and I perched on a stool at the breakfast bar. As usual, the place was full of toys; hardly surprising as Bev was a registered childminder. A couple of toddlers played with shape sorters and soft toys. A baby sat in a highchair, loudly complaining that Bev wasn't spooning the food into her mouth fast enough.

I noticed a stuffed frog among the clutter. It resembled the one I had given Christopher a couple of years earlier. 'Is that Steve?'

Bev grinned. 'It is indeed Steve the frog. Christopher outgrew him and Carly wasn't interested, so I added him to the communal toybox.'

When I went to work later, I would have to tell Steve Patton that his namesake was still going strong.

'What's this?' I went over and picked up a box that had been left on the armchair.

'It's an *Ansafone*, one of those modern answering machines. It was Terry's idea; you know what he's like for gadgets.'

I pulled the machine out and scrutinised it. 'I bet this cost a bit.'

'It was a bit expensive, but it's crazy here when I'm busy with this lot, and it gets worse when my own kids come home from school. Terry thought I might be losing business when I don't answer the phone. With that machine, I can pick up any messages and ring them back when it gets quieter. I'm the only registered childminder that has one, so far.'

'Your husband is full of good ideas,' I said.

'It would be a good idea if I could figure out how to get the stupid thing working,' Bev complained.

'Where are the instructions?' I tapped the *Ansafone*.

'That's my other problem,' Bev said. 'I can't find them. I suspect one of these little cherubs has had them and probably shoved them into the bin or something.'

I examined the machine. Three lights, several buttons and a compartment for the small cassette tape: similar to the mini cassettes we used for dictation machines at the station.

'It looks like it plugs into the phone socket and you can set it to come on after so many rings. What's the date? I'll see if I can set it up.'

Beverley laughed. 'I thought if you needed to know the time, you ask a policeman; or woman, in your case.'

'The time I can do, but I lose track of the date. I have to keep looking in my diary,' I said.

'It's Wednesday 22nd of March. Do you need the year?'

'1978. I'm not that far out of it,' I laughed.

I couldn't see how to set the machine to the date, or even if I needed to set the date. There was a little number display, but that could be for just counting the messages.

'I'll go into the hall and see if I can plug it in. Perhaps it'll be clearer then,' I said.

'Not in the hall.' Bev nodded meaningfully at the two children, who were advancing on me. 'Flashing lights, buttons and small children do not mix. Take it to our bedroom. I'll keep it up there when I get it going anyway.'

I went up to Bev's bedroom and knelt beside the phone socket she had had put in beside the bed. Another of Terry's good ideas. No more racing downstairs to answer the phone. I made a mental note to see about getting a bedside phone for myself. I rigged the answering machine in a way that seemed most logical and tried to get it going. A red light came on, but the tape didn't move. Maybe the red light remained on to show it was connected; or perhaps it was charging or something.

'We could do with someone calling to see if it works,' I called down the stairs. With that, the phone rang, and Bev answered it in the hall. I watched the machine, but nothing seemed to move on it. I pressed a few buttons, but again nothing seemed to happen.

I returned downstairs. 'You answered the phone too quickly. I think you need to let it ring out before it turns on. Do you want me to go to the phone box and ring you?'

'Not to worry; I'm no worse off than I was. I'll get Terry to take a look when he comes home,' Bev said. 'I'll get that kettle on, now madam has got a full tum and a clean bum.'

I glanced at the wall clock. I had half an hour before I had leave to get ready for work.

*

At 2:40 pm I made my way to parade, the briefing every block at every police station had before going out on patrol. In the old days, it had been an actual parade and police officers were inspected and marched to their beats. Now, it was more of an assembly, and the only time in the shift that the whole of B Block would be together. Today, the parade would be different; we were going to meet our new inspector. Alan Bowman, our station sergeant, had bridged the gap after Gary left.

As I passed the sergeants' office, on impulse, I put my head around the open door. No sign of Alan Bowman who would normally deal with station business. However, Shaun Lloyd, our patrol sergeant was there. Someone else was sitting over by the key cabinet but I was focused on Shaun.

'Hey, Shaun, any chance of four hours' time off this evening?' I could finish at seven, get myself a takeaway on the way home and settle back into the flat.

Shaun looked up and grinned. 'I think that's okay but I'd better clear it with the Inspector.'

I hadn't paid much attention to the other person there. I looked at him and was surprised to see a familiar face.

'Benno!'

He looked a lot smarter than the last time I'd seen him, when I had worked with him on a previous operation to bring down a porn ring. His hair and moustache were neatly trimmed.

He grinned. 'Hi, Sally.'

'This is Samantha Barrie, sir, not Sally,' Shaun said.

'We've met before, haven't we, Sal,' Benno said.

'We have. We took part in Operation Elstree. You weren't with B Block then,' I said to Shaun. Then I noticed the pips on Benno's shoulders. 'You're our new inspector? While we had been using aliases, I had never been told Benno's real name. Now I knew where the name Benno had come from.

'I am, so be kind. I've seen you in action when someone has pissed you off.'

10

I laughed. 'This is one good egg, Shaun.'

'Glad to hear it,' Shaun said.

'So, how about my four hours off, Benno?' I caught myself. 'I must remember to call you "sir" from now on.'

'I think that's okay,' Benno— Inspector Benjamin—replied.

'Brilliant. Thank you, Be...boss.'

Alan Bowman, the station sergeant, came into the office, carrying the enormous parade book. He was working his last week of shifts before retirement, and he would be missed by everyone.

'All right, Sam,' Alan said. 'Have you met our new inspector?'

'They already know each other,' Shaun said.

'Operation Elstree,' Benno added. *Inspector Benjamin* added. I had to remember his new rank.

Alan knew all about that operation. 'Right, then. Get yourself to the control room. We'll be there shortly.'

'On my way, Sarge.' I hurried to the parade room at the end of the corridor.

The parade room was one of the few rooms in the station large enough to hold a whole block. It was a smelly, dingy, musty place with poster-covered walls that hadn't seen a lick of paint in decades. The high windows hadn't been cleaned since before I had arrived at Wyre Hall and the cobwebs and bird poo were piling up, blocking a lot of light. Sometimes, the caretaker had a go at it with a long-handled broom, but it really needed a good, deep clean. A job that would probably involve scaffolding. The force seemed to have a policy of cleaning the outside of police stations in rotation. It had to be our turn soon.

Ken Ashcroft was already in his seat in the rows arranged behind the large table that the drivers sat at. I took my own seat next to him. I felt the usual little pang when I thought about Steve Patton, who would normally sit on my other side. He was recovering from a bullet in the chest, collected when he had tried to rescue me from a moving light aeroplane. A nice little guilt bundle to add to my pile of guilt bundles. One day, when I felt really strong, I'd sit down and open each parcel on the pile and deal with it. One day…

'All right, Sam?'

'Not bad,' I replied.

'Heard from the boss?' he asked.

'He's settling down I think. He's not the boss any more,' I reminded him. 'We can call him Gary now.'

'Not when he comes back. And with that sort of experience under his belt, he'll be a Chief Inspector in no time.'

'He's planning on going back to the CID when he gets back,' I said. 'He'll be a DI. To start with, anyway.'

'Is Webby leaving?' Ken asked.

I snorted. 'DI Webb will be here forever. No, Gary will have to go to another division when he gets back.'

We both acknowledged Andy Broad, who sat down in Steve's seat on my other side. He was one of our new recruits, but would continue to be referred to as a "sprog" until we got another recruit. I had been the sprog for almost all of my two year probation. I had begun to wonder if I would be the first sprog to be confirmed as a constable, so I was relieved when Andy and Charlotte had arrived, shortly before my probation ended.

Andy was just nineteen and starting to fill out. Puberty had been kind. His lovely, caramel complexion, inherited from his Jamaican mother, was clear and smooth and the skin around his green eyes, inherited from his white, British father, was unlined. I could see the publicity department wanting to use him in recruitment advertising. In fact, I could see any modelling agency wanting him, but he seemed oblivious to his exceptional looks.

'I just met the new Inspector,' Andy said.

'He's a good bloke,' I said. 'I've met him before, during an operation.'

'Did you notice how small his pips are?'

Ken and I exchanged a look. Neither of us was going to ask.

Andy continued. 'They're half the size of the ones Inspector Tyrrell had. If I ever become an inspector, I want pips as big as your fist, that glint in the sun.' He thumped his shoulder to emphasise the point. 'I bet they've switched to a cheaper manufacturers. By the time I get to be an inspector they'll just be embroidered onto an epaulette.'

'I'll let you know when I get there,' Charlotte called from the other side of the room.

'I'm sure you will, Charlie,' Andy replied.

Charlotte glowered at Andy. She hated being called "Charlie", and Andy knew it.

'I don't know how she manages to tune into conversations the way she does,' Andy whispered to me and Ken. 'She must have bionic hearing, or maybe she lipreads.'

I had often thought that lipreading would be a useful skill for a police officer. Maybe there were classes somewhere. I should look into it.

The door opened and we all stood as Alan Bowman led Shaun Lloyd and Inspector Benjamin into the parade room.

'As you were,' the Inspector said.

We all sat and parade began with introductions.

'Gents, and ladies, allow me to introduce our new boss, George Benjamin,' Bert said.

Most of us made friendly noises. A couple of the older ones eyed him suspiciously. They couldn't complain at his lack of service; almost everyone had less service than them.

'I'm glad to be here,' the boss said. 'I expect I'll get a chance to have a chat with each of you over the coming days. Meantime, it's business as usual.'

Having worked with Benno, I thought he'd fit in fine once he found his feet. He wouldn't have the autonomy that he'd had as a detective sergeant working undercover, and I wondered if he'd miss that. As far as I knew, he was unknown to the rest of the block, so the responses to his greeting were muted, but friendly.

Parade got underway. I got my usual beat. The sprogs were

still with their tutor-constables: Phil Torrens—the Mike Two driver, and my old tutor-constable—in Andy's case, and Frank Morton—Mike One's driver—in Charlotte's case. Frank was a bit of a dinosaur with some outdated opinions, so I sometimes wondered how Charlotte would fare with him. I had no worries about Andy; Phil was great and anyone he tutored would do well.

*

After parade, I went to the tiny, glass-partitioned control room to collect my radio and do my test call before going out on patrol. Ray, the radio operator spun around his chair around and handed me a sheet.

'Job just came in on your patch, Sam.' He drew on his ever-present cigarette and blew a stream of smoke towards the brown-stained ceiling. 'Clarence Avenue. Mrs Thompson.'

I scanned the sheet and my stomach fell to my shoes.

Ken read the sheet over my shoulder. '*"Dead baby under a hedge."* Bad luck, Sam.'

Shaun Lloyd came over and peered at the sheet. 'Andy needs the experience, Phil, so you go too.'

'A dead baby!?' Andy gulped.

I recognised his expression. It was the moment reality hit, and you realised that training school truly was in the past and you actually had to go out and deal with more than shoplifters and drunks. Every probationer had had it. Most got over it, some didn't. They didn't last long.

Phil put his hand on Andy's shoulder. He had used that same gesture on me a few times, and I had always found it calming. It told me that he had my back, and I would not have to face whatever the problem was on my own.

Derek Kidd, the other operator, put down the phone. 'Boss informed and on his way. CID also informed.'

Benno—Inspector Benjamin—came into the control room.

14

'When did this come in?'

I checked the time on the sheet. 'Four minutes ago, sir.'

'Just assess the situation to start with. If there really is a baby there, call it in and secure the scene,' he said. The inspector turned to Derek. 'Ring CID and give them the heads-up.'

That was par for the course. If this really was a dead baby, the CID would need to be informed and a detective—a "jack"—would have to attend, along with SOCO—the Scenes Of Crime Officer—who would photograph the site and gather up evidence.

'Already done, sir,' Derek said.

Derek might be a pain in the neck sometimes, but he knew his job.

'Come on, Sam,' Phil said. 'Let's get this over with.' He led Andy and me into the yard.

Chapter Two

Andy sat in the back of the panda car and I took the front passenger seat. Travelling out with Phil felt familiar and comforting. He had been my rock during my turbulent first year and slightly less turbulent second year. I still went to him if I needed guidance.

'This must have been a terrible shock for the caller,' I said as we drove.

'Yeah. Not the sort of thing you expect to find under your privet.' Phil turned into Clarence Avenue, a pleasant road of larger mid-war semis. All the roads in this area had been named after royal residences: Buckingham, Sandringham, et cetera. It still held an air of elegance, despite the encroaching '60s-built council estate.

I looked over my shoulder to speak to Andy. 'Did they teach you the tongue pressing trick at training school?'

He shook his head. 'What's that?'

'If you feel close to tears, as can happen with some jobs, press your tongue as hard as you can against the roof of your mouth. It stems the tears somehow,' I said.

'Better still, suck your tongue a little at the same time,' Phil added. 'And make sure you keep your lips closed or you'll look like you're snarling.'

Andy's mouth moved as he practised the manoeuvre.

'That'll be Mrs Thompson.' Phil pointed to a plump lady of indeterminate age who was waving frantically in our direction.

'Oh, It's Terry's mum,' I said.

'Who's Terry?' Andy asked.

'My cousin Beverley's husband. His mum's a nice woman and quite sensible. I've only met her when they married and at the kids' christenings. I didn't know she lived here.'

Phil pulled up and we got out.

'Thank goodness you're here. Quickly, come and look.' Mrs Thompson grabbed my arm and pulled me into her front garden. 'I was doing some weeding and I saw it. Poor little thing couldn't have been here long.' She dabbed a tissue against her eyes. I anticipated I would have to use the tongue pressing trick; Mrs Thompson was already upset, and a blubbing cop was the last thing anyone wanted to see.

'Don't you worry, let us deal with this,' I said and gently but firmly guided her towards the house. 'You've had a shock. Why don't you put the kettle on and make yourself a nice hot drink with lots of sugar?'

She must have known I was trying to get her out of the way, but she nodded and went inside.

Phil, Andy and I got onto our knees and peered under the hedge. There was the usual detritus that you got in hedges: dead leaves, an old nest, sweet wrappers from passing children. Then I saw it lying there; tiny arms pulled in and matchstick legs pulled up towards its oversized head.

I straightened up and took a deep breath to calm myself. 'Here! It's not full term; it's only about six inches long. How far along is that?'

Phil wiped his top lip. 'About four or five months, I think. Hellfire, if someone has miscarried, they should see a doctor. Why dump it here though?'

Andy remained at the far end of the hedge, looking on with trepidation while Phil crawled over to me and looked under the hedge. He reached in and pulled the baby out and held it towards me.

I recoiled. 'Phil!'

'We're supposed to secure the scene,' Andy said.

'Relax! It's a rubber alien doll. They're all the rage; my oldest girl has one.'

Andy edged towards us. 'It looks real. No wonder poor Mrs Thompson freaked out.'

I turned and saw Mrs Thompson standing on the doorstep watching us. I waved her over. 'There's nothing to worry about; it's just a toy.'

She scuttled over and put her hands over her cheeks. 'Oh no. I feel such a fool.'

She wasn't the only one.

Phil heaved himself to his feet and dusted off his knees. 'Don't worry, Mrs Thompson, you did exactly the right thing ringing us. It is quite lifelike. Both the young 'uns here thought it was real when they saw it.'

Now she was calmer, Mrs Thompson peered at me. 'You look familiar.'

'I'm Samantha: Beverley's cousin, Mrs Thompson.'

'Oh, of course. Samantha Barrie. I haven't seen you since Carly's christening. I'd forgotten you'd joined the police.' She patted her glowing cheeks. 'Please don't tell Beverley I've been so silly.'

'Mike Two. From Mike Sierra One, do you have an update?' Ray's voice crackled over the radio. The fact that Ray referred to the boss by his call sign indicated that he was on patrol and probably on his way over to our location; likely with Shaun, our patrol sergeant. Neighbours were already peering from their windows, another police car turning up would whip them to a frenzy of curiosity. Not what Mrs Thompson needed.

'4912, it's just a toy. All in order. False call, good intent,' I transmitted. It was important to log that the call was made with good intent. Mistakes happened, and we needed to make sure that those callers would not be afraid to call us again. 'Do you want me to remain with Mike Two?' I asked.

After a few seconds, Ray transmitted, 'Negative. Patrol as normal.'

'Roger.'

Phil held the doll out to Mrs Thompson, who stepped backwards. 'No, no. Throw it away, I don't want to touch it.'

Phil put the doll into his pocket. 'All right. Take care now, and don't hesitate to call us if you need us again.'

'Thank you. Nice to see you again, Sam. Call in for a cup of tea if you're passing, all of you.' Mrs Thompson waved as we went back to the car.

I would take her up on that; not today, but in the future. It was always nice to have somewhere to stop off for a cuppa.

'What are you going to do with that thing?' I asked Phil.

'I'll clean it up and give it to my youngest girl. She's been jealous of her sister.'

I chuckled. 'I'll leave you and your new friend to get acquainted.'

'Roger that, ma'am,' Phil joked.

Phil and Andy drove off, and I wandered over towards the park. Ray sent Mike Two to check out some nuisance youths. Andy would be relieved, but he needed to get some more serious jobs in before he went solo. If he had to be held back a couple of weeks to get his jobs in and Charlotte didn't, he'd never hear the last of it.

I walked up Sandringham Boulevard and down Kensington Road towards the park. I was getting to know people and building memories in this area now; not all of them good. I paused in Kensington Road. A *"For Sale"* sign had appeared in the garden of number ten. I wondered who had organised the sale and where the proceeds of the sale would go, as the former residents were dead and had no family. It wasn't my business. I walked on.

*

I didn't go for first refs as I was knocking off at seven. Instead, I worked through then stopped off at Chiu's chip shop on my way home. It was close to the station, and a favourite with B Block.

I pushed open the door and stood in line. Even though I was wearing my civvy coat and no tie, the black tights and flat, black lace up shoes were a giveaway and I got some looks from the other customers. Nobody said anything, for which I was grateful. I was off duty and just wanted to buy my evening meal.

'Hello!' Eric Chiu, the owner, was a wiry man just a little older than me. He always sounded pleased to see his customers. Since his living depended on them, he probably was.

'Hello, Eric. Can I have a sweet and sour chicken with chips please.'

He scribbled my order onto a sheet and passed it to an older Chinese woman, who was supervising the frying. No sign of Cathy, his wife and business partner. She had recently had a baby.

'How is Cathy?' I asked.

Eric said, 'She is recovering. My mother is helping me until Cathy can return.'

I smiled and nodded at the older woman. She stared back. Okay then. She scratched her cheek and turned away from me. I noticed her arms were marked with old scars. Perhaps that was to be expected if she was used to working in kitchens.

'What did you name the baby?' I asked. Last time we had spoken, they couldn't decide on a name.

'We named her Rose.'

'That's a lovely name,' I said.

Eric leant forward and dropped his voice. 'We saw it in a book. English Rose. Also the flower of Peking is the China Rose. My mother comes from Peking so it seemed fitting, but she doesn't really like it.'

'How is little Rose?' I asked.

Eric's smile slipped a little. 'I don't know. She looks different. A doctor said she is Mongol. We are seeing another doctor soon,'

Downs Syndrome was fairly common and I knew that many afflicted children lived mostly normal, if shortened lives. I also knew of such children so severely affected that they could barely function.

'I hope the other doctor will have good news for you,' I said. I also hoped he would use a more enlightened term than *"Mongol"*.

'Thank you,' said Eric. He turned to the customer behind me and beamed. 'Hello!'

I stepped to one side to wait for my food.

*

Back at the flat, I changed into my jeans and a loose t-shirt. I sat at the table overlooking the sea and forked pink, sticky chicken into my mouth. It was a bit blowy outside, and white topped waves slapped against the sea wall. I had been alone in the flat many times, but never had the emptiness been so total. Gary would not be walking in at any moment, and I would be going to bed alone and waking up alone. I wished that I had had a letter from Gary, but he had warned me before he left that the post from Hong Kong was patchy at best.

I gathered the rubbish from my meal and took it to the rubbish chute. Each floor had an access hatch to the rubbish chute that ran from top to bottom of the building. All the rubbish landed in a large metal dumpster bin on the ground floor.

My thoughts turned to Eric and Cathy Chiu. They had adopted their first names when they came to England. The health certificates on display in the chippy gave the names Eric Chiu Yang Bao and Cathy Chiu Li Na. I didn't properly understand the Chinese naming system. I knew the family name came first, which would make Eric's Chinese name: Chiu Yang Bao, and Cathy's: Chiu Li Na. I didn't know if that was coincidence or if a woman normally took her husband's family name, and I really didn't understand why they had taken English names when they had perfectly good names already. Gary was still Gary even though he was in Hong Kong. Maybe they felt they had had to do that to fit in.

I didn't want to go back to the quiet in the flat yet; a walk along the prom would perk me up. I nipped back to the flat and put on my coat, then went downstairs and stepped outside. It was dark but not too cold. I could see the lights of the amusement arcade and a small fairground in the distance. I would walk there and maybe buy a freshly cooked, sugary doughnut. Despite having just finished my meal, my mouth watered in anticipation.

I had only just stepped outside when a woman called across from a house opposite the flats and strode towards me with purpose.

'You're a policewoman,' she said. It wasn't a question.

I hated anyone recognising me as a police officer when I was off duty. 'Can I help you?'

The woman pointed to a car parked on the road. 'That car.'

I looked across the road to the Ford Escort. 'What's wrong with it?'

'You need to get it moved.'

'It's not my car,' I said.

'I know that. You need to find who owns it and tell them to move it.'

There were no yellow lines or dropped kerb or parking restrictions, and there were no double markings in the centre of the road. Her path was not blocked and the registration did not ring any bells. Perhaps I was missing something. I went to the car and looked at the tax disc. It was good for another four months and the registration number matched the plates. A quick glance confirmed it wasn't parked over a hydrant. I couldn't see any problem with the car.

'There is no reason to move the car. It's parked properly, it's not causing an obstruction and it's taxed.'

The woman shifted her weight to one foot and folded her arms. 'It's outside my house.'

'Do you own the road outside your house?' I asked. I knew what the answer would be, but I smelt a complaint brewing so I asked anyway, just to be certain I had covered all bases.

'What do you mean?' she said.

'Unless you pay rent for or have bought the lease on the piece of road outside your house, it is not for your sole use. This is a public road and as such the public can use it.'

'They can't park outside my house!'

'Look, no one has the right to a patch of road on a public highway, even if it's right outside their house; unless they have paid for it, or it's medically necessary. Then the council will mark it off to prevent other road users parking there. It is annoying but that's the way it is. Good evening to you.' I began to walk towards my hot doughnut, but the woman followed me like an annoying, yappy chihuahua.

'It might not be insured; it wouldn't be allowed to park if it wasn't insured.'

'It shouldn't be on the road if it isn't insured,' I agreed. 'However it is taxed and as you need to show the insurance to get a tax disc, it is reasonable to assume it is insured.'

'It might be stolen.'

I paused 'Perhaps, or it could be someone visiting somebody around here. You will have to ring the control room so they can do a check on the number. I'm off duty so I can't do that here.'

'I'll do that. I'll ring and tell them there's a stolen car outside my house and you refused to do anything about it,' she said. 'It would be a different matter if it was outside your flats, wouldn't it? You would call your mates and they would be here with blue lights to move it. Bloody coppers: never help where it's needed.'

Oh yes, definitely a complaint coming in. I doubted it would go far though.

'That would be a different matter because The Crags has a private car park that residents pay for. I'm sorry I'm not telling you what you want to hear, but that's how it is. There's nothing I can do here.'

The woman stormed off into a house opposite the flats. I shook my head; there was no telling some people. I resumed my quest for a doughnut.

It was a pleasant walk to the arcade. I got my doughnut, and another for later back at the flat. I watched the rides at the fairground, which always looked better at night with the coloured lights, and then strolled along the seafront back to the flat.

I turned into our road and pulled up sharp at the sight before me. The car that had annoyed the yappy chihuahua woman had gone, but her own car was no longer on her driveway. It was parked across the entrance to our car park. Nothing could get in, or out. Now I would have to take action, and I just knew it wouldn't go well. I considered ringing the local police to report an obstruction, but I didn't want to antagonise the neighbours so I would deal with this myself. I strode up the path and knocked loudly on the door. Eventually, the annoying, yappy chihuahua woman opened it and smirked at me. She knew why I was there but wanted to play.

'Is that your car?' I asked, knowing full well it was her car.

'Why, yes it is,' she replied.

'Would you mind moving it?' I asked.

She eyed the greasy doughnut bag I was holding. 'Oh, but my car is taxed and insured and I am parked on a public road. So no, I don't want to move it,' she said.

I sighed. 'It is right across the car park entrance. You've blocked it for everyone in the flats and, as I explained earlier, it's a private car park and we residents pay for the privilege of parking there. That is an obstruction.' As if to prove my point, a car tried to get into the car park but had to move up the road.

'So?' she countered.

My patience snapped. 'So, if you don't move it, I will ring my mates who will send a truck to tow it away. Then they will send the bill for removal and storage to you.'

'Send them. I won't pay.'

'Then they will dispose of the car and send you the bill for that too and, if you don't pay up, they'll send in the bailiffs. You have ten minutes then I pick up the phone.' Smiling brightly at the incandescent woman, I walked back down her path.

'It's eating greasy rubbish that's made you so fat,' she called after me.

I suppressed the urge to raise two fingers at her. Just as well, because when I turned back she had a Polaroid instamatic pointed at me. Devious cow, trying to provoke a reaction to get grounds for a complaint. I smiled for the camera but inside I was fuming. Did she keep the damned thing next to the front door?

'Just for the record, my weight is within normal parameters,' I said to her and walked through her gate with my head held high.

'Is that your car?' the blocked driver called to me.

'No, sorry.' I gestured over my shoulder with my thumb. 'This is the woman you need but she's refusing to move it,'

'Bitch!' shouted the annoying chihuahua woman.

'Shift your damned car right now!' shouted the blocked out driver.

I didn't hear her response.

I returned to the flat and put my doughnut on a plate. My hands shook quite a bit. I had noticed that happening recently, especially after confrontations.

Fifteen minutes later, when I looked, chihuahua woman's car was back on her path. I mentally shrugged. It was probably adrenaline from the row downstairs. Gary had noticed "my nerves", as he termed it. and had questioned whether he should leave for Hong Kong at all; but I had reassured him that I was fine and a few days with my mum was all I needed.

I would run a check on her tomorrow; if she was going to engineer complaints, she deserved a card in the system as a warning for those who would visit her in the future.

Chapter Three

I arrived at work early next day to check out the neighbour before parade started. I didn't know her name, so went into the report writing room, rang the collator at Odinsby—the division that covered our road—and asked what he had on the address.

It turned out that her name was Tracey Quinn and she was a frequent caller: mostly rubbish jobs complaining about her neighbours. A couple of calls from her neighbours complaining that she had been peering through a gap in the fence and shouting at their children as they played in their own garden. I was glad I didn't live closer to her.

Interestingly, I was not the only police officer she had tried to set up, although I was the only one who had been off duty. Her technique was to start off in a reasonable manner then, if she could not get her own way, she would provoke a negative reaction and use that as the grounds for complaint. Not a criminal act, but still time consuming for the boss and worrying for the officer concerned. I thought it was time someone advised her about her conduct, but it was not my division and therefore not my place. I briefly updated the collator about the incident the previous night, making sure I mentioned the camera that was probably stored next to the front door, and he promised to add it to the card.

'Someone trying it on?' Trevor, the Mike Three driver, asked from the doorway. I bit back my instinctive jibe about him creeping around eavesdropping. I was feeling a bit on edge, which I attributed to the incident the previous night.

'Tried and failed,' I said. 'Did you overhear what happened?'

'Yeah, I'd have told her to knob right off.'

'Then you'd have had a complaint,' I said.

'So might you, yet. People like that don't let the truth get in the way of a good complaint,' Trevor said. 'Anyway, it's ten to. Don't forget it's Alan's last parade. Are you going for the drink after work?'

'I wouldn't miss that.' I picked up my bag and walked with Trevor to the parade room. I would miss Alan—we all would—but I had been told that Bert Mason, his replacement, was a decent bloke.

Ken barely acknowledged me when I sat next to him.

'All right, Ken?' I asked.

'Yeah, not bad.' He was evidently distracted and not in the mood to chat.

'What's up with Ken?' Andy whispered from my other side.

'Not sure,' I replied.

The door opened and Alan came in followed by Inspector Benjamin and Sergeant Lloyd. Everyone gave a cheer and he bowed.

'Thank you everyone, but I don't want a big fuss.'

We settled down and parade continued.

*

About five, Ray sent me to a *"Youths Causing Annoyance"* job in Devon Road. *YCA* was the cover all term for incidents ranging from kids playing football in the street to teenagers rampaging through gardens. Mr Paxton was a regular caller and his complaints centred on the playing field behind his house.

To save time, I walked past the playing field where children were playing on the swings and roundabout. They seemed to be having a good time. A couple more children played a game of frisbee on the grassed area. None of them were over ten; nothing rowdy happening here. Devon Road was also quiet when I arrived. I knocked on the door of number fifteen.

'Mr Paxton.'

'Do something about those children on the field.'

And hello to you too, I thought. 'What is the problem?' I asked.

Mr Paxton dipped his head irritably. 'They are too noisy and they are there every night,' he said.

'What are they doing?' I asked.

'Playing with one of those frisbee things,' he replied. 'If you go now instead of asking me damned stupid questions, you'll catch them.'

'Catch them doing what, Mr Paxton? It is a playing field. Children go there to play.'

'I want you to move them.'

My patience had been thin at the best of times recently and I felt it snap now, but still I tried to keep a lid on it. I was aware that my heart had started to race, and I gripped the strap of my handbag to stop my hands shaking.

'Would you prefer them to play on the street and kick a football at the windows?'

'Of course not, stupid woman. But neither do I want them screaming and shouting behind my house.'

I bit back a sharp retort. I deliberately kept my voice calm and said, 'Are they throwing things into your garden?'

'No, why?'

'I might have gone to ask them to move away and be more careful. But no, Mr Paxton I will not remove children from a playing field. A space specifically reserved for them to play on.' I cocked my head to listen out for the noise. 'They are not being unreasonably noisy in my opinion. In fact, I walked past the field on my way here and I saw children having fun and not being the least bit rowdy.'

Mr Paxton visibly shook as he looked at me, chewing his lip in annoyance. He evidently was not used to being denied.

'When I rang last night, police came and moved drunken teenagers from that copse at the end of the field,' he barked.

That was a bit of a problem area. The local teenagers gathered in the copse to smoke Lord knows what, and to drink alcohol. They could get very rowdy.

'That's different,' I said. 'These aren't drunken teenagers. These are young children, playing on a playing field. Please tell me if I am wrong.' I gripped the strap of my handbag even harder as I watched Mr Paxton trying to process this information. He almost hopped from foot to foot in frustration.

'I am going to report you for neglect of duty.' His voice shook with suppressed rage. 'A constable is supposed to work for the community. You are lickspittle.'

That did it; the lid came off. 'The community, yes; an intolerant little despot like you, no. I will not move children who are playing where they should be, and I will be submitting a report about your unreasonable demands. If you hate children so much, why did you buy a house by a playground?' I turned and walked away from the stuttering man. I knew I had earned myself a complaint but I was too annoyed to care. I updated the control room, adding a personal opinion or two, and resumed patrol carrying on a mental chunnering about the Mr Paxtons of the world. I shouldn't allow my feelings to show as I did, but I was only human and I had a short fuse at the moment.

I was still brooding when Ray called me on the radio. He was crackly, which was not unusual in a built up area.

'Can you make seven Sunderland Place? Sudden death.'

'Roger. Do we have any details?'

'…seventy. Doctor informed and en route.'

'Roger.' I had missed most of the message, but I got that the deceased was seventy and the doctor was attending to confirm life extinct. That would do for now; I could sort out the rest when I got there.

I walked quickly towards the address, a short road of bow-fronted, terraced houses. I heard control inform the patrol sergeant and Inspector. That was normal; the sergeant would attend and would only ask the inspector to attend if there was a problem. Although a doctor was required to confirm life extinct, they could not issue a death certificate giving the cause of death if they had not recently seen the patient. The coroner had to be informed, and that was our job.

I arrived at the house and tapped on the open door. I was surprised when a red-eyed Eric Chiu answered; I had assumed they lived close to the chip shop. I guessed it was his mother who had passed away, although she had looked well enough when I had seen her and a good deal younger than seventy. I pushed aside all thoughts about Mr Paxton.

'Hello, Eric. I got a call to attend here,' I said. Obviously, I'd had a call but I had to open the conversation somehow.

The distraught man nodded and beckoned me to come in. I stepped inside the tidy hallway and looked around.

'She's in here,' Eric said, his voice cracking.

I followed him into the back room. Like in so many houses, they kept the front room free and lived in the rear room with a tiny kitchen off it.

Cathy sat weeping in a fireside chair, nursing the baby who was wrapped in a pink blanket. 'Please don't take her yet; let me hold her longer,' she pleaded.

Eric's mother came in from the kitchen and stared at me.

Realisation dawned. I blinked back the tears that welled in my eyes and knelt in front of Cathy.

'What happened?' I asked.

Eric pointed to a cot in the corner of the room. 'Rose fell asleep in her cot. I went into the back and Cathy washed up dishes in the kitchen while my mother watched Rose. When Cathy came back in about twenty minutes later, Rose was still asleep and so was my mother. Cathy made us a drink and brought mine out and we chatted for a short time then she went back inside. I heard her scream and I rushed in. Rose was dead.'

A noise at the doorway drew my attention. 'That's probably the doctor.'

Eric brought the doctor into the room. It was getting crowded so I moved away to allow him to see the child. I stood by the doorway and turned away from the tragic scene. Sergeant Lloyd came in through the open front door; I went down the hall to fill him in on the details.

'Are you okay, Sam? You look pale and you're shaking.'

I hadn't been aware of that. 'I'm okay, Sarge. I just didn't realise it was a cot death until I got here. I thought Ray said seventy. The transmission was breaking up. He must have said seven weeks.'

'What's their English like?' he whispered.

'Good, but Cathy misses some words if you speak too quickly. I don't know about the grandmother, I haven't heard her speak,' I replied.

We went into the back room. The doctor straightened up and pursed his lips to let us know what we already knew.

'Right then, we'll have to let the coroner know,' said Shaun. 'Mr and Mrs Chiu, your baby has to go to the mortuary so the cause of death can be established in a post-mortem examination. Don't worry; it's standard procedure in cases like this.'

Cathy clutched baby Rose to her. 'No!'

Eric held out his arms and spoke in their own language. Rose half turned away from him.

Eric's mother barked a few words then marched over to Cathy, pulled Rose from her arms and thrust her into mine. Automatically, I held the child close to me. I looked down at the tiny face, so peaceful she could have been sleeping. Rose did have the features of Down's syndrome but they were not severe and sort of blended into the normal newborn features. I could see how Eric was confused about her condition.

Cathy howled, leapt to her feet and snatched the baby back from me. Eric wrapped his arms around the mother and child and both wept big, loud, wet sobs. Grandmother stood to one side watching them, dry-eyed. The whole sequence must have only lasted a few seconds but I knew this was a memory I would carry for all my life. My tongue started to go numb because I was pressing it so hard and so long against the roof of my mouth.

After a couple of minutes, Cathy wiped a hand across her eyes and allowed Eric to take Rose. He kissed the baby's head then held her out to the doctor.

The doctor gently shook his head. 'You can keep hold of her until the undertaker gets here.'

Meanwhile, Cathy stared at the grandmother. There followed a quickfire exchange between them that I couldn't understand. Eric snapped something at them and both quietened down.

'What was that, Eric?' I asked.

'Everyone is upset,' he replied.

'Understandable. What is your mother's name?' I asked.

'Yang Hui Ping,' he replied. 'Why do you need to know that?'

'I need to put the names of everyone present in my report,' I answered. Remembering the family name came first, I asked, 'Is that okay Mrs Yang?'

'My mother doesn't speak English. I will explain to her,' Eric said.

Fair enough. I didn't need to speak to Mrs Yang at that point.

'What language do you speak, Eric?' I asked. 'Is it Mandarin?' I had once read somewhere that there were many dialects and languages in China and surrounding areas, but Mandarin was used everywhere.

'We do speak Mandarin, but we use Cantonese normally. Most people from Hong Kong do.'

And he was fluent in English. Three languages. I was impressed. It put my school French to shame.

The undertaker arrived. He was a sympathetic and professional man, well suited to his work. He carefully took Rose from her distraught parents. I followed him to the mortuary to complete the paperwork while the doctor tended to Eric and Cathy.

*

At the mortuary, I gently undressed baby Rose and with shaking hands, placed her clothing into property bags. Her parents could have them back once the coroner had released the body, if they wanted them back, not everyone did. Shaun and I worked in silence, logging each item, even the nappy. The mortuary attendant remained quietly in the background.

I wanted to weep at the injustice of a tiny baby in these surroundings, but I mentally removed myself from the situation and made heavy use of the tongue pressing trick while I concentrated on the requirements of the job. It didn't matter how much training anyone had, nobody could deal with this situation and not be upset. Even Shaun's eyes glistened. With a normal sudden death, we might have made use of the famous police dark humour. We wouldn't have been callous, but often it was a case of having to laugh or you'd cry and if you ever started to cry, you'd never stop. Here, neither of us felt inclined to speak much.

'Is it worth noting that the nappy isn't very wet?' I asked. 'I mean, it could just be that she had had her nappy changed a short time previously.'

'Note everything,' Shaun replied. 'Even if it isn't useful to the coroner, it's better to have too much information than too little.'

I jotted a note on the property card.

I lifted Rose to pull the nappy from underneath her when something caught my eye.

'Is that a bruise?' I said to Shaun.

He came to the other side of the trolley and rolled the child towards me. 'Looks like it.'

'It's a fair size. How could a child this young collect a bruise like that?' It was almost half the width of Rose's back.

Shaun and I looked at each other. I didn't want to believe what we were both thinking. I didn't want to believe that Eric or Cathy would harm Rose. There had to be another explanation.

'Could this be a birthmark or something?' I suggested, although I had never seen a birthmark like that.

'We need the boss and the jacks,' Shaun said.

The mortuary attendant stepped forward. 'Problem?'

Shaun pointed to the baby's back.

The mortuary attendant peered closely. 'I'm sure I've seen something like that before. It's got a name but I can't remember what. I'll leave a note for the doctor; he'll know.'

'Even so, we need to be sure.' Shaun gently replaced the baby onto her back then went outside to radio the results to the control room.

I stayed beside Rose and whispered to her. 'We will find out what happened, sweetheart.' I stroked her little head, which was already feeling cool, and pulled a sheet across her. I didn't try to stop the pent-up tear that escaped and ran onto my cheek.

Chapter Four

Once the CID had been informed of the bruise on Rose, I was surplus to requirements. So I returned to the station and spent an hour completing the sudden death form, also a statement for the file the CID would be compiling when and if they investigated Rose's death.

I dropped the form into the submissions drawer, and was about to resume patrol when Alan came out of the sergeants' office.

'I thought I heard you. I want you to work the front desk till knocking off time.'

'I'm okay to go out again, Sarge,' I said.

Alan folded his arms. 'Maybe you are, but I want you to work the desk.'

'Yes, Sarge,' I said and turned away.

'Don't take this home, lass.'

I turned back. 'Sarge?'

'We get to see the rough side of life and it's easy to let pent up feelings out on those at home. Try to leave work in work.'

'Wilco,' I said. I must have looked worse than I thought, although I appreciated his attempt at comfort.

A woman came in. Alan returned to his office and I went to the desk.

'Can I help you?'

The woman broke down and recited a tale of how her dog had slipped the lead and had run off. I made sympathetic noises as I took details, but I wanted to shake the weeping woman by the shoulders and shout, 'A seven week old baby is lying in a cold mortuary!'

Instead, I promised to ring if the dog turned up.

When she left, I sat at the desk, closed my eyes and let my head fall backwards. I had so little patience anymore. Everything irritated me, when normally I would easily cope and move on to the next thing.

I opened my eyes and saw Ray, the radio operator puffing on a cigarette as he watched me from the door of the control room.

'All right, Ray.'

He came over and I saw Derek move smoothly to cover the radio in Ray's place.

'The question is, are you?' Ray said as he stubbed his cigarette out in the metal ashtray on the counter.

'Oh, I'm fine,' I said.

'No you're not. I've noticed you've been a bit edgy recently. You sounded quite sharp on the radio after that YCA, and you clenched your jaw so hard as you spoke to that woman, you practically spat sparks. We've had a phone call from Mr Paxton moaning about you. I also heard that a complaint came in about you from when you were off duty. Want to talk?'

'Nothing to talk about,' I said.

'No? Not about your friend being seriously injured and your abduction and near murder not very long ago. Or about your fiancé working abroad? Not about anything from your past? Not about a dead baby?'

I glared at Ray. 'No! I don't want to talk about any of it. The off duty thing is a load of rubbish from a vindictive cow about a legally parked car. Mr Paxton is a whinger.'

'Nothing is happening about the neighbour and I doubt that anything will come of Mr Paxton's moaning,' Ray said. 'But it's not good to keep things bottled up. If you don't want to talk to me, how about that counsellor you were seeing?'

'Only a few people know about that,' I hissed. 'I want to keep it that way. People will think I'm a complete nutcase.'

Ray sat opposite me and leant on his elbows. 'In 1966, I had a nervous breakdown. I was off work for three months and took tablets for over a year. My doctor told the bosses that it was caused by the stress of my job, and I went along with that. Actually, it was caused by not being able to be myself. I couldn't tell anyone I prefer men and was actually in a relationship, which I still am, because it was illegal then. Things were legalised the following year, but the damage was done and even now, we don't come to work functions together because the need to be discreet, even secretive, is still strong.'

I knew Ray was homosexual and I had never had a problem with it. 'You shouldn't have to hide away.'

'No, but that's the way it is. When I came back to work the bosses were kind and tried to help my situation, without knowing what my situation really was. I accepted a role in the control room to "reduce my stress" and here I am still, although I would argue that the control room is also stressful.'

'You had a good reason to be stressed. I don't,' I said.

Ray slapped one of his large hands on the table. 'You have excellent reasons to be stressed. Apart from your personal life, this whole job is stressful. But my point is, I had nobody to talk to: you do.'

'Thanks, Ray.'

'You look terrible. I think you need to take some leave before you burn out,' Ray said.

'Not after all the sick leave I had to take in the last year. We've got a couple of rest days from tomorrow. I'll make sure I rest.' I gulped. 'Thanks for caring, Ray.'

Ray smiled. 'Your sickness has almost always been because of some injury you collected on duty, not because you were scowing. Think about it, Sam. We all get stressed sometimes, and bad sickness record or not, you are entitled to take your leave.' He returned to the control room.

Maybe Ray was right and I did need some time away, proper leave, not just time to recover from some injury. I'd put in a leave request before knocking-off time. I'd also visit Steve and reassure myself that he continued to get better, and I'd avoid my annoying neighbour.

The front door crashed back and Cathy Chiu ran into the front office, closely followed by Eric speaking urgently to her in their own language.

I stood up. 'You should be at home, Cathy.'

She pushed Eric aside and ran to the desk. 'My baby was murdered. My mother-in-law hates her. She killed my baby.'

Eric also came to the desk. 'My wife is mad with grief; she doesn't know what she's saying,'

'I do!' Cathy shouted, followed by a volley of what I now knew to be Cantonese.

'Please, both of you, sit down. I need to ask someone to come and speak to you,' I implored.

Eric tried to take Cathy's arm, but she shrugged him off and plonked herself onto a plastic chair. Eric watched her for a moment, then sat a few seats away.

Derek looked out of the control room. 'Everything okay?'

'Derek, can you ask one of the jacks to come down. The parents of that baby death I had earlier are here, and the mother is alleging that the grandmother killed the child.' I dropped my voice and sidled closer. 'The child did have a huge bruise on her back.'

'Eamon and Mike have picked that job up,' Ray called from the radio.

Derek rang upstairs and asked for Mike Finlay. He quickly explained the situation and replaced the handset. 'He's on his way.'

'Tell the boss and Alan too, just to keep them in the loop,' Ray said.

I heard Eric and Cathy shouting and returned to the desk. 'Please stop shouting, you're disturbing the whole station,' I said. 'DS Finlay is coming to see you in a few minutes.' As I spoke, the door at the side of the waiting area opened and Mike Finlay came in.

'Mr and Mrs Chiu, I believe you want to talk to me,' he said.

'No.' Eric pointed at his forehead. 'My wife is mad. She has not been right since Rose was born. You cannot believe her.'

Mike turned to me. 'Sam, I need a female to sit in. Can you tell Alan you need to leave the desk?'

Alan came out of the sergeants' office. 'No need, I heard.' He went across the front office to the control room. 'Will you be okay to see to the desk while the lass sits in with Mike?'

'No problem, Alan. If it gets busy, I'll ask one of the other foot patrols to come in,' Derek said.

'Actually, Alan, that's something we need to talk about. We haven't had anyone covering the desk permanently for months. We have to keep borrowing foot patrols, which isn't ideal. We need someone on the desk all the time,' Ray said.

'Aye,' Alan agreed. 'I'll pass that on to Bert.'

I left Alan, Ray and Derek discussing the foot patrol shortage, despite the surge in recruitment, and joined Mike in the corridor at the foot of the stairs.

'Do Cathy and Eric know we've seen the bruise?' I asked.

'We haven't spoken to them yet. Webby wants us to wait for the pathologist's report so we can say if it had anything to do with the baby's death. Don't mention it yet; let's see what comes out here.'

'Okay, Mike.'

Mike went back into the front office. 'Mrs Chiu, would you come with me please.' Cathy came to the door and Eric also stood up. 'No, Mr Chiu, we'll just speak to Cathy for now. We might want to speak to you afterwards.'

'But I am her husband,' Eric protested.

'Please sit down, Mr Chiu,' Mike pointed to the seat and Eric sank onto the hard plastic. Mike closed the door on him and led Cathy to the interview room.

'Sam, would you get Mrs Chiu a cup of tea please, and one for Mr Chiu as well?'

'I don't want a drink; I want you to lock up my husband's mother,' Cathy cried.

Tea forgotten, I sat down and Mike began the questions.

'Mrs Chiu, why do you think your mother-in-law killed Rose?'

'She hated her because she was not normal and she was a girl.'

'Why do you think that?' Mike asked.

'My mother-in-law was cross when Rose was born; she wanted me to give Eric a boy. I told her that maybe we would have a boy next.' Rose pulled a tissue from up her sleeve and wiped her eyes. 'Then the doctor told us that Rose was Mongol. I didn't understand at first but I have read what that means now. Eric's mother told us to put Rose in a home and try to have a boy. We had a terrible fight about it; Eric was cross with me.'

'Why you?' I asked. I know Mike had told me to just sit in, but I was being drawn in by the story and the question just popped out.

'I should be respectful to his mother. Even if I think she is wrong, I should not shout at her.'

I remembered Yang Hui Ping's cool demeanour when I was at the house, and the almost brutal way she had taken the baby and passed her to me. Maybe there was something in this allegation. I would speak to Mike afterwards.

'I understand there might have been some cultural differences...' Mike began. He caught Cathy's confused expression and continued. 'Some differences in how you and your mother-in-law think about things. Even though Hong Kong is a British colony, your mother-in-law might be more traditionally Chinese while you have adapted to living in England.'

Cathy nodded. 'We have tried to fit in. That is something else my mother-in-law does not like.'

'You think that because of your mother-in-law's traditional views, she might have harmed Rose?' Mike asked.

'She was alone with her. I was in the kitchen. When I looked at Rose, I thought she was asleep, but now I think she was dead then. My mother-in-law was asleep in the chair. I think she was pretending.'

'Why would she pretend?' Mike asked.

'To hide that she had killed Rose! But I know she did kill her, so she must have been pretending,' Cathy said.

'How do you think she killed Rose?' Mike asked.

'She stopped her air.' Cathy pinched her nose.

'Stopped her air? You think your mother-in-law suffocated Rose?'

'Suffocated.' Cathy stumbled over the word. 'Yes, suffocated, to make us think Rose died in her sleep.'

'Have you ever seen your mother-in-law mistreating the baby, perhaps being a bit rough, even unintentionally?' Mike asked.

'No, she would not do that if we were there,' Cathy said.

'Were you always there?' Mike asked.

Cathy was not stupid. She stared at Mike. 'My baby was hurt?' She gasped. 'My baby was hurt!'

Mike's ears grew red, he had let slip a pretty big part of the investigation. 'There's a mark on her back.'

'Rose was born with a mark on her back,' Cathy said. 'Maybe my mother-in-law gave her another mark that I don't know about,' Cathy became more agitated. 'She hurt my baby and took her breath away.'

I caught Mike's eye. I could tell that he realised he had planted another idea into Cathy's confused mind.

'The coroner will see the mark and will be able to tell us if it is a birthmark,' Mike said.

'You must arrest her!' Cathy cried.

'Cathy, as soon as we have evidence of the cause of Rose's death, we will let you know. What you have told us today is not solid evidence, it's only your opinion. We will need to speak to your mother-in-law about these allegations. Meantime, we need a statement from you.'

'Yes, I will give a statement then you will go to arrest her,' Cathy said.

41

'I can't promise that,' Mike said.

I don't think Cathy heard him; she was muttering about Mrs Yang's arrest. Mike caught my eye and I stared back, neither of us knew what to say, so we stuck to routine and took the statement, which was rambling and disjointed and proved nothing.

Afterwards, Mike showed Cathy back to the front office.

Eric jumped to his feet. 'You can't believe her. My mother would not hurt anyone. Having Rose has muddled her thinking.'

'She hurt Rose! They told me!' Cathy shouted at Eric.

Eric froze. 'No!'

'That's not what we said, Cathy,' Mike said quickly. 'Eric, Rose does have a mark on her back and we are waiting for the pathologist's report. Let's see what comes up there.'

'She was born with a big mark on her back. Here.' He pointed to his lumbar region, the spot where Rose had the mark. 'My mother is a good woman. She would not harm anyone,' Eric declared. 'You will see.'

'Cathy, why don't you sit down for moment while I speak to Eric,' Mike said.

Cathy sat quietly on a hard plastic chair in the front office and Mike took Eric through to the corridor. He didn't bother going to an office.

'Eric, I would like to call an ambulance for Cathy. She is evidently in need of medical help.'

'No, I will take care of her. I will ring the doctor,' Eric said. 'You believe my mother would not do such a thing?'

Mike exhaled. 'Please understand, we have to investigate these allegations and we will need to speak to your mother. It all hangs on the pathologist's report.'

Eric nodded. 'It will prove that my mother did not hurt Rose.'

'I hope so,' Mike said. 'We have to follow protocol so you must be patient.' Mike glanced towards the door. 'Promise me, Eric, that you will ring your doctor as soon as you can and ask them to see Cathy. She is suffering.'

'Yes, I will,' Eric said.

Mike showed Eric back to the enquiry office.

'Good day, Mr and Mrs Chiu.' Mike closed the door to the front office and turned to me. 'The pathologist's report might be a few days yet. The inquest even longer. We need to get the mother in for a chat.'

'She doesn't speak any English, so we'd need an interpreter,' I said. 'I can tell you that Mrs Yang was remarkably unaffected by Rose's death when I was there. She snatched the baby off Cathy and almost threw her at me.'

'You know grief affects people differently. Maybe there was a cultural thing going on about crying in public or something like that. One thing I am certain of: Cathy is suffering more than the baby blues. I hope Eric does get a doctor to see her.' Mike ran a hand through his hair. 'Right. I'll let Webby know.'

*

At knocking-off time, as normal, we all gathered outside the bridewell. Inspector Benjamin signed our pocketbooks, then— instead of rushing for the door—we walked across to the police club to drink our goodbyes to Alan. He had an official do organised at the club on our long weekend, when friends, family, old and new colleagues could celebrate his freedom as they termed it. I couldn't help but feel that Alan regarded his retirement with regret rather than excitement, but he was as old as he could be and still be a police officer. Steve would be disappointed to miss something like this. To make matters worse, we'd both miss Alan's official do because it was Steve's brother's wedding that day.

'Do you want a drink, Sam?' Ken asked.

'Coke, please. I'm driving,' I said.

'We're all driving, so cokes all round then, and an extra-large whiskey for Alan,' Ken said.

Steve forgotten, I sat with my block mates and listened to Alan reminisce.

Chapter Five

The following day I called in on Steve, who was convalescing at home. He was sprawled on the sofa, still in his pyjamas but looking a lot pinker than he had been when I last visited him. I brought him up to date with the B Block news, missing out the baby Rose story, and listened to his news, such as it was.

Mrs Patton, Steve's mother came in with a tray of tea and biscuits and placed it on the coffee table.

'I know you like chocolate bourbons,' she said.

'I do, thank you, Mrs Patton,' I replied.

'Don't forget, Richard's wedding is a week on Saturday.'

'I already have my outfit,' I replied.

'I tried that woman in the market you recommended: Karen Fitzroy. She made me a lovely blouse to go with my suit. The colour and fit are perfect, and so reasonably priced. I couldn't find anything like it in the shops,' Mrs Patton said.

'I told you she was good,' I said. 'Spread the word. She hasn't long started up and she's keen for customers.'

'I've already told everyone at the Women's Institute about her. She can expect several orders to come.' Mrs Patton returned to the kitchen and left us alone.

I was doing my best to drum up business for my friend Karen. I wondered what the WI would think if they knew that Karen was an ex-prostitute who had recently made the transition to earning a living from her formidable sewing talent. It was nobody's business and I hadn't told Mrs Patton, or even discussed it with Steve.

'Are you going to be strong enough to be best man?' I asked Steve. 'I can imagine a stag night with a bunch of marines would be pretty wild.'

'Of course. To be honest, I feel fine now. I still have to go for check-ups, but I think I'll be discharged back to my GP next week.'

'So you're suffering from *Plumbum Oscillans?*' I laughed at Steve's confused expression. 'It's a phrase I picked up from Mum. They use it sometimes at the surgery she works for. It's Latin for "swinging the lead".'

'Well, I haven't got a plum bum nor am I swinging the lead. In fact, once I'm back with my GP, I don't think it'll be any time before I'm back at work. Light duties of course.'

'You know I was only teasing you?' I fretted.

'Yeah.'

'Have you seen anything of that nurse, Emma Seton?' I asked.

Steve's cheeks grew pink. 'We've spoken on the phone a few times.'

'So why haven't you asked her out yet?'

'I'm waiting until after Richard's wedding. You're my plus one and Mum would kill me if I didn't bring you. Besides, it would be awkward if Emma came too.'

'Good. She seems nice.'

We chatted over tea a while longer, then I declined an invitation from Mrs Patton to stay for my evening meal. I ate so many meals there, they were going to start charging me.

I did as I had promised Ray; I rested over our days off. I watched more television than was good for me and got stuck into a couple of books I had been promising myself I would read. Ray was right; I needed a proper break. I was glad I'd booked a few day's leave.

On the Friday, despite the early hour, I felt invigorated as I took my place in parade.

Ken was quiet again. I nudged him.

'All right?'

'Yes thanks.' His smile didn't reach his eyes. I'd get him alone later and force the truth from him.

Inspector Benjamin, Shaun Lloyd and another sergeant came in. We all stood up.

'As you were,' Inspector Benjamin said. 'I'd like to introduce Albert Mason, Alan's replacement. Some of you will already know him.'

'All right, you lot,' Sergeant Mason said.

We all responded, some more loudly than others.

I knew Sergeant Mason was known as Bert, and that was as far as it went. He was about five foot ten inches tall, and almost that in circumference. His round, red face and white moustache made me think of Father Christmas. It was just as well fitness was not such an issue for station sergeants. He seemed a friendly chap; he just wasn't Alan.

'I'm glad to be here. I understand I have some big shoes to fill, but I'll do my best,' he said. 'On an operational level, I know you tend to keep to the same patches, but I like to mix things up a bit. So, I've had a chat with Inspector Benjamin and starting tomorrow, you drivers will remain the same for now and the two probationers will continue to accompany their tutors, but the foot patrols will be rotated across the town.'

That was different. It would be interesting to cover a different area, but I'd miss my walk through the park and being able to drop in on Karen or Mrs Thompson.

Parade continued and I got my usual beat, possibly for the last time in a long time. I hoped nothing too bad would happen, it would be a pain trying to make enquiries while I was covering another area.

After parade, we jostled for our turn to test call.

'Did you see the size of the new bloke? A walking heart attack that one if you ask me.'

I turned to Charlotte, my barely-restored patience suddenly very low. I really needed my leave.

'Nobody was asking you. Show some respect.' I turned

away and spotted Bert Mason standing at the door between the sergeants' office and the front office. His gaze was fixed firmly on Charlotte's back.

'WPC Leader, would you come into the office please,' he said.

'We're all constables now...' Charlotte turned around and her voice trailed away. 'Yes Sergeant Mason.'

So, Santa had a hard side. Not a bad thing and useful to know. He went into the office with Charlotte, no doubt to discuss his fitness regime. I mentally shrugged my shoulders and went out.

On my way to my beat, I walked past Chiu's chip shop. A handwritten notice on the door stated, *'Closed due to bereavement'*. I walked on thinking about baby Rose. Had she been killed by her own grandmother simply because she was a girl with Down's syndrome? Cathy was convinced, but her evidence was all supposition. Eric insisted that Cathy was mad, but then there was that big bruise. The post-mortem would have taken place while I was on rest days. I couldn't wait to hear what the pathologist had said.

*

At refs, Ken was sitting at the formica table, staring into space while Andy chatted away with Phil and Ray who were trying to play snooker. Now was my chance to find out what was wrong.

I sat beside him. 'What's up, Ken? You've been quiet.'

Ken furtled in his pocket then handed me a wedding invitation.

'Please be discreet. We can't invite everyone.'

I glanced at the date then shoved mine into my handbag.

'That's only next month. I thought you were waiting for Gaynor to finish her probation,' I said to Ken.

'We were.' Ken went over to Phil, Andy and Ray and handed them invitations. They immediately put them into their breast pockets. Andy came to sit with us, finally leaving Ray and Phil in peace.

'She's up the duff, isn't she?' Andy said.

'Wind it in,' I warned Andy. This was serious.

'Yes,' Ken hissed. 'Our parents are not happy.'

'Why?' Andy demanded. 'It's not like you were going to leave her in the lurch. You're engaged!'

'Yeah, but she doesn't qualify for maternity leave. She'll have to resign.' Ken put his head in his hands.

'Does the boss know?' I asked.

Ken nodded. 'I told him earlier. He was really good about it.'

I patted Ken's arm. 'You're still following your plans; just a bit earlier than anticipated.'

'That extra time would have meant that we could have had a house on that new estate. We've looked at cheaper housing but, even though we've got the deposit, we can't afford a mortgage the size we would need on one wage. Also, Gaynor could have taken maternity leave. Hell—who knows—maybe by then they'd have introduced part time working, which would have made it easy for her to return. Now, she'll have to start from scratch if she wants to come back. That's if they'll have her.'

Ken had a valid concern. The brass thought policewomen should be above reproach.

'What's that, you've got your girlfriend into trouble?' Trevor's voice came from the kitchen. None of us had heard the kitchen door open, which was unusual. Trevor had a habit of sneaking around; that's how he usually got the gossip first. Ken's news would be across Wyre Hall, if not the whole division, by the end of shift.

'Great! Supergob's here,' Ken groaned.

Trevor came into the refs room and appeared unaffected by Ken's assessment. 'You know you can get rid? Apparently it's a simple procedure, very safe.'

'Piss off, Torchy,' Ken snarled.

'Wazzer,' I added.

'Just saying.' Trevor stood up and went to the snooker table, but Phil and Ray replaced their cues in the rack and came and sat at the table with us. Trevor practised potting balls by himself.

'We would never even consider an abortion,' Ken said.

I didn't think I could either, but I did think abortion had its place, in certain circumstances. Inconvenience was not one of them.

'You know what he's like. Ignore him,' I said.

'Why did you call him Torchy?' Andy asked.

'He never goes out, like the Olympic torch,' I replied on Ken's behalf. 'You must have noticed how often he hangs around the station.'

Andy sniggered. 'That's a good one.'

'Ken, you're not the first and you won't be the last to be in this fix,' Phil said with the gravitas of a judge. 'Most of us go on to have successful marriages.'

We all gaped at Phil. Steady, sober, principled Phil, tutor, mentor and de facto big brother to us all.

'You had to get married? I had no idea,' I said.

Phil shrugged his broad shoulders. 'It's not something I broadcast. Jo and I were engaged, but like you, Ken, we had to bring things forward. It'll be all right, you'll see. Even your parents will forgive you when they meet their grandchild.'

Ken smiled for the first time that day. 'Thanks, Phil.'

'Do you have any regrets, Phil?' I asked.

He thought for a moment. 'I think my only regret is that Jo didn't get a church wedding like we were planning. All girls dream of a church wedding.'

'Do they?' I countered.

'Long dress, fancy hair, flowers, walking down the aisle. Girls love that stuff. Jo was too embarrassed to wear a traditional wedding dress, so we married in the registry office at the town hall. She wore a turquoise mini dress with white boots and a floppy, white hat. Very modern then. She carried a homemade bouquet of flowers. Then we went to the church hall by her parents' house for the reception. Our parents clubbed together and gave us a weekend in London for our wedding present, which served as our honeymoon.'

We all stared silently at Phil, but he was lost in his memories.

I broke the silence. 'You're getting married in a church, aren't you, Ken?' A registry office or a church were the only options and I was sure I'd seen a church on the invitation.

'Yeah, we managed to get in at St Michael's, mainly because we wanted a midweek ceremony to fit in with our rest days.'

'She can carry a big bouquet to hide the bump,' Andy said.

'She's only a couple of months along, she'll get away with it,' Ken replied.

'If you're going to go for police housing, I'll give you a hand with the application,' Phil said.

Ken beamed. 'Thanks, Phil. We will probably go for a police house to start off with. It's quite short notice, so I don't suppose we'll have much choice about location, but once we're in, we can always apply for a transfer if we don't like it. Even though they'll stop some of my pay, we could still save a bit each month and buy our own place eventually.'

'That's the spirit,' Phil said.

Ken seemed a lot brighter as we gathered our things together ready to resume patrol, Phil had a knack for making things better. Now he had passed his sergeants' examination, it was only matter of time before he was promoted and moved on. I'd miss him, we all would.

Chapter Six

Ray held out a job sheet when I went into the control room to get my radio. 'A toddler has been taken to the general hospital with a heroin overdose.'

I took the sheet from him. 'How the hell did something like that happen?!'

Ray shrugged.

Derek said, 'It was the sister in casualty who rang. It doesn't sound good.'

'I'll come with you,' the Inspector said as he squeezed into the tiny room. 'Derek, can you get on to CID, give them the heads up.'

'Will do.' Derek picked up a phone and dialled the extension.

Inspector Benjamin and I left for the hospital, about a five minute drive away. I decided that I wouldn't stress any more about thinking of the boss as Benno. As long as I remembered to call him "sir" or "boss" to his face, it would be fine.

We pulled into the car park outside the casualty and walked across to the entrance. A woman, skinny and stroppy, sat smoking a cigarette on the seat outside the department. She stood up and threw down her cigarette as we approached.

'Oh, here they come, Pinky and Perky. Stinking pigs. Oink oink.'

'Watch your mouth,' Inspector Benjamin said.

'Fuck off.' She followed that up with a series of grunts.

'Is she high?' I asked the boss.

'Probably,' he replied to me. He turned back to the woman.

'Consider yourself lucky we're busy with something else at the moment, or you'd be on your way to the bridewell.'

'Fuck off, bacon breath.'

We pushed through the heavy plastic strips across the entrance that were supposed to allow easy access whilst keeping the weather out of the department, but actually beat people around the head and shoulders as they fell back. The woman followed us in, grunting and oinking.

'We shouldn't put up with that. I'm going to take her in,' I whispered to Inspector Benjamin.

'I would agree normally, but hold fire and if she's still here when we leave, you can have her,' he whispered back.

A sister came out of an office. 'Oh good, you're here. I'm Sister Lomas, please follow me.'

'Fat bitch!' grunting woman bellowed.

The sister was stick thin so I guessed it was aimed at me. I hoped she would still be there when we came out, we'd be having words.

'Try to ignore Maureen; she's cross we won't let her past the waiting room.' The sister turned into a side room that contained a large metal cot, a chair and the ubiquitous metal table. 'This is the child I rang about. Shane Clough. Two years old. Home address, 3 Clipper Street. He has ingested heroin.'

Clipper Street was in one of the grimmer areas of town, known locally as the "Ship Streets", as each street was named after a type of sailing vessel. Heroin was becoming a real problem in the town but this was the first time I had heard of a child getting hold of it. Shane lay quietly under a cover. It was wrong; he should have been making noise, playing with a toy or running around, not lying so still, attached to a beeping monitor.

'Is he going to recover?' the boss asked.

'Probably, but it was touch and go for a time.'

'What will be the long term effects of a heroin overdose?' I asked.

'Uncertain yet,' the sister said. 'The problem is that heroin is an opioid and slows things down. He went into respiratory arrest, so brain damage is a concern. There might be other ongoing problems with his heart and lungs, but we won't know for some time.'

Poor little mite. Inspector Benjamin's lips were a thin, hard line as he gazed at the child.

'How did he ingest the drug?'

'It was in powder form and he got at the bag. He's inhaled some and we believe he's swallowed some. We can't be sure exactly how much has entered his system.' Sister Lomas said.

The Inspector said, 'We'll need to speak to the parents. Meantime, I'm initiating child safety protocols. Sam, tell Ray to contact social services.'

I radioed in the update whilst listening to Benno talk to the sister.

Sister Lomas said. 'He's going to intensive care at the children's hospital in the city when he's more stable, but I don't trust his mother not to try to kidnap him.'

'In that case, she needs to be kept away, and any other family too,' Inspector Benjamin said.

'Maureen won't like that,' Sister Lomas said. 'She's already been on the phone trying to round up reinforcements. We've got security on standby in case of trouble.'

'Is that awful woman outside his mother?' I asked.

'I'm afraid so. Ah, here's Dr McKay,' the sister said.

A short, white-coated woman with steel grey hair came into the room and shook hands with us. She had a good, strong grip and a direct manner. I liked her on sight. I'd feel safe if she were my doctor.

'Thank you so much for coming. I take it Sister Lomas has explained things to you?'

'She has,' Inspector Benjamin said 'We've instigated child safety protocols and informed social services. The sister has advised us that Shane will be sent to the Children's Hospital. Until then, this is an approved place of safety. We just need to keep the family away until he can be transferred.'

'The mother is outside,' Dr McKay said.

'We met her.' The boss grimaced. 'A difficult woman by the look of it.'

'You might say that.' Dr McKay shook her head.

'Was the child brought in by ambulance?' the inspector asked.

'Yes—'

Noise of a disturbance came from the waiting area. The boss and I went out, closely followed by Dr McKay and Sister Lomas. Maureen was sweeping magazines to the floor and shouting as she tipped over the chairs. A huddle of people were pressed back against the far wall. An older man, possibly a porter or cleaner, approached the enraged woman but she shoved him to the floor.

'Hey!' A young male doctor ran at her but was floored by a punch to his nose. He tried to stem the blood with his hands as he rolled away, out of reach of her kicks.

Maureen picked up a wooden chair and brandished it.

'Radio in for backup,' Benno said to me.

I made the call as the Inspector strode over to the offender, then I trotted after him whilst listening to Ray directing patrols to assist us. The cavalry was coming.

At the same time, Dr McKay said to a nurse cowering in a doorway. 'Have security been called?'

'Yes, Doctor,' she stammered.

Dr McKay, pulled up to her full four foot eleven and puffed out like a belligerent bantam, tried to follow us.

'Doctor, it would be better if you were to stay away. You might be injured and you're needed here,' I said.

'Rubbish,' she shot back. 'She's hurt one of my doctors. I've tackled worse in my time.'

I didn't doubt it. 'Let us deal with this, help is on the way. You see to the injured man.'

Reluctantly, she nodded and returned to the doorway from where she directed the nurses to assist the injured doctor and the porter / cleaner into treatment cubicles. I hoped I would be as feisty as I grew older.

'Stop that now!' Inspector Benjamin barked at Shane's mother.

Maureen paused with a chair above her head. I kept an eye on it in case I had to dodge out of the way. Maureen had a look of sheer glee on her face. I had noticed how high tension situations often attracted people like her. Maybe it was the adrenaline rush, or the chance of being seen as part of something bigger than their drab lives.

'What's this about?' the boss asked.

'They stole my baby,' she shouted, then smashed the chair down onto the floor, shattering wood, leaving her with a chair leg in each hand. That was criminal damage, to add to the charges she was amassing. 'I AM SHANE'S MOTHER! I HAVE RIGHTS. I DEMAND TO SEE MY BABY BOY,' she bellowed.

'You can't keep a mother from her child,' ventured a woman from the small crowd pressed against the wall.

Another woman called, 'She should be able to see her baby.'

'Not happening,' I called back. 'He's been placed under police protection because somehow he managed to get hold of heroin and almost died.'

The crowd of onlookers gasped. I probably shouldn't have disclosed that, but, so what.

Maureen apparently didn't notice the change of sympathies.

She pointedly looked at my epaulettes. '4912. I'll remember you, baby snatcher.'

'He'll have a better upbringing than with you,' called a third woman from the wall.

'YOU WHAT?!' yelled Maureen. She flung a chair leg at the woman and the crowd scattered. Where the hell were security? A little backup would be helpful.

Inspector Benjamin grabbed her arm. 'You are under arrest for—'

Maureen clouted him across the face with the remaining chair leg. Benno staggered back a pace, holding his mouth. I grabbed Maureen as she ran towards the outspoken woman and grappled with her as she went for my eyes with her nasty, dirty nails.

'You are under arrest—' My words were lost in a confusion of noise as practically the whole of B Block and several security men piled into the waiting room.

Five minutes later, order had been restored. Maureen was taken to the bridewell. Nurses and security bustled about, picking up chairs and binning ripped magazines and people began to relax. Police personnel resumed patrol, the porter / cleaner had been declared fit and came out to help the tidy up.

Dr McKay came out of the young doctor's treatment cubicle, leaving the nurses to dress the doctor's wound.

'His nose is not broken, but I would like to see that woman charged,' she said.

'It will be added to the charge sheet,' I assured her.

Dr McKay eyed Inspector Benjamin. 'Let me take a look at that lip.'

'No, it's okay. Thanks for asking,' he replied whilst backing towards the door.

Dr McKay got a glint in her eye, the one that I suspected wayward nurses and junior doctors got and didn't ignore.

'I wasn't asking. Sit down.' She was a woman used to obedience. The boss sat down.

Dr McKay peered into his mouth. 'Hmm. You need stitches. Follow me.' She went into a treatment cubicle. Benno stared after her. Half a minute later she poked her head out. 'I'm waiting.'

'Off you go, sir. I'll wait here,' I grinned as he trailed into the treatment room.

*

Inspector Benjamin pouted all the way back to Wyre Hall. It wasn't his fault; his lower lip was badly swollen and the stitches

Dr McKay had given him didn't help. Mike Finlay and Eamon were waiting for us in the bridewell and grinned when they saw him.

'Another happy customer?' Mike asked. The boss glared.

We all refused to look at each other because it would only take one to start laughing to set us all off. Coppers can be brutal to each other. It's how we show we care.

'Already in hand,' Mike said. 'We've carried out initial checks on the prisoner.'

'Her name is Maureen Clough,' Eamon said. 'Prolific shoplifter and a few D-and-Ds on the system. She's been an addict for a number of years. One child has already been removed by social services and has been adopted. Shane was born addicted and had to go through withdrawal therapy after he was born.'

'Poor little lad,' I murmured.

'Yeah, not a pleasant thing for anyone. Especially hard in a newborn,' Eamon said.

'How was she allowed to keep him?' I asked.

'You'd have to ask social services that,' Mike said. 'Maybe they thought as long as they were supervising her, it would be okay.'

'Boss, can I borrow Sam to interview Maureen?' Eamon asked.

'*Thure*.'

Trying to stifle a chuckle at the inspector's lisp, I followed Eamon into the interview room, while the bridewell officer went to get Maureen. I knew the drill: keep quiet, watch the prisoner for anything out of the ordinary. Only ask questions with permission, as long as they are relevant and haven't already been asked by the interviewing officer.

Maureen came in with the bridewell officer and was instructed to sit down, which she did without argument. Eamon did the usual introductions.

'Maureen, we want to talk to you about a couple of things,' Eamon began. 'Apart from the public order offences—'

'The wha'?' Maureen interjected.

'Public order offences. The kick-off at the hospital,' Eamon clarified.

'That wasn't me,' Maureen said.

'We'll be reviewing the security tape, but I have it on good authority that you were involved. That aside, I want to talk to you about how Shane managed to overdose on heroin.'

'It wasn't my fault,' Maureen whined.

'How so?' Eamon asked. 'A two year old gets hold of heroin? How is that not his parent's fault?'

'I left the bag on the table. He shouldn't have climbed up.'

Sadly, this wasn't the worst thing I had heard as a police officer, but it was still pretty awful.

'Did you try to keep Shane away from it?' Eamon asked.

'Wha'?' Maureen said.

Obviously protecting her child was an alien concept to her.

'So you just left it there?' Eamon said.

'Yeah.' Maureen chewed on the side of a fingernail and looked around, evidently getting bored.

'Tell me what happened,' Eamon said.

'I had some heroin and fell asleep. Junk always makes me sleepy. When I woke up I saw Shane lying on the floor. The bag was open. I put Shane on the sofa and waited for him to wake up.'

Eamon shook his head. 'You didn't think he needed an ambulance?'

'Like I said, it always makes me sleepy so I thought he'd be fine once he'd slept it off.'

If Eamon had rolled his eyes any harder, he'd have been looking at his own brain. 'So, you fell asleep, leaving your two-year-old child unsupervised, with a bag of heroin on the table. Then you left him to "sleep it off"?'

'Yeah.' Maureen sniffed loudly and wiped her nose on her sleeve then folded her arms on the table. A nauseating smear of snot glistened on her cuff. I tried not to look but it kept drawing my eyes.

Eamon exhaled loudly. 'Who called an ambulance?'

'That was her next door. She popped around and saw Shane on the sofa. She said that his breathing was funny. I told her he'd be okay, but she rang the ambulance.'

A chimpanzee would take better care of Shane than this woman could. I pondered the ethics of compulsory sterilisation for certain members of the population.

'The ambulance came and took Shane to the general?' Eamon asked.

'Yeah, then Pinky and Perky showed up, and suddenly I can't see my own child.' She suddenly lunged across the table; filthy, yellow claws went for my face. I slapped her hand away.

'Did you see that? She just fucking assaulted me. I want to make a complaint!'

I snarled. 'Please do. I'll add it to my pile of "don't give a damn".' Which sat alongside my pile of guilt. The guilt pile was bigger.

Eamon gave me the side-eye. I took the hint and stayed quiet.

'Maureen, you just tried to assault Constable Barrie. You need to stay on your own side of the table or I'll 'cuff you to the chair,' Eamon warned her.

Maureen jabbed a finger towards me. 'Constable Barrie. 4912. I'll remember you. You'd better keep one eye over your shoulder because one day I'll have you and you won't be able to steal no more babies.'

Eamon stood up and Maureen shrank back.

'That's enough. I'm stopping this interview. You can go back to the cells and we'll try again when you've calmed down.'

The bridewell officer escorted her away, but she continued shouting and complaining about me assaulting her and stealing her child.

'Why has she focused on me? I wasn't even there when the baby was brought in,' I said. 'And I just reacted from instinct when she went for me.'

'Don't worry,' Eamon said. 'I saw, and I heard her threaten

you.'

Good enough.

'It's not like you to bite back when a prisoner has a go at you,' Eamon said.

'We all have our limits, Eamon. I just thought about that poor little boy lying in hospital and snapped.'

He watched me for a moment. 'You are under stress at the moment, I suppose. Go and do your statements and I'll bring Mike up to speed.'

I didn't argue or ask Eamon why he thought I was under stress. Poor Shane. I really, really hoped the social services would remove him permanently. Anywhere would be better than living with Maureen.

Chapter Seven

Next day, I didn't hear any more about little Shane. I called into the collator's office to speak to Irene: our collator and Eamon's wife.

'Did Eamon manage to interview that witch?' I asked.

'I take it you mean Maureen Clough.' She laughed. 'He got a female DC and tried again after you had gone home. Not very successfully, I might add. Maureen's currently lodged in one of our luxurious accommodation units with twenty-four hour security, an open-plan, metal toilet and crash-mat hard mattress.'

'She's headed for Crown Court, for sure,' I said.

'Remand court first,' Irene reminded me.

I hoped the magistrates would deny her bail.

'What did you do that's pissed her off so much?' Irene asked.

'Nothing! Really, nothing. She was barred from seeing the child before I even got there.'

'Sam!' Bert Mason called.

My heart lurched. What had I done? 'Got to go, Irene.'

I stepped into the corridor. 'Here, Sarge,'

Bert peered out of his office and grunted. 'DI Webb has a person coming in for interview, he's asked for you to sit in. It's a Chinese woman, Yang Ping or something like that. He said you know her.'

'Ah, yes, Mrs Yang. I dealt with an infant death. She's the grandmother,' I said.

'I heard,' Sergeant Mason said. 'This job can be shit sometimes.'

No arguments from me in that department. This job could be total shit, but it could also be absolutely, bloody brilliant.

I went into the CID office. It was always useful to hear how a case was going before starting an interview. I knew I wouldn't be asking questions, but I might pick up something relevant if I knew the facts.

'Sam, m'darlin', what brings you here?' Eamon Kildea's honey-smooth, Irish voice trickled down my spine.

'DI Webb wants me to sit in on an interview. I think it's about Rose Chiu. Did we get the report from the PM?'

'We did indeed. That bruise you saw is actually something called a Mongolian Spot. It's quite common in Asian people, ' Eamon said.

The mortuary attendant had been right.

'I've never heard of it,' I told him.

'Me neither until yesterday.'

'Is it because Rose had Down's Syndrome?' I asked. 'Eric told me that the doctor had told them that Rose was a Mongol.'

'Their doctor must be old then, because that term isn't used much anymore. I don't think Down's is connected to the mark or everyone who had Down's Syndrome would have it, wouldn't they?' Eamon said.

I shrugged. 'I don't know.'

'Thanks for being so prompt, Sam,' said DI Webb as he came over to us.

'That mark was not a bruise, sir?' I asked.

'No, a birthmark. It seems the child died of sudden infant death syndrome. The coroner is happy to go with natural causes.'

'A cot death,' I said. Webby nodded. 'Why are we interviewing Mrs Yang if it's classed as natural causes?' I quickly tagged on a 'sir'.

'We need to explore what Cathy Chiu is saying. Depending on Mrs Yang's answers, we might need a second PM.' DI Webb turned to Eamon. 'Has the interpreter arrived?'

'Yes, sir. She's been given a cup of tea and is awaiting our arrival.'

'Let's get on with it, then.'

We went downstairs and into the interview room. A Chinese woman sat sipping black tea from one of the blue, china cups that we kept for the Superintendent and special visitors. It even had a matching saucer.

'Thank you for coming. I'll fetch Mrs Yang now,' DI Webb said.

He went into the front office where Mrs Yang sat with Eric.

'Mrs Yang, would you come with us please?' DI Webb held the door open.

Eric stood up and Mrs Yang followed suit.

'You remain here, Mr Chiu,' DI Webb said.

'My mother speaks no English. I can help,' Eric said.

'Don't worry; we have an interpreter,' DI Webb said.

Eric said something to his mother and she nodded.

'This way please.' DI Webb led Mrs Yang to the interview room and introduced her to the interpreter. Mrs Yang sat down and the two women spoke together for a minute or so, then the interpreter switched to English.

'Mrs Yang speaks both Mandarin and Cantonese. For your records, we will speak together in Cantonese.'

It didn't matter to me what language they used, but with that phrase added to the record, if something did come of this investigation and it went to court, Mrs Yang couldn't then claim that she had not understood what was happening.

'Thank you,' DI Webb said. 'Mrs Yang, is it all right if we ask you some questions?'

The interpreter spoke rapidly to Mrs Yang. This was the first interview I had sat in that had required an interpreter, and I found it fascinating to listen to the sounds, so unlike our language.

'I am happy to answer any questions you have.'

It also sounded odd to me that the interpreter answered as if she were Mrs Yang.

'Thank you Mrs Yang. Firstly, are you aware of the allegations made by your daughter-in-law?'

Mrs Yang listened to the interpreter and replied quite forcefully.

'I know what she said and I deny this allegation strongly. I did not kill the child,' the interpreter said.

'Can you tell us what happened when you were looking after Rose on the day she died?' DI Webb said.

Mrs Yang stared at DI Webb and me as the interpreter spoke. She didn't seem to feel the least bit uncomfortable about it, unlike me. Perhaps staring wasn't considered ill-mannered in Hong Kong. I'd ask Gary when he next rang.

Mrs Yang's reply seemed to go on for some time. Eventually, the interpreter said, 'I was sitting with the baby, who was sleeping after having her nappy changed by her mother. I fell asleep in the chair and woke up when the mother screamed.'

DI Webb nodded and wrote down what he had been told.

'What happened then, Mrs Yang?' DI Webb asked.

The interpreter and Mrs Yang spoke together again, then the interpreter said, 'My daughter-in-law accused me of killing the child. I did not.'

'Mrs Yang, it has been suggested that you had hoped for a grandson and were disappointed when Rose was born.' DI Webb waited the interpreter to speak to Mrs Yang. 'It has also been suggested that you told Mr and Mrs Chiu to give Rose away, and thought Rose's death was a good thing. Do you have any comment on that?'

The interpreter did her thing, then listened as Mrs Yang gave a lengthy reply.

The interpreter said, 'It is always sad when a child dies, but sometimes a death is not a bad thing. The child was born with something wrong with her, so I knew that she would always be a burden to my son. I did suggest that they give her away so their future son will not be hindered by his imperfect sister. She could have gone to a home for children like her.'

64

Wow! That was harsh. I turned a wide eyed stare to DI Webb.

He rubbed his hand over his chin. 'Mrs Yang, such an attitude seems callous to us. Can you explain it please?'

Another exchange between the women, then the interpreter said, 'I have seen children like the child before. They have wretched lives and their parents suffer too. The child would never have been able to marry and would have remained a burden to her parents as they aged. They probably will have a son and he would have had to take care of his sister as well as his parents as they aged. Also, when he comes to look for a wife, a girl's family would not want him to marry their daughter because of his imperfect sister. I am not happy that the child died, but it is for the best.'

Poor little Rose. Who could say how badly she would have been affected; she might have been able to live an almost normal life. However, *almost normal* wasn't good enough for Mrs Yang. Then I caught myself. Was I being too judgemental? I had never had the experience of raising a disabled child, and hopefully never would. Perhaps if I did have that experience, my opinion would alter and I would agree with Mrs Yang's hardnosed viewpoint. Perhaps losing Rose was like ripping off a plaster: painful at first, but better in the end.

I nudged DI Webb. 'May I ask a question?'

He nodded and I said, 'Mrs Yang, I notice that you have not used Rose's name once, You just refer to her as "the child".'

DI Webb glanced at me but said nothing and turned back to Mrs Yang, who was listening to the interpreter.

'It is my experience that it is better not to become attached to babies who are likely to leave you.' The interpreter replied.

'And that includes not using their name?' I asked.

Mrs Yang nodded when the interpreter spoke to her.

The interpreter said, 'I thought that my son would send her away as I suggested, so I did not try to bond with her.'

I said, 'That seems sad to me when Rose was named in your honour. Eric told me that the Chinese Rose is the flower of

Peking,'

The interpreter spoke and Mrs Yang snorted then released a stream of impassioned Cantonese.

The interpreter said, 'It is not an honour. That place has bad memories for me. My baby girl died there. I fled to Hong Kong with my son during the famine.'

A famine in China?! I had thought that famines only happened in places like Biafra. I recalled our school collecting silver milk bottle tops to raise money to send to Africa. I had no idea how milk bottle tops raised money, but footage of fly-covered victims of the famine had been all over the television and posters of swollen-bellied babies around the school urged us to gather as many as possible. So we did.

This wasn't just something on the television. Mrs Yang was sitting right in front of me, a living, breathing person.

'Your baby starved?' I was horrified.

'She was born like the child. We had so little food we were barely able to keep my son alive. We could not waste food on her. My husband made me give her to his mother and she took her away less than an hour after her birth.' The interpreter paused for several seconds as Mrs Yang spoke, then continued. 'I used my meagre milk to help nourish my son, even though he was too old to breast feed. My husband was right, we had to concentrate on our son, but I could not forgive him or his mother. I took my son and left. My son was, and still is, my priority. Everything I have done, has been for him.'

'Is Eric's father still in China?' DI Webb asked.

'I don't know. Maybe he is dead. Lots of people died in the famine,' Mrs Yang said through the interpreter. 'I told Eric he died. In Hong Kong, I told them I was a widow.'

'Didn't they check?' DI Webb asked.

'Too many dead people, too many refugees,' the interpreter relayed.

'Mrs Yang. Did you kill Rose to help Eric?' DI Webb asked.

'No, I did not kill her but I think he is better off now she gone,' the interpreter said.

DI Webb pushed his chair back. 'Mrs Yang, I can tell you that initial reports suggest that Rose died of natural causes, but the investigation is ongoing. We might need to speak to you again.'

Another exchange between the women.

'Am I going to go to prison?' the interpreter asked.

'Based on the evidence we have now, you will not be charged with anything and you are free to go. It could be that the mother is grief stricken and is not thinking straight.'

The interpreter interpreted and Mrs Yang nodded and said something that sounded like, 'Sheh sheh.'

'Thank you,' said the interpreter.

The two women left and DI Webb and I returned to the front office. I remained silent because I couldn't think of anything to say after that interview.

'Don't let it play on your mind,' DI Webb said.

'I didn't know there had been a famine anywhere outside Africa,' I said.

'The Great Leap Forward. Late fifties. Millions of people died,' DI Webb said.

I was dumbfounded. Twenty years was not that long ago and I had known nothing about it.

'What about her baby? She must have known her mother-in-law was going to kill her. Doesn't that make her culpable?' I asked.

'Here, yes, but...' DI Webb sighed. 'China was a very patriarchal society. It still is, though not quite as much these days. Mrs Yang would not have been able to go against her husband's instructions. That she left him and took Eric was almost an unthinkable rebellion. Even if her husband and his mother are still alive, we don't have jurisdiction. The local police would have to deal with it, and I don't think the death of a girl child with health problems, in a famine nearly twenty years ago will be high on their agenda.'

'She knows what it is like to lose a child, but she was so

unfeeling at the scene and now she says that Rose would have been a burden. Even if she didn't kill her, she's a hard one,' I said.

'There's worse than death,' DI Webb said.

'What's worse than death?' I asked.

'Life,' replied DI Webb. 'A life lived in pain, hopelessness, regret and despair is worse than death.' He went into the sergeants' office and closed the door.

I stared at the closed door for a moment. When I thought about it, Webby was right, death was the end of everything, including suffering. I felt that he had given me a piece of a jigsaw and now I could see more of the bigger picture. Mrs Yang had had to make the most terrible decisions. Life had hardened her and Eric became her reason for living. To her, putting Rose into care was better than what she had had to do. Rose's death solved the problem and saved any more argument. My brain couldn't cope with more thinking about this, so I went to the control room.

'Do you want me to go out for the last couple of hours?' I asked.

'I would prefer you to stay at the enquiry desk,' Derek said.

'Righto.' Through the glass partition, I spotted Webby walking up the corridor. He must have left the sergeants' office from the other door.

'Put the kettle on, before you do,' Ray said.

I went into the little cupboard-sized telex room behind the control room and examined the brown stained mugs. If tea did that to ceramic, what did it do to teeth?

'These are disgusting. When did anyone last clean them?' I brought them out to show Ray and Derek.

Ray made a show of considering my question. 'When did you last do them?'

'About a month ago!' I cried. 'I think I'll skip a tea for now. Do you think Bert will want one?'

'Will Bert want one what?' Bert asked as he came into the control room.

'A mug of tea,' I replied.

'Bert certainly does want one. Strong, and sweet.' He grinned at me. 'By the way, I think you can take over the front desk permanently. Let the guys deal with the mean streets.' He said the last like he was the narrator in an American detective series.

'Yes, Sarge,' I muttered and slunk into the telex room to make the tea. I didn't mind covering the desk once in a while, but taking it permanently was hardly a move that would enhance my career. Also, nice as Bert was, he evidently hadn't got the memo about policewomen being the same grade as policemen. So, this was my life for now. Desk duties, tea maker and mug cleaner.

Once everyone, including the inspector, had a drink, I sat at the desk to make up my pocketbook.

The door flew open and Cathy ran to the desk. There was no sign of Eric and I wondered if he knew she was here.

I stood up. 'Cathy, what is it?'

'She is at home! Why is she at home? She killed my baby. She hurt her! She should be in prison.'

I pointed to the tiny interview room next to the desk. 'Cathy, go in there. I'll get someone to speak to you.'

'No! You speak to me now. Why did you let her go?'

Derek popped his head out from the control room.

'Derek, could you ring CID and ask someone to come and speak to Mrs Chiu?' I asked.

Derek nodded and picked up a phone.

Cathy banged her palms on the desk. 'Tell me why you let her go?!'

'Cathy, the pathologist's report said that Rose died of a cot death. She wasn't murdered.'

'No! You said she hurt Rose. She killed her!' Cathy shouted.

'Rose wasn't hurt, Cathy. The mark we saw was the birthmark you told us about,' I said.

Bert came out of the sergeants' office. 'Mrs Chiu, come and sit down in the office.'

Cathy surveyed him for a moment, then went into the tiny

interview room. Bert indicated for me to join him in there.

In the small office, Cathy sat down and Bert sat on the other chair. I stood by the door.

'Cathy,' Bert began gently. 'The pathologist has said that your little baby died of sudden infant death syndrome. It's a horrible thing that happens sometimes, and nobody can explain it properly.'

'My mother-in-law was arrested; why did you let her go?'

Bert shook his head. 'She wasn't arrested. Because of what you told us, we asked her to come in to answer some questions, and that is all. She answered the questions and there was no reason to arrest her.

'She said that it was a good thing that Rose died.' Cathy's despair was plain to see.

'That does not mean she killed her. Cathy, I'm sorry but Rose's death was just one of those bad things that happen sometimes.' Bert shifted in his seat making it creak. 'Many years ago, my little boy, Leslie, died of the same thing. He was four months old. Just got his first teeth.' Bert paused then swallowed. 'I promise you, Cathy, that in time you will be able to remember your Rose and smile just as I remember my Leslie and smile.'

I stared at Bert. People had things in their past that I had no idea about. I had been so wrapped up in my own dramas that I never gave it a thought. I felt a bit guilty. Even though there was nothing I could do about other people's troubles, I should remember that I was not the only one with problems.

Eamon put his head around the door. 'All right?'

'I was just explaining to Mrs Chiu why her mother-in-law was allowed to go home,' Bert replied.

Eamon squeezed in past me. 'Oh Cathy, m'darlin' it's an awful thing that happened, but little Rose died peacefully, asleep in her own cot. She wouldn't have been frightened.' He was using his lovely voice to full effect and it seemed to be working. Cathy was visibly calmer. He continued, 'We are certain that your baby wasn't harmed.'

'Could my mother-in-law have taken her air to make it look like she died of this sudden infant death syndrome?'

'You mean, could she have suffocated Rose,' I clarified. Cathy nodded.

'There are signs that the pathologist would have recognised if Rose had been suffocated,' Eamon said.

Cathy played with her fingers for a moment then nodded again.

'Go home, m'darlin', and rest.'

'Did the doctor come and see you the other day?' I asked.

'He gave me tablets. Tablets will not bring back my baby.' Cathy stood up and turned to leave. She paused a moment and turned back. 'You have sons now?' she asked Bert.

'A son and a daughter. Two grandsons and another grandchild on the way,' Bert replied.

Cathy nodded, seemingly satisfied and left.

'What was that about?' Eamon asked.

'Ancient history,' Bert said and wandered back into the sergeants' office.

Eamon turned to me but I didn't think it was my place to say anything if Bert hadn't chosen to explain things to Eamon. I shrugged and returned to the front office.

Chapter Eight

I called off at Woolworth's on my way home and purchased sweets and a dozen mugs with various patterns. Tomorrow, I'd replace the worst of the mugs in the telex office with these. I chose a mug with the most garish pattern on it. There could be no doubt that that was my mug, but to be certain I'd keep it in my locker.

From Woolworth's, I went to Beverley's place. I felt I needed a lift and what better than playing Lego with little kids. I didn't want to get the neighbours talking, so I took off my tie and unpinned my hair to make me look less like a policewoman.

At Beverley's house, Christopher and Carly ran down the path to greet me. I suspected their enthusiasm was because I usually had sweets for them.

'Hi, Sam,' gushed five-year-old Carly as she eyed my bag.

Eight-year-old Christopher played it cool. 'Hi.'

It was jelly babies today. They took the sweets and disappeared into the back garden. I followed and let myself in through the back door. Bev was already making tea. She plonked a mug of builder's in front of me and took the other stool so she could still keep an eye on the small children she minded.

'Am I okay to give the little ones sweets too?' I asked. 'They're only jelly babies.' Bev nodded so I handed a small bag of sweets to each of the minded children too.

Bev watched me over the top of her mug. 'Need to talk?'

'Is it that obvious?' I asked.

'What's happened.'

'Our new sergeant has put me in the office permanently because I'm female,' I said.

Bev poured the tea. 'Is it so awful being in the office? No more trailing around in the rain and no more getting injured. Auntie Liz will be happy about that.'

I hadn't thought of that. 'Mum will be pleased,' I agreed.

'Tell me,' she said, 'Did you have a run in with someone about an illegally parked car a few days ago?'

My jaw sagged. 'A couple of weeks ago. How did you know?'

'Judith, one of my mothers, was moaning to me about useless police and how a policewoman refused to move a stolen car her sister reported. I know Tracey lives near your flats so I wondered if it was you.'

My annoying neighbour was the sister of one of Bev's clients. Small world.

'The car wasn't stolen. I was off duty and she was horrible. It's probably best that Tracey doesn't know we're related; I don't trust her not to use that somehow,' I warned her.

Bev chuckled. 'Apparently, you called her names and threatened to arrest her over nothing, then set a neighbour on her. Judith says her sister's made a complaint.'

I took a sip of my tea. Like Trevor said: some people don't let the truth get in the way of a good complaint. This woman sounded like she could cause a lot of trouble.

'What actually happened was, I was off duty and she collared me as I was going out. She demanded that I move a car simply because it was outside her house. She didn't like me telling her there was nothing I could do, so she parked her car across the entrance to our car park. Another driver wasn't happy he couldn't get in and I threated to get her car towed if she didn't move it.'

'So no name calling?' Bev asked.

'She called me fat to provoke a reaction and then tried to photograph me. I didn't give her the satisfaction of a compromising photograph.' I took another mouthful of tea.

Bev let her eyes wander over me. 'You're not fat. You've always been more Marilyn Monroe than Twiggy.' Beverley glanced towards the children, leant towards me and lowered her voice. 'Tracey and I had a bit of a spat a couple of weeks ago and I almost gave Judith notice over it.'

'Go on,' I said. Bev had never given anyone notice so this must have been bad.

'Judith asked me to take…' Bev nodded towards one child who was engrossed with a toy car and oblivious to our conversation. '… Jonathan at weekends too. I told her I wasn't registered for weekends and had no intention of getting registered outside of my existing hours because I wanted to spend weekends with my own family. She seemed to accept it and that was that as far as I was concerned.' Bev swallowed another mouthful of tea. 'A couple of days later, Tracey came to do the pick-up and had a big go at me. She argued that Judith works all week and needs the weekends free to get on with the house and do the shopping, and I have all week sitting at home to do that.'

I laughed, but Bev shook her head.

'It got a bit heated. She said I had the evenings for my children, you know, when they're asleep. She demanded that I change my registration to take him. When I absolutely refused, she changed tack and told me that I had to do whatever Judith said because she employed me. I reminded her, not for the first time, that I was self-employed and Judith was just buying my services, so Tracey said I was a parasite living on the backs of working mothers.'

'That was nasty. I would have given notice at once,' I said.

'I can't blame Judith for what Tracey says. Anyway, I pointed out that I was also a working mother who happened to work from home. I mentioned it to Judith when I saw her, but she told me that Tracey had told her I had threatened her that I was going to give Jonathan notice. All lies. Judith and I talked and sorted things out, but I told her that I was not prepared to have Tracey do the pick-up again unless it was an emergency. It might be coincidence, but I got a spot visit from the social services the following week.' Bev finished her tea.

'You get spot visits anyway,' I pointed out. 'It comes with the job.'

'Yes, which is why I can't point a finger at her.'

'Tracey certainly follows a pattern. If she can't get her own way, she gets personal, just like she did with me.' I rinsed my mug under the tap and left it on the draining board. The phone started to ring, which made me think of the answering machine. 'Did you ever sort out that answering machine?' I asked.

Bev snorted. 'Terry said he'd look at it sometime.' She answered the phone.

One of the minded children's mothers arrived and Bev ended her call and gathered the child's things together and saw her out.

'One down,' she said when she returned.

I got onto the floor and helped Jonathan build a tower. He was a bright little boy and delighted in our game.

'He loves building things. I can't make up my mind if he's going to be an architect or a bricklayer,' Bev said.

I stood up. 'Right, I'm going to see Mum. I'll help you build another tower next time, Jonathan.'

Jonathan knocked the tower down and giggled as the bricks scattered.

'He might be a demolition expert. See you, Bev.'

'See you, Sam.'

I drove over to Mum's and ended up having my tea with her. Bev was right; Mum was delighted that I was in the office.

'Quite right. I always thought that young women should not be walking the streets alone, especially at night.'

'They pay me to do that, and I have a radio,' I argued.

'Women are not as strong as men,' Mum insisted. 'Look how often you've been hurt. Women belong in the office.'

I picked up an imaginary phone and held the invisible receiver out to Mum. 'It's the nineteenth century. It wants its attitude back.'

Mum sighed. 'I know you'll never agree with me, but I'm

never going to be sorry you're in the office.'

I sighed. We'd just have to agree to differ.

'Steve is going back to work,' Mum said. Evidently she had reached the same conclusion as me and was changing the subject.

'Eventually,' I said.

Mum smiled. 'No. I met his mother. He'll be back on light duties for a while quite soon.'

That was good news for me. Light duties meant office work and limited shifts. Once Steve was back, I would be freed from the enquiry desk. I didn't tell Mum.

*

As I turned into The Crags' car park, Tracey came out of her house. Had she been looking out for my return? I was starting to feel stalked.

She crossed the road and stood at the entrance to the car park. I got out of my car, leaving the mugs on the back seat so I didn't forget them in the morning, and walked to the door, trying to ignore her.

'I'm surprised to see you still in uniform,' she said.

I glanced down at my police skirt and black clad legs. There was no denying I was in uniform. I felt my jaw creak with the effort of smiling.

'Your complaint was recognised as the vexatious and malicious lie it was, Tracey.'

She cocked her head. 'How do you know my name?'

I thought for a moment. What sort of trouble could she cause for me if I revealed that I had checked up on her? I decided that if she was happy to put in complaints about me, I was entitled to check up on her.

'I looked on our systems when I made a note of your complaint about the car. I was right, you know.' Okay, I didn't need to add the last bit, but I enjoyed it.

Tracey's mouth tightened. 'Well, we will just have to hope

that you don't do anything that warrants another complaint. A complaint that they will take more seriously.' She turned on her heel and went back to her house.

Was that a threat? It certainly sounded like a threat to me. I took a step after her to confront her, but had second thoughts. It would be another excuse for her to complain about me and there were no witnesses around. I muttered to myself as I went inside. I hesitated by the lift; it was only a few floors up and this was a chance for a bit of exercise to go with the healthy eating plan I had started, so I trudged upstairs, still muttering about Tracey.

In the flat, I took off my coat and went into the bedroom to change into my jeans. I went to close the curtains and spotted Tracey in the car park, photographing my car. I grabbed my own camera from the top of the wardrobe and took a photo of her, photographing my car. She then hurried away. I was at a loss to explain what she was going to do with that. My first instinct was to go over and confront her, or to photograph her car; but then, would I be playing into her hands somehow? I looked down at the polaroid photo I had of her. I had managed to get a clear shot of her face so she couldn't deny it was her. It might be useful sometime for something. I jotted the date and time on it, put it in an envelope and popped it in the kitchen drawer, just in case.

I went downstairs and out to my car to make sure she hadn't done anything to it. Everything seemed in order. I spotted the caretaker by the big bins.

'There was a woman here a short time ago, I saw her hanging around my car. Did you see her by anyone else's car?'

He came over. 'I didn't see her, but I'll keep an eye open for strangers. What does she look like?'

I described Tracey and pointed out her house to him.

He nodded. 'I'll call the police if I see her hanging around the cars.'

Happy I had done what I could for now, I returned to the flat.

Later on, I had just settled in front of the television with a cup of tea and a slice of toast when the phone rang. It was crackly when I answered it but, through the static, I heard Gary's voice. Suddenly, I had tears running down my face.

'Are you crying?' Gary asked.

'No,' I lied. 'I have a cold.'

'Oh dear. How are things apart from that?'

'Fine. Alan's gone and Bert Mason has arrived. He seems okay. Your replacement, George Benjamin, is Benno from Operation Elstree.'

'I know,' Gary said.

'Why didn't you tell me?' I demanded.

Gary laughed. 'I didn't want to spoil the surprise. How's he settling in?'

'It hasn't been long, but I think he'll be okay. In other news, Steve is coming back to work soon. Ken and Gaynor have brought their wedding forward because Gaynor's pregnant. I'll probably go with Steve.'

'Bloody hell, I thought Ken was more sensible than that,' Gary said.

'It happens,' I replied. 'Never mind the boring stuff here, tell me about Hong Kong.'

'There's too much to talk about in a phone call; it costs a fortune so I can only stay on for a few minutes. I've been moved out of the hotel and put in an apartment near to work. The rent is reasonable. I don't think anyone apart from millionaires can afford to buy out here. Get paper and pen and I'll give you the address.'

I grabbed a pen and pad I kept near to the phone and wrote the address down, checking the spellings a couple of times.

'The markets here are incredible,' Gary said. 'They actually advertise *"Genuine Fakes"*.'

'As opposed to *"Fake Fakes"*,' I quipped.

'I think it means it isn't genuine designer stuff, but it's so good, you wouldn't tell. I can get a suit made very cheaply. You'd love it here.'

'I'll have to start saving for a ticket to visit you,' I said.

'I miss you,' Gary said.

'I miss you too.' I sniffed loudly.

'Did you get my letter?'

'No.'

I heard Gary sigh. 'They did warn me that the postal service here can be unreliable.'

'More like non-existent,' I said.

'Apparently it's even worse on the mainland. What time is it there? I guessed about eight.'

'You're right. It's ten past.'

Gary chuckled. 'It's tomorrow here. Right, have a hot toddy, bath and an early night. I'll try to ring again soon. As soon as I get a proper phone number, I'll let you know. Love you.'

'I love you,' I said. Then I heard nothing but static so I put the phone down.

I thought I'd feel happy after speaking to Gary, but instead I felt desolate. He was so far away. I wasn't hungry anymore. I threw away my toast and took his advice, as far as the bath and early night went. Tomorrow was a new day.

*

Next day, instead of going to parade, I went straight to the enquiry office. The night enquiry officer had nothing to pass on to me, so he scarpered. I sat at the little table and watched the night control room staff do the handover with Ray and Derek.

Sergeant Mason came out of the sergeants' office and crossed the enquiry office to the control room.

'All right, Sam?'

'Yes, Sarge. Do you want me to take first refs as normal?'

'Yes, you might as well,' he replied.

I was happy at that; at least I'd be scoffing with the usual crowd. I checked the folder for any new warrants. The night officer should have added the details to the parade book for the morning shift. I read the visitors' book to see if anyone interesting had come in; they hadn't. I was bored so I wandered through to the control room and read through the overnight telexes, but there wasn't very much of interest there either. The night control room staff would have sent copies to the relevant departments for the morning.

Almost out of habit, I flicked on the kettle and got the new mugs from their box.

'Ooh, posh,' said Ray as I put a new mug in front of him.

'The new mugs are only for B Block so find a hidey hole for them, let the other blocks sort themselves out.'

'Tea doesn't taste right if it doesn't come from an old mug,' Derek complained.

I grabbed his mug away. 'Fine, give yourself tannin poisoning then.'

'Don't be touchy; I was just saying.'

'How about saying, "Thank you, Sam for worrying about our health and using your own time and money to buy us nice new mugs".'

'Thank you,' Derek said.

I returned the new mug and went into the telex room to get the teas for the sergeants and the Inspector.

'Must be the time of month,' I heard Derek say to Ray.

'Not my monthlies, just the wazzer by the phones.' I snapped as I went past to the sergeants' office.

When I got back to the enquiry office, Ray popped his head around the door.

'Did you book any leave?'

I knew what he was telling me, but Derek could be really aggravating.

'Yes, I did.'

'Good.' He went back into the office and I followed.

'Sorry I was a bit sharp,' I said to Derek.

'Sorry I was ungrateful,' Derek said.

The rest of the block surged into the office for their radios. I retreated to the enquiry office, where nothing much happened all morning, apart from a couple of bailees who came in to sign on as per their conditions. The clock dragged around to scoff time and patrols started to return to the station. It was with much relief I went on my break.

In the refs room, Andy sat with Ken and me at the large Formica table. Phil and Trevor were playing snooker. Unexpectedly, Charlotte came in.

'You're normally on the opposite break from me. Why are you scoffing now?' Andy asked.

It was a reasonable question. We now had Mikes Two, Three and Frank from Mike One in, which meant Mike Four was the only panda out. Not good.

'Frank has got to go somewhere, so Sergeant Mason said I was to come in, have my scoff now and go out with Mike Three later,' Charlotte replied. 'I'm with you after scoff, Trevor,' she called to him. He put a thumb up in acknowledgement.

'Has John taken over Mike One?' I asked. John Batt was a foot patrol, on the other side of town from me. He had had his driving course and was used as a spare driver. The problem was, he wasn't a tutor-constable.

'I suppose so. Frank said he normally takes the spare pandas,' Charlotte said. 'I suggested to Shaun that I was ready to patrol alone, but he refused.'

'I'm not surprised,' I said. 'You need to do your time in company to get all your jobs in before going solo.'

Charlotte shrugged, 'Some are ready earlier than others.' She opened her bag and pulled out a small square of material and laid it on the table. We watched as she laid out a plastic plate and a knife and fork with the care of a butler laying the table for a banquet at Buckingham Palace. When she had done that, she transferred a salad from a Tupperware pot onto the plate. The rest of us would have just eaten straight from the pot on a bare table with the cutlery in the station kitchen drawers.

'Is that it? No meat, or cheese or egg?' Ken asked.

'I don't eat or use any animal products,' Charlotte said. 'Humans need to stop exploiting animals. Also, it helps keep my weight in check.'

She dribbled dressing from a small bottle over her meal while eyeing my cheese sandwiches. Was she coveting them or was she judging me for eating them? I smiled at her; I would play nicely, although I suspected that she didn't give tuppence about animal welfare. Weight control would be the major influence for her dietary choice.

'I didn't realise that there was more than one type of vegetarian,' I said.

'I don't suppose you did.' Charlotte speared half a tomato with her fork and ate it. No further comment, no discussion about vegetarianism, and a definite air of judgement.

'How do you get protein and calcium?' I was genuinely interested.

'I don't expect you to understand.' Charlotte ate another half tomato.

'I went to the grammar school, so try me,' I said as pleasantly as was possible through gritted teeth. She wasn't the only one who had had a good education, I just hadn't gone to university. I was too busy recovering from a traumatic experience.

Charlotte surveyed me for a moment. 'Have you heard of tofu?'

I nodded. 'Bean curd.'

Charlotte blinked. Ha! One point to me.

'That's how,' she said.

'Peanut butter is a source too,' Ken said.

'Most nuts are,' Charlotte said. For a moment she actually sounded as if she had climbed down from her pedestal and had accepted that we were not just ignorant yokels. I had a thought and peered under the table. 'Your shoes are leather, and our handbags are leather.'

'And the belts,' Ken said.

Charlotte scowled and I could almost hear her scampering back up her pedestal.

'I had little choice. The joining instructions specified leather shoes, and I did suggest to stores that they made handbags in plastic or canvas for people like me, but they laughed in my face.'

I smirked. I could imagine that would have been their reaction to such a request. They didn't encourage individuality.

'You don't want plastic shoes in this job. Your feet will sweat and stink and the plastic will crack very quickly,' Ken said.

'And canvas shoes don't offer much protection.' I sighed. 'I suppose you do have to live in the real world and make compromises sometimes.'

Charlotte didn't deign to answer, which I took as a victory for Ken and me. Then I felt guilty. She was only a sprog after all.

'Did you join up straight from university?' I asked, to guide the conversation to a safer direction.

'Oh, no. I joined the civil service, straight in as executive officer, because of my degree.'

Okay, Charlie, you have a degree, we get it, I thought.

'What did you do before you became a policewoman?' she asked me.

'After A levels, I went to live in Canada for a couple of years,' I replied.

'Really? What did you do there?' She actually sounded interested.

'I worked in my uncle's restaurant.'

She paused before speaking and I felt her judgement come down on me like a ton weight.

'Do you find that working as a waitress prepared you for life in the police?' Charlotte asked. Why did it always sound as if she was belittling me? And why did she assume that I was a waitress? Okay, I was, mostly, but there was more to it that that because it was a family business and I was family.

'It taught me patience and how to deal with difficult people without escalating the situation.' I replied. And it got me functioning in the outside world after the most traumatic period of my life, the scars of which I still carried, but I was never going to discuss that with her.

'I can see how you'd want to do that when you were just a waitress, but I wouldn't worry about escalating the situation now. The public need to know who's in charge.'

Just a waitress! I would not show her she had annoyed me, but she did need a warning about her attitude.

'That type of policing won't go down well in this town,' I said.

'Then it's about time the plebs learned their place,' Charlotte said.

I bit into my sandwich to stop myself throwing it at her. Phil would never have tolerated me speaking like that. Why hadn't Frank got to grips with her superior attitude. I had never worked with Frank so maybe this was also his attitude.

'What's your degree, Charlotte?' I asked though a mouthful of bread and cheese.

'I got a 2:2 in History,' she replied.

'Do you find having a lower second in History is useful in the police?' I deliberately emphasised the *"lower"*.

She smirked. 'Any degree opens the door to promotion.'

'Have you had a sudden death yet, Charlie?' Andy asked. The types of jobs they attended were a concern to sprogs. They had to complete a tick sheet to ensure they covered pretty well everything before they were let out alone.

'Yes, of course I have. Frank calls part of our area, *"The Elephants' Graveyard"* because there are so many nursing homes. Also, you know I prefer to be called Charlotte. It's more professional.'

There were a lot of nursing homes in Mike One's area, but I thought the name was disrespectful. I was glad I had got Phil to puppy walk me.

'Charlie sounds friendlier that Charlotte,' Andy said.

'My focus is on progressing my career, not making friends. I intend to be an inspector within four years and Chief Constable, eventually.'

Everyone went quiet for a few seconds. Whether or not she noticed the discomfort I couldn't say, but Charlotte packed up her bag and left the room.

'The arrogance is strong in this one,' said Ken, paraphrasing a character in the newly released Star Wars film.

'I'd hate to be on her block,' I said. 'She wouldn't care about the people under her, except to step on them on her way up the promotion ladder.'

'In four years' time, you might be a sergeant to her inspector,' Andy said.

I shuddered. 'I think I would turn down promotion if it meant working with her as my boss.'

Wasn't Charlotte a spider?' Trevor said from the snooker table.

'Yes, a barn spider in *'Charlotte's Web'*,' I replied.

Laughter travelled around the table like a wave. We all knew what nickname Charlotte was going to get. Whether she liked it or not, she would be Spider for the rest of her service.

Chapter Nine

Staying in the office was never going to be my first choice, but it wasn't too bad. Sometimes it was so busy, one of the control room staff would come and help out, if they weren't too busy themselves. Other times, it was so quiet I could almost hear crickets and I was sure I saw tumbleweed out of the corner of my eye. At those times, I'd remind myself that Steve was coming back soon, and he'd probably be given the office until he was deemed fit to patrol again. Meantime, tomorrow was Steve's brother's wedding and then I had a whole week off to look forward to.

I toyed with the idea of using the quiet time in the office to revise for the promotion exams later in the year. Now I was through my probation, I would be eligible to sit them and, although I would not have enough experience to consider promotion just yet, it would get the theory requirement out of the way so, when the time came, I could concentrate on the interview boards. On balance, I decided that revision was a good idea. I went to the bookshelf and selected a *Baker and Wilkie's* textbook.

'Get the kettle on, Sam,' Derek called from the control room.

I sighed, pushed aside the book and went to fill the kettle.

'Did you ever hear any more about that little lad that overdosed?' Ray asked.

'No, Mike and Eamon are dealing with it and haven't updated me. Last I heard he had been transferred to the children's hospital in the city. Have you heard anything?'

'I might have.' Ray grinned and leant back in his chair with his hands behind his head.

'Go on, tell me,' I urged him.

'The mother went to court and went guilty for the public order and assault offences. She was less inclined to plead for the child cruelty and neglect offences..'

'So what's happening?'

'Mike told me that it's going to Crown Court as a bundle. She's been denied bail and is currently residing at the remand centre.' Ray lit another cigarette.

'That's brilliant. Is Shane still in hospital?' I asked.

Ray's face darkened. 'Sadly, yes. He'll be there for a while yet.'

'But when he does come out, he can go to another family and have a decent upbringing.' I was delighted.

'Mike says that he might never be able to leave the hospital. He might have survived, but they're still assessing the damage. He's an extremely sick baby.'

That put a downer of everything. I finished making the teas and went back into the enquiry office, where I tried to get up the enthusiasm to revise for the exams.

*

That night, I couldn't sleep. I turned on the telly, but there was nothing on apart from the Open University lectures. For want of something better to do, I watched one. It wasn't terrible, well, the camera work and the stilted delivery were, but the subject was fairly interesting. This got me thinking about Charlotte and her degree. She positively wallowed in her graduate status, something Gary never did, even though he had also joined as a graduate entrant with a first.

From what I understood, a 2:2 was acceptable, but not out-of-this-world great. I could have had a degree by now if I'd gone to university, but I'd had other priorities at the time so I only had A Levels.

A little thought scratched at the back of my mind. If Charlotte

87

could get a degree, so could I. Almost immediately, the thought died. I worked shifts and that would make regular attendance at a university difficult. Then I watched the credits roll up on the programme, listing when it would be shown again. The answer was right in front of me. The Open University! I had no idea what degree I could do, but I remembered Charlotte saying that any degree opened doors to promotion. Then I also remembered that I was starting to revise for my sergeants' exam. How would I fit it all in? Not to worry; I wasn't committing myself. I'd get the information then have a think about it.

I scribbled the address that came on screen, and promised myself I'd send off for information. I giggled to think of me telling Charlotte I had a degree, completely forgetting that it would take me years and we'd probably be serving in separate places by then. Feeling a whole lot better, I went back to bed and slept like the dead.

*

Richard's wedding went without a hitch. Steve was best man and made an excellent job of it, considering his weakened state. I noticed Richard didn't tease him as much as usual; maybe he was finally growing up and his marriage was not doomed from the outset, as per Steve's prediction.

Once Richard and his new wife left to start their honeymoon, the DJ wound down the party with slower music. Guests started to dwindle. I went outside to cool off on the terrace. Steve was already there, leaning on a railing and sipping on a pint of bitter.

'All right, Steve?' I leant beside him.

'All right.'

'People are starting to leave. I'll be getting off shortly.'

'You haven't danced with me yet,' Steve said.

'I didn't think you'd be up to it,' I replied.

'I have been busy, but I'm always up for a dance.' Steve put his beer on a table, wrapped his arm around me and we did a little shuffle to the music right there on the terrace. The music stopped and Steve pulled me to him and kissed me.

I pulled away. 'What the hell was that?!'

Steve shrugged. 'I wanted to kiss you.'

'Steve, we talked about this when everyone thought we were an item. I thought we agreed you and I work better as friends.'

'How do we know, if we don't try?' Steve countered.

'I'm engaged!'

'To a man who has taken a three year posting on the other side of the planet, leaving you behind,' Steve shot back. 'I'd never do that.'

'He asked me to go with him but I didn't want to resign! Anyway, that's irrelevant; I'm off the market.' I brought my breathing under control then patted Steve's arm. 'Let's put this down to you mixing alcohol with your medication. If you remember this tomorrow, you'll cringe. Ring Emma: she's nice and she likes you a lot. I'm going to find your parents and say goodnight.' I turned and went back inside to say my goodbyes.

*

The phone woke me up. I looked at the clock and was shocked to see it was almost ten. I got up and padded off to answer it, but the phone went off before I could pick it up. Typical. Oh well, they'd ring back if it was important. There was a lot to be said for getting a bedside phone like Bev and Terry had. I'd have to get around to making some enquiries.

I went into the kitchen and flicked on the kettle. When I had got back the previous night, I had sat and thought about Steve for a while. He had tormented me when I had first arrived at Wyre Hall but over time we had forged a friendship that I valued. A friendship that would be threatened if he pulled another stunt like last night.

The phone rang again, and this time I got to it before it went off.

No greeting at all and my mother was crying!

'Beverley's been arrested. She's accused of killing one of the minded children.'

I sagged against the wall as the breath left my body. 'No, that can't be right.'

'She's been taken to High Lake police station.' I could hear Mum's breath coming in short gasps.

'Bev would never hurt the children,' I said.

'I know. Sam, what do we do? Terry is at the station waiting to find out what's happening, his mum has the children.'

'Tell me exactly what you know.'

'On Friday, one of the minded children wasn't well. Bev tried to get someone to collect him but they were busy at work. Bev took him to the hospital. It turns out he had a fractured skull and he died.'

'Which child?' I asked, my voice shaking.

'Jonathan.'

I remembered his laughter, his sweet smile and delight in building and rested my forehead against the cool wall.

'Are you still there?' Mum asked.

'Yes.' I gulped. 'There is nothing we can do at the moment. I wouldn't be allowed to become involved with this case even if it wasn't in a different division from mine.'

'Tell me the worst; what will happen?' Mum asked.

'Firstly, I'm not sure she will have been actually arrested. She's probably just been brought in to answer a few questions to clear up any misunderstandings,' I said.

'You mean helping with their enquiries, like you hear on television?' Mum said.

'I think so. Bev will be questioned about Jonathan's injury. The mother will also be questioned and anyone else who has a connection. There will have to be a post-mortem and evidence will be gathered from that. All this takes time.'

'Will it be murder?' Mum asked.

'Depends on the evidence,' I replied. 'For murder, they

have to prove intent or malice aforethought and that's difficult sometimes. Sometimes an act of omission, such has not taking steps to prevent the death is evidence enough, but she took him to the hospital so that's not the case here.'

Mum sniffed. 'So, in the worst case scenario, they might try to go for manslaughter. That's not as serious.'

Serious enough—the maximum sentence for manslaughter was also life—but Mum was stressed enough.

'Secondly, nobody will be charged until there is sufficient evidence to prove an offence. Bev won't be charged at all if the coroner rules it was misadventure or something along those lines. Probably the poor boy's had an accident and the hospital have been obliged to inform the police. Once they have investigated it will likely come to nothing.'

'Okay. Thanks. I'll tell Terry when he rings again.' Mum put the phone down.

I replaced the handset and, for a few seconds, I stared blindly at the wall. I had no doubt about Bev's innocence, but I also knew the legal system and, if the evidence pointed at her, she could end up charged if the verdict was not accidental death.

The phone rang again making me jump. I automatically picked up the phone.

'Hello.'

'Hi, Sam,' Gary said. 'Where were you earlier?'

'One of Beverley's minded children has died and she's being questioned,' I blurted out.

A moment's silence. 'Bloody hell. Do you need me to come home?'

'No. I love you for offering but there's nothing to be done. The truth will come out in the end.' I had to believe that. I had to let everyone believe that.

'Sam, I know you will want to try to help, but don't rush in. You must keep your distance. It's not your division and you're too close to Bev to be objective. Let the local jacks deal with this without interfering,' Gary said.

'You are lecturing me from six thousand miles away!'

'I know you. You won't be able to resist having a little dig around. You have form for it. Just don't jeopardise the investigation,' Gary replied.

'You're not my boss anymore! If you're just going to make assumptions and criticise me, I'm ending this call right now!' I went to slam the phone down but hesitated, then I put the handset back to my ear. I could hear Gary breathing.

'Still there?' Gary asked.

'Yes.'

'I don't mean to upset you, but you can't blame me for warning you off,' Gary said.

I thought back to the times I had rushed in on my own, but this was too close to home. I wouldn't get involved.

'All right,' I said. 'Let's talk about something else.'

'Let's talk about this if you need to,' Gary said.

'Like you said, we just have to let the local CID deal and wait for the outcome.'

'How was the wedding yesterday?' Gary asked.

Inside, I was dying with heartache and fear, but I pushed it down and embraced the new topic of conversation. 'Good,' I said in my fake bright voice. 'Steve thinks they won't last a year, but Richard seemed different, more adult.' I wondered if I should stay quiet about the kiss, but if it came out later, it might look like I was trying to hide something. 'Steve kissed me.'

'Did he? Remind me to punch him on the nose when I next see him,' Gary said.

I chuckled. 'He was drinking and I think it reacted with his tablets. He's going to be mortified if he remembers today. I didn't kiss him back, in case you were wondering.'

'In that case, I forgive him.' Gary grew quiet. 'Sam, I know it's hard being apart like this, but if you do decide to… kiss Steve back, or anyone else, just tell me.'

'I love only you.' I felt Gary's smile over the line. I don't know how, but I definitely did.

'It's getting late here, so I'm going to bed now. I wish you were with me.'

'Me too,' I whispered. 'Sleep tight.'

The phone line went dead and I replaced the handset. I needed a cup of tea, then I would go to Mum's and wait for news on Bev.

*

It was late afternoon before Beverley got home. Mum and I drove over there as soon as Terry rang us after collecting the children.

Bev sat, visibly stunned, as Mum bustled around making cups of tea and preparing something for the evening meal while Terry took the kids to the park.

'How was it?' I asked. Banal, I know, but I had to start somewhere.

'Not so bad,' Bev replied. 'At least I'm home.'

'Have you spoken to your parents?' I asked. Bev's parents lived on the south coast near Portsmouth.

'Not yet. I'll do it later.' She lapsed into silence again.

'It's standard practice to question everyone involved after something like this,' I said.

'I told them the truth, but I don't think they believed me.' Bev stared off into space. 'Tracey told me on the phone that Jonathan had fallen at her house that morning.'

'I thought you two weren't speaking.'

'Judith and her husband were away overnight to attend a function somewhere. I don't know where. They left Jonathan with Tracey and she brought him that morning, on her way to work. She left me her contact details in case of problems. Judith was supposed to have collected him at normal time.'

'But I thought you and Tracey weren't speaking,' I repeated.

'Needs must sometimes, and the children must come first. When Jonathan became ill, I rang and rang and begged Tracey to come and get him to a doctor. Eventually, she admitted he had

had a fall at her house. If she had told me that he'd fallen earlier, I wouldn't have waited so long before phoning an ambulance. Judith would have come at once but I couldn't ring her because I didn't know where she was.' Bev looked out of the window at a woman coming up the path. 'And here's Alma, the social worker who deals with childminders. No prizes for guessing why she's here.'

The doorbell rang and Bev answered it.

I stood up when Alma came into the room. 'I'll go and help Mum.'

'No, please stay, Sam,' Bev said.

'This is quite delicate so it might be better if your friend leaves,' Alma said.

'Sam is my cousin and I want her to stay,' Bev insisted. 'I can guess why you're here.' She sat down and indicated for Alma to do the same. I also sat back down.

Alma perched on the edge of the armchair as if ready to flee at any time, and took a sheaf of papers from her bag. 'We have been informed of an allegation made against you.'

'Jonathan died.' Bev played with the fringe around the edge of a cushion.

'Yes, apparently from an injury caused whilst in your care,' Alma said.

'That isn't the case. His aunt told me that he had fallen whilst at her house, but she brought him to me anyway, without letting me know. She only admitted it later on.' Bev hugged the cushion to her.

Alma looked at the papers she held. 'We can only go on the report we have. It seems that you may have been distracted and allowed him to go upstairs unsupervised.'

'That's ridiculous. You know from the spot checks that I keep a gate on those stairs at all times when I'm minding, and I only care for the number of children that I am registered for,' Bev cried. 'I've passed every spot check I've ever had.'

'This isn't the first complaint that we've received that you are too distracted to properly care for the children,' Alma said.

'What! When? Aren't I entitled to know when a complaint has been made about me?'

'You were visited.' Alma blinked quickly, signalling her confusion.

'That last spot check,' I said to Bev.

'It wasn't a spot check, was it?' Bev said.

'No it wasn't, and you should have been told about the allegation,' Alma agreed. 'Anyway, we have allowed the police access to our records—'

'Where they'll see the other allegation against me, an allegation I didn't know about and therefore I could not defend myself,' Bev cut in.

'I'm afraid we have no choice but to revoke your registration,' Alma continued.

'You'll be able to reinstate her when this is all sorted out, won't you?' I asked.

Alma didn't answer me. She stood up. 'I'm sorry, Beverley.'

'So am I,' Bev said. 'I'll show you out.'

They went into the hall and stood speaking for a few minutes. Mum peeped out of the kitchen.

'Is it safe to come back in?

'I think so,' I said. 'Bev's registration has just been revoked.'

'Oh dear.' Mum sat on the sofa next to me.

Bev closed the front door after Alma and came back in, wiping tears from her cheeks. 'Well, that wasn't entirely unexpected.' She exhaled loudly. 'I don't even have to contact the other parents; they've already done that for me. Isn't that kind.'

We sat in silence for a minute.

'I've done a cottage pie for tea,' Mum said.

'Thanks, Auntie Liz.' Bev smiled, then gasped. 'Sam, do you think this will get into the paper?'

I didn't have to answer; the local rag would fall on a story like this and Bev knew it.

Mum said, 'The coroner will rule it an accidental death and

nobody will be charged with anything and that poor little boy can be given a proper funeral.'

Bev tried and failed to raise a smile. 'He was such a sweet child.' She covered her face with her hands and cried for the little boy who loved building things.

Chapter Ten

Bev being Bev, she played down her predicament when she spoke to her parents and refused their offer for them to travel up to the Peninsula to be with her. She then forbade any of us to contact them with the true seriousness of the situation.

'I don't want them to worry,' she said.

'They'd want to support you too,' I argued.

'What's the point? They can't change anything, so why make them worry more than necessary.' She refused to budge on her stance. At least I had my leave, and could be there for her for a few days.

I didn't rest much during my leave. I spent a lot of time with Beverley, who had gone into a slump following Jonathan's death. I let Christopher and Carly have a sleepover at the flat so Bev and Terry could have a night out to unwind a little.

The weather wasn't great, but not unusual for spring. The children and I wrapped up, walked to the beach in the afternoon, played on the sand and paddled in the freezing water, then we walked to the fun fair and the amusement arcade and spent a couple of hours there shoving pennies into flashing machines. Then, following a fish and chip tea in a little café on the seafront, we walked slowly back to the flat.

Carly was yawning by the time we reached the junction of our road. I saw Tracey in her front garden. I considered approaching her and offering my condolences, but a little voice in the back of my mind suggested that it would not be a clever idea.

'I don't like her,' Carly said. 'She never smiles at us and I heard her tell Mummy she has too many children.'

'Then let's pretend we haven't seen her and keep walking. Maybe she will have gone inside when we get back.' I suggested.

The children trudged on and I looked across to Tracey, who was looking in our direction. I didn't want her to know I was connected to Beverley; I didn't know if that would cause a problem, but I didn't want to chance it.

After ten minutes it was obvious that Carly was flagging, so we turned back and approached the flats from the other side. Tracey was nowhere to be seen. Good. I hurried the children into the building before she had a chance to see us and come over. I had to assume she was watching all the time, which was a bit disturbing, especially now I had the children with me. I didn't want them to witness Tracey having a go at me.

*

Beverley heard no more about Jonathan that week, so I slowly relaxed. She still hadn't had her registration reinstated, but I expected that would happen once the social services had received the police report.

I had spent a few days avoiding Tracey, but in the end I had to get on with my life. If she approached me, I would offer my sympathies and that would be that. On my last day of leave, I was walking out to my car when I saw Tracey cross the road. I inwardly groaned and hoped that maybe she was not coming to the car park. No such luck; she came in and made a beeline for me. I spoke before she had a chance to say anything.

'I heard about your nephew. I'm sorry.'

Tracey stared at me for a moment. 'Thank you.'

I went to turn away but she said, 'I want to know what is happening with the case.'

If the family were waiting for a result, that meant the case was ongoing and no decision had been made. It was possible that Judith had had the results and had not shared them with Tracey, but I killed the thought as soon as it popped up. Of course Judith would tell Tracey. They were sisters. I had convinced myself that the pathologist would see that Jonathan's death had been accidental, but now I had a nasty squirm of anxiety in the pit of my stomach. The pathologist's report should have been back by now, even if the coroner had not yet made a ruling. Maybe the police were casting the net further and were checking out Beverley by interviewing the other minded children's parents as well. Perhaps they were speaking with Tracey's workmates about the calls that Bev had told me she had made.

I faced Tracey. 'I don't work in this division so I have nothing to do with it. You need to speak to the officer dealing. Your sister should have been given contact details.'

'I think she has them.' She paused for a moment before speaking again. 'You haven't been to work for a while.'

'I've been on leave,' I replied. I definitely felt stalked. Maybe I would mention it to Irene when I was next at work. She would do a card for the system and advise me if I should make a formal complaint.

'Oh. I hoped you had been sacked.'

Charming! I cracked a smile. 'Sorry to disappoint you.'

'Why were you with those children the other day?' Tracey asked.

My first instinct was to tell her to shove off and mind her own business, but I wanted to avoid confrontation, especially after my last comment, so I replied, 'They're my cousins.' Actually, first cousins once removed or something like that but I wasn't going to get into a discussion about my family with her.

'I see. So you are connected to my nephew's murder.'

'I am not connected to the case,' I reiterated. 'Also, from what I have heard, this is not a murder.'

'My nephew was killed. That's murder.' Tracey looked me up and down. 'And now I know why it's taking so long. You're all closing ranks and protecting her.'

Uh oh, I smelt a meltdown. 'That is not true,' I replied. 'And, as I told you, I am not from this division.'

'Yes it is!' Tracey's voice grew louder. 'I bet you knew she was dangerous all along, and lied to the social services so she could mind children. You knew she was dangerous but lied about it and now she's killed a baby. You're all lying to protect her and to protect yourselves. You won't get away with it. I'll make sure people know all about your lies. I will make sure that killer is convicted.'

Bev had become a childminder while I was still in Canada and I had had no connection to the police. I wasn't even used as a reference, but sometimes you meet a level of delusion or paranoia, or plain stupidity so great that you just know it is pointless arguing. This was one of those times.

I got into my car and spoke to her out of the window. 'Nothing you have said is true. Anyway, if you will excuse me, my mother is expecting me.' I left Tracey and drove out of the car park. She picked up a stone and threw it after me. It hit the rear windscreen but didn't damage it. I didn't stop; it wasn't worth the hassle. In this mood, Tracey would only use it against me, somehow.

I decided not to mention anything to Beverley; I wanted her to enjoy some peace of mind until we knew exactly what the coroner had ruled. One thing I was certain of, was that Tracey Quinn was mentally unwell and had probably been unwell before Jonathan died, which would account for the aggression and paranoia. However, I didn't feel I could bring up my concerns because it really would look as if I was trying to muddy the waters around the investigation.

*

Next day, I returned to work and went into the enquiry office because nobody told me not to. I felt more rested but worry about Beverley weighed on me. I told myself that it would do me good to be back in work. Keeping busy would distract me from dark thoughts.

'Fancy a cup of tea?' I asked Ray and Derek.

Derek put the phone down and scribbled on a job sheet. 'Ambo attended at 7 Sunderland Place. They're requesting our attendance.'

Ray took the sheet and scanned it. 'The Chius. You know them well, don't you, Sam?'

'Fairly well, because of baby Rose. What's happened there?' I asked.

'It's a bit vague; something about mother being ill. Everyone's still in parade. You go, it might be good for them to have a familiar face to deal with,' Ray said.

'I'm still working in the office.' I glanced at the door to the Sergeants' office.

'I'll square it with Bert,' Ray promised.

I took the job sheet, fetched my hat and jacket from my locker, and walked to the address.

When I got there, the door to number 7 was open, so I stepped inside and called out a greeting. One of the ambulance crew peered out of the living room and gestured for me to go back outside. I complied and he followed me.

'What's going on?' I asked.

'A woman has been suffocated with a pillow by the looks of it. The doctor has confirmed life extinct.'

'Eric's mother, or Cathy, his wife?' I asked.

'Middle-aged, fifties,' he said.

'Sounds like Eric's mother,' I said.

'You seem to know the family.'

'Their baby died of cot death a little while back and Cathy has been struggling mentally. She accused her mother-in-law of killing the child.'

'So she could be suffering some kind of post-partum psychosis, which drove her to take revenge?'

'Are you saying that Cathy did this? Have you found some evidence?' I asked.

He shrugged. 'No, but it's a strange coincidence isn't it.'

'Where is Cathy? Is she okay?' I asked.

'Don't know and don't know,' he replied.

'How's Eric?' I asked.

The ambulance man sighed. 'He's just closed down and isn't responding to anyone.'

Hardly surprising. Eric had lost his baby, his mother and now his wife had lost her mind. When found, Cathy would be placed under arrest and probably end up in a psychiatric unit for a long time.

'I need to let our Control know what's happened,' I said. 'Do you have a description of Cathy?'

'Sorry, love. She was gone before we got here.'

I radioed in an update then went inside the house.

The doctor was talking urgently into the phone. Eric sat on the same armchair that Cathy had sat in the last time she had held Rose. He stared ahead, but I could tell he wasn't seeing anything.

I touched his hand. 'Hello, Eric. I need to see Mrs Yang.' Nothing, not a flicker. I looked to the doctor who bobbed his head towards the stairs. 'I'm going upstairs, Eric. I'll be back shortly.' Again, no response, so I went upstairs anyway.

Mrs Yang lay on a green eiderdown. A blood smudged pillow lay beside her and a small trickle of blood had dried around her nose. The half-open eyes were the real giveaway. The whites had turned almost black as the blood vessels in the eyes had burst. This was the proof that Mrs Yang had been suffocated. Rose hadn't had that.

I radioed in my observations then left the room and closed the door behind me. It hadn't been the most secure scene before I had got there, but there was little I could do about that.

I heard Ray acknowledge Mike Sierra One and Mike Sierra Two; Shaun and the boss would be here shortly. Scenes of Crime and CID undoubtedly would be arriving soon after that. I went downstairs and everyone turned to me.

'I must ask everyone to stay out of the bedroom for now. CID will arrive soon, so you cannot move the deceased until then.'

I crouched beside Eric. 'Where is Cathy? Can you tell me what she's wearing today?'

He turned to me in slow motion. 'Cathy?'

'Yes, Eric. Where is she? Can you tell me what she's wearing?' I asked.

'Pink.'

'A pink dress, a pink top or a skirt?'

'A pink dress and black boots.'

I radioed in a description, but most people on B block had bought food at the chip shop and knew Cathy by sight.

The doctor knelt beside Eric. 'I don't like to leave you like this after such a shock. I'm to leave you a prescription for something to help for a few days.'

Eric surprised everyone by abruptly standing up. 'I'm going to look for Cathy.'

'That's not a good idea,' the doctor said. 'Why not let the police…'

Eric walked out of the room.

'Eric, please wait,' I called after him but he walked out of the house. I told control what had happened. I heard Ray pass it on as a "concern for welfare" observation. I was a little concerned for Cathy's welfare too. I had no idea where she was and now a traumatised Eric was looking for her. What would happen if he found her?

I had to trust that the rest of the block would be looking out for the Chius. I had enough to do with the crime scene at the house. then I would have to go to the mortuary, collect Mrs Yang's property, and even though the CID would investigate, I had to start the paperwork.

*

I was at the hospital, sorting through Mrs Yang's property, when

I heard Ray responding to a caller on the radio. I looked at my watch and saw it was almost scoff time. I had been so busy I had lost track of time.

'Roger Mike Two. Mike Sierra Two from control,' Ray transmitted.

The radio beeped as Shaun in Mike Sierra Two replied.

'From Mike Two, he has found Eric Chiu at the rear of the chippy. Can you RV with him please?' Ray transmitted.

The radio beeped again.

A minute's pause then Ray transmitted, 'Mike Two, Ambulance en route.'

The radio briefly beeped then there was silence. I felt pleased. Phil was the most compassionate and practical cop ever in my eyes. Eric would be all right with him. I hoped he would be able to tell Phil where Cathy was.

I determined that there was nothing more I could do where I was, so I radioed up for a lift back to the station for my break and a couple of hours of paperwork.

*

Phil came in as I was going back out. Normally he reffed at the same time as me, but he'd taken Eric to the hospital, which had taken time.

'How did you guess he was at the chippy?' I asked him.

'People in crisis or despair often go back to where they've been happiest. I took a gamble,' Phil replied.

'What was he doing?' I asked.

'Just sitting there,' Phil replied.

'Did he say anything?'

'Mostly mumbling about dreams and fate.'

'Nothing to help with locating Cathy?' I asked. She had now been circulated as the suspect in Mrs Yang's murder.

'Nothing I could make out. He's deeply traumatised. The hospital has given him a bed. He'll be assessed tomorrow morning.'

Yes, that was for the best. Three months ago, everything in his world seemed so happy, the future was bright, now everything was dust. How quickly things could change. Poor Eric and Cathy.

Chapter Eleven

I hadn't spoken to Steve since Richard's wedding because Beverley's predicament had overtaken everything, so I dropped in the following day. We shared an awkward little hug.

'I thought you weren't talking to me,' he said.

'As long as there's no repeat performance, we're fine,' I said.

'Why didn't you phone me?' he asked.

'I meant to, but something has happened… in the family. You could have phoned me, you know.'

'I thought you were angry with me, so it seemed better to wait for you. Then the longer it went on, the more it looked like I was right.' He paused for a moment. 'You don't look especially rested. What family stuff?'

'My cousin is a childminder. One of the children died of a fractured skull. She's been questioned about it. It's all rubbish but processes have to be followed.'

'How can someone prove that an accident didn't happen with them? That could have turned out so badly for her,' Steve said.

I didn't tell him it still might. I didn't want to think about that.

'I thought you were returning to work. I was surprised when you weren't there.'

'The hospital said I had to leave it another three weeks or so. The good news is that I've been discharged to my GP.'

'That's great!' I really meant it.

'Erm, I've asked Emma to come to Ken's wedding with me. I know we normally go to things like that together but I thought you were angry…' Steve's voice trailed away.

'That's great too. She's a nice girl and really likes you.'

'You don't mind?' Steve asked.

'Of course not. I'll be with people I know.'

'Mum was a bit miffed. She had you lined up as the next Mrs Patton,' Steve said.

I laughed. 'I'm sure she'll like Emma when she meets her. I'll have a word and tell her I approve if you like.'

'Don't you dare! Good God, my mum and my best friend conspiring together. I have no dignity left.'

'Speaking of marriage, how's Richard?' I asked.

Steve shrugged. 'He seems to be okay.'

'You still think it'll be all over in a year?'

Steve snorted. 'It's Dick the Berk, he won't be faithful.'

'He seemed more mature, so I hope you're wrong,' I said.

'Time will tell,' Steve said in a tone that told me he had decided on the outcome.

'Okay then,' I said. 'I only dropped in to make sure we're all right and that you're going to spring me from the front office soon.'

'No worries on both counts,' Steve said.

I accepted his offer of tea and chocolate bourbons and we chatted for an hour or two. Everything felt normal again. I was glad.

*

The local newspaper came out again the following day. Mrs Yang was this week's front page news. A picture of the closed chip shop added a sense of pathos to the article, which asked for sightings of Cathy to be reported to the police.

I went for a cuppa with Mum and we sat at the kitchen table with the paper between us.

'Tragic,' Mum said. 'I had a touch of the baby blues, but nothing like this.' She closed the paper. 'When I was in hospital having you, they kept us in for two weeks, not like now. The woman in the next bed to me went into psychosis. She thought she was in a hotel and the babies in the little cots were monkeys. She was frightened of them and decided to leave. She was found wandering in the hospital grounds in the early hours, barefoot and in her nightie. Lucky it was summertime. The staff had to remove the child to the nursery to be looked after. I heard from gossip at the baby clinic that he went home with his dad and his nan. The mother went onto the psychiatric ward and, when she was allowed home, she had no memory of what happened. She never had any more children; her husband didn't want to risk it happening again.'

Would Cathy remember blaming Mrs Yang for Rose's death, I wondered. Would she remember demanding her arrest and would she remember killing her? Tragic didn't begin to describe the situation.

*

Three weeks passed and there was no sign of Cathy Chiu. Not a single sighting. Eric returned home, and Eamon and Mike kept in touch with him, but I was stuck in the office dealing with the random incidents that happened. Occasionally I heard snatches of conversations and gossip so I was able to keep abreast of events, but I was feeling left out.

During this time, Andy and Charlotte were allowed out solo. Andy was like an untethered puppy, hyper with excitement, but Charlotte was cooler; in fact, she complained that her specialness had not been recognised and she'd had to complete her time in company. I don't think she realised that we all laughed about it behind her back.

As expected, she disliked her new nickname even more than she hated being called Charlie, which made us use it even more than we normally would.

'Don't knock it,' I told her. 'Charlotte's Web was one of my favourite books, and the spider is a pretty cool character.'

'A spider though,' Charlotte objected.

'I get it: you won't be happy until we're all calling you, Ma'am,' I said.

'Exactly,' Spider said. 'Feel free to practice anytime you wish.'

I had the feeling she wasn't joking.

At home, I received an information pack from the Open University. I read through and liked what I saw. I needed to complete at least six units of increasing complexity to build up enough points to graduate with a degree. Doing one a year, it would take me six years. I could do more, but that seemed a bit of a stretch with work and the promotion exams. I wondered if I should postpone taking promotion exams for a year or two. It wasn't as if there was any rush.

When Gary called again, I told him about my plans for a degree.

'I think it's a great idea,' he said. 'Have you decided on a subject?'

'Not yet, I don't have to decide a particular subject to start with, so I could just start with something that would interest me.'

Gary chuckled. 'I don't think they do chocolate studies.'

I chuckled too. 'Shame, they should. Not maths, I'm useless at maths. I might do a sociology-based foundation unit, which opens the way to loads of interesting courses.'

'And you'll be able to continue even if you come to Hong Kong eventually,' Gary said.

I hadn't thought of that, but it was a valid point. I really had to get around to thinking more about the future: specifically, Gary's and my future.

I didn't want to make a big fuss about my plan at work, not least because I would have to wait until September to begin my studies, and I didn't want Spider to get all superior about it. What I did want was to get more than a 2:2, just to rub her nose in it.

109

Of course I told Steve and Ken, with dire warnings of their fate if they told anyone else.

'You'll be about thirty before you're finished,' Ken said when I told him about it.

'I'm going to be thirty whether I take a degree or not, so I might as well do a degree,' I replied.

'What does the boss say about it,' Ken asked.

'He's supportive; and I told you, we can call him Gary now.'

'No, he'll always be the boss,' Ken said.

So, now I had a timetable. If I was going to take the promotion exams, I needed to get any studying done between now and September, and then I needed to concentrate on the OU. No problem.

*

Steve returned to work and took the front office, freeing me to go back out on patrol. I went to the parade room for the first time in ages and took my usual seat. The door opened and we all stood up as Inspector Benjamin, Shaun and Bert came in to start parade.

'Still no sign of Cathy Chiu yet,' Bert said before he gave out the duties. 'Bear in mind she's mentally unstable if you happen to come across her.'

'She'll be halfway across to Ireland by now,' Frank said. 'And I don't mean on a ferry.' Spider nodded her agreement.

So much time had passed, I didn't disagree: many of our *mispers*—missing persons—ended up in the river. Some washed up, others were caught in the current in the middle of the river and were swept out past the estuary and into the Irish Sea, destined to remain forever on our *misper* list. We'd never know how many went that way.

'Maybe. But for now, we're still keeping an eye out for her,' Bert said.

'Shouldn't we organise a search, Sarge?' Andy asked.

'If we knew where to centre it, we would,' Inspector Benjamin said. 'We don't have the staff to be able to start a search over the whole of the Peninsula. We'll have to wait for a definite sighting to come in.'

'Or a report of a body,' Frank muttered. 'It'll be a mess after all this time in the water. The skin will be like blancmange.'

'If there's any left,' Charlotte added.

'Thank you, Francis and Charlotte, that'll do,' Bert scanned the room. 'If everyone's ready, I'll give out the duties.'

I sat, pen poised ready to jot down my beat, refs and anything of note I might need. I was given my usual beat out by the park. Whether it was coincidence or Bert's idea of rotating the beats had fallen flat, I would have to find out later.

*

At refs, I picked up *The Clarion* that someone had left behind. One step up from the local paper, it covered the whole Peninsula and surrounding areas. I settled down at the Formica table picked up a sandwich and opened the paper. On page three, positioned discreetly by another article about local councils dealing with traffic outside schools, the headline punched me in the gut.

"Childminder questioned in baby death."

It wasn't a big write up, just an inch or so of one column credited to a journalist named Anne Leigh. It simply described how Jonathan had died of a fractured skull in hospital and how his childminder had been helping police with their enquiries. It named the town, and I knew it wouldn't take much to work out who the childminder was. I couldn't imagine the investigating officers at High Lake would be impressed either. Word was spreading. How long before the nationals got hold of it.

I raced across to the phone and dialled Bev's number.

'Bev, it's Sam. Have you seen *The Clarion*?'

'Yes.' Bev's voice sounded thick and hoarse. She'd obviously been crying for ages. 'I didn't think the police would release anything yet. People are going to work out that it's me.'

'It hasn't come from the police. If you read to the end, it says that they contacted the police and they refused to comment,' I said.

'Then who?' Bev wasn't really asking, more thinking aloud. 'Why haven't the police let me know what's happening? This is going to make me look guilty.'

'The police will continue their investigation and anything that appears in the paper won't influence it,' I said.

'Other people will be influenced though. You know what it's like when the public has a hate figure, and nobody is hated more than child killers. They'll read this and decide I'm guilty without even thinking about it.'

'It doesn't matter what everyone else thinks,' I said. 'We believe you and when the investigation is over, everyone else will have to believe you too.'

'I wish I had your faith in the system, Sam.'

I wished I could say something to make her feel better. I had to cling to my belief that the system would work and Bev would hear nothing more about it, but I knew that sometimes evidence could misdirect investigators. I fervently hoped that this would not happen here.

We ended our call with promises to keep in close contact.

I couldn't get directly involved, but I could give Bev pointers and advice on the processes. I switched my brain to police mode, sat down at the table with a pen and paper and started to list the direction the investigation would likely go.

I wrote the names Judith, Bev and Tracey on one side of the sheet. Judith had been away so I wrote a note next to her name. Perhaps Jonathan had been injured before she had dropped him at Tracey's house, but then he would have shown symptoms before he was with Bev. I crossed a line through Judith's name, it was highly unlikely she was connected to the injury.

Tracey had firmly pointed a finger at Bev, therefore Bev was a suspect and it was correct that she had been questioned. Tracey would also have been questioned and, as far as I knew, had dodged any blame. Bev had told me that Tracey had admitted on the phone that Jonathan had fallen at her home. Why would Tracey deny this? The most obvious answer was because she was afraid of the consequences. I jotted a few words next to her name, then turned the thought on its head. What if Bev was lying to me? Why would she do that? She was scared of the consequences, the same as Tracey. As I thought it, I didn't really believe it, but I was not Cousin Sam here, I was Constable Barrie and I was trying to be impartial. Bev lying was something I had to consider. I added a note next to Bev's name.

I strongly suspected that it had been Tracey who had contacted the paper. She had made threats during her rant at the flats. She was the aggressive sister; Judith just seemed to go along with her. Why would Tracey contact the paper? Because she knew that they would probably run the story as far as they were allowed before charges were laid. and that would gain public sympathy. I wrote another note against her name.

If Jonathan had fallen at her home, had any offences taken place? Accidents happened all the time. Had she sought help at once I didn't doubt that, tragic as the outcome was, Tracey would not have been charged with anything. However, by refusing to come home when Beverley asked, she caused a delay. Whether that delay caused Jonathan's death, or whether he would have died anyway, I couldn't say. That was a decision for the coroner. If it had contributed to his death, Tracey could argue that it had been unintentional and we would find it hard to prove intent, which would rule out a murder charge but could tip the balance towards a charge of manslaughter. Had Tracey realised that? It was something else to consider. I jotted another note.

The most obvious thing to me was that Bev had to somehow find the evidence that Tracey had told her about Jonathan falling on the stairs. The jacks at High Lake would get the phone records, but that would only show that calls had been made. If the records proved that Bev had made a number of calls to

Tracey's workplace, that could be proof Bev tried to get her to come home for Jonathan, but it wasn't definite proof.

I sighed. The best proof, barring Tracey suddenly admitting everything, would be a record of that phone call. Dammit, why had Bev discarded that answering machine? But even if she hadn't discarded it, Tracey would have had to phone Bev and Bev would have had to allow the phone to ring long enough for it to kick in to get the evidence she needed. It was so unlikely it was not worth thinking about.

I'd share my thoughts with Bev, but that was a much as I could do for now.

Steve came in and sat beside me.

I pushed the paper towards him.

'Shit,' he breathed. 'Who let that out?'

'Not us, that's for sure. I think it was the child's family,' I replied.

'They need advising that they could be jeopardising the investigation,' he said.

'Not our division, not our place,' I said.

Steve took a deep breath. 'I suppose you're well out of it.'

'I'm not out of it, Bev's my cousin. I just can't take part in the investigation.'

'At least they haven't named her,' Steve said.

'It's not going to take Einstein for locals to work it out though,' I replied.

Steve patted my shoulder. 'I'll make us a nice cup of tea to have with our scoff.' He disappeared into the kitchen. I threw the paper into the bin.

*

The Clarion's offices were near to Wyre Hall, so when I went out again, I called in and asked to speak to Anne Leigh. I was treading on dangerous ground, but I was too angry to care if anyone considered it interference or not.

114

'I'm sorry, nobody of that name works here,' the receptionist replied.

'She wrote a short article in this week's paper,' I said.

The receptionist smiled. 'Oh, that means nothing. We sometimes take stuff from freelance journalists and even the public if it's interesting.'

I wanted to tell her not to believe everything Anne Leigh said, but I had already overstepped the mark.

'I'll let my boss know she doesn't work here. Thank you.' I left the building and then it hit me what a foolish thing I had done. If my visit got back to Anne Leigh, it could be twisted to seem like intimidation. I might have made things worse for Bev. There was good reason I needed to keep away from the investigation, and I needed to remember that.

*

On my next rest day, I went to Beverley's again. Terry was in work and the children were in their school. I didn't want to crowd Bev, but I didn't want her to be left alone either. We passed the afternoon chatting, drinking coffee and sharing observations about life in general and specifically, the investigation.

'I swear, everyone went quiet when I approached the school,' she said.

'You need to remember that you have only been questioned,' I said. 'Let's be optimistic, maybe they are on their way right now to let you know it was a terrible accident and they're closing the case.'

Bev pointed upwards. 'Oh look, there goes another pig at thirty thousand feet.' She grinned. 'That wasn't a dig at your job by the way.'

'I didn't take it as such.' I smiled back.

Bev looked at the clock and stood up. 'Time for the school run.'

'I'll come with you,' I offered.

115

'No, you stay here. I won't be long. Bev picked up her bag and went for the children.

While she was gone, I prepared more tea and got out two tubes of Smarties I had brought for the children. Bev said I had to stop spoiling them, but I enjoyed it and I knew she didn't really mind.

The kettle boiled and there was still no sign of them. The school wasn't far and I had expected them back within fifteen minutes. I made my own tea and sat sipping it whilst imagining reasons for their lateness. I wasn't worried, she had probably got into conversation with someone, or had needed to speak to a teacher.

After forty minutes, I heard the front door opening and jumped up to greet Christopher and Carly. Instead of rushing at me and waiting for their sweets, they trailed in with barely a word and went straight into the dining room.

'What's happened?' I asked Bev. 'Is that a black eye on Christopher?'

Bev slammed her bag onto the worktop and flicked on the already boiled kettle. 'Some little toerag in his class told him that I was a murderer and I was going to go to prison. Christopher stood up for me and it resulted in a fight. I got called into the head teacher's office and, instead of taking action against the kid that started it, he's suspended Christopher. He didn't even listen to me when I told him I had only been questioned and not arrested.' She flumped onto one of the stools. 'If that wasn't bad enough, someone in Carly's class is having a party and everyone got an invitation except for her. I can put up with the other parents giving me the cold shoulder, I can even pretend I can't hear them talking about me, but I will not put up with my kids being targeted.' She sighed. 'I suppose there's no point in planning a party for Carly's birthday; nobody will come.'

'Oh, Bev.' I didn't have the words.

Bev gazed off into the distance. 'There was a woman with a camera at the school gates. She took my photograph as I came out, after speaking to the head.'

'I hope you said something to her,' I said.

'I told her to get lost but she followed me with a tape recorder and kept snapping and shouting questions.' Bev lowered her voice. 'I finished up telling her to eff off and went into the phone box to pretend to call the police.'

'Why didn't you call them?' I asked. 'The kids must have been terrified.'

Bev gave a bitter laugh. 'Because I didn't think they'd be interested. I'm a suspected baby killer, remember? Even if nothing comes of this, the other parents at school are always going to be suspicious of me.'

It seemed the human race hadn't developed very much past the witch hunter days, when mere suspicion could doom a woman.

I cocked my head towards the other room. 'Can I give the kids their sweets?'

Bev got up to make the tea. 'Yeah, go ahead. It might make them feel better. I'll bring the drinks in.'

I went into the dining room and held out the Smarties. The children took them but remained quiet.

I sat down at the dining table. 'Don't listen to the other kids. You know your mum would never harm anyone.'

'Darren Lovell said it was in the paper and that means it's true,' Christopher said.

'Sometimes the paper gets its facts wrong.' I so wanted to make him feel better.

'Then why isn't Mum allowed to look after the little kids anymore?' Christopher asked.

'Your mum wouldn't be able to help the police if she was busy looking after the little ones,' I replied.

The children accepted that and settled down to eat their sweets.

Bev brought the teas in and sat opposite me. 'I think I might take them out of school.'

'Isn't that playing into their hands?' I asked.

Bev shrugged. 'But it's plain we're not welcome. I think it'll save a lot of bother overall.'

'If you think that's best,' I said.

'Want to stay for your tea?' Bev asked.

'Tell you what, I'll go to the chippy and get us all tea: my treat,' I said.

The children looked happier than they had since they came in, and called across orders for a battered sausage and a fishcake. I agreed to everything. I'd have bought them anything to make things right for them.

Terry came in. Beverley looked at the clock and frowned.

'You're back early.'

Terry sighed. 'I was called into head office and told it would be better if I took some leave until all this blows over. Hi Sam.'

I waved silently.

Bev went pale. 'They're forcing you out because of me?'

'They're calling it "leave".' He spotted Christopher. 'What the hell happened to Chris?'

Bev sent the children upstairs to play. 'Darren Lovell did it because Christopher defended me when Darren called me a murderer.' Bev put her hands over her face and wept. 'It's not fair: the kids and now you.'

'I hope you complained to the teacher,' Terry said.

'I didn't get the chance. When I went to collect them, I was called to the Head's office and he's suspended Christopher. Also Carly has been left out of a birthday party. The whole class was invited except her.'

'Bloody hell!' Terry punched the wall in frustration, which shocked me. Normally he was the mildest of men.

Bev wiped her eyes. 'I think we need to talk about what to do.' I went to stand up but Bev said, 'I can say what I'm thinking in front of you, Sam. Terry, I think you and the kids should go to your mother's and it would be best if I didn't go with you. I'll tell the school tomorrow that we're withdrawing the children.'

'We'll get into trouble if we don't send the kids to school,' Terry said.

'We'll home school them and hire a tutor for the bits we're not good at until we can enrol them at another school,' Bev said.

Terry rubbed his chin. 'It's not right that you have to live apart from me and the kids.'

'It's for the best, Terry. The kids have been bullied today and it might get worse. Once everything is sorted out, you can come back.'

Terry chewed his lip for a moment then nodded. 'Okay, if you think that's best.'

'I think you should go as soon as possible. Today, in fact. When they realise I'm no longer at the school gates, they might come here.'

'Who might come here?' Terry asked.

Bev examined her nails. 'A woman—a journalist—followed me taking photographs. I told her to get lost. I had to go into a phone box and pretend to ring the police before she left us alone.'

'Which paper?' Terry demanded.

'I don't know. I don't know,' Bev cried.

Terry gritted his teeth. 'She'd better not show her face around here. I'll give her what for.'

'And she'd use it as evidence that we're a violent family,' Bev said. 'Bad idea.'

'Where will you go?' Terry asked.

'You can go to Mum's,' I said. I knew Mum wouldn't mind.

'I don't want to bring trouble to Auntie Liz,' Bev replied. 'I'll stay here for now. If things get bad, I'll book into a B&B or something.

'Come to Ma's with us,' Terry said.

'I don't want to bring the press to her door either.'

'You know Ma would send them off with a flea in their ear. I'll go and ring her.' Terry was grinding his teeth as he went into the hall to use the phone.

I said to Bev. 'Give me a description.'

'No, Sam, you can't be involved,' Bev said.

'I can't be involved because you are family, but I can pass things on to High Lake.'

'Okay,' Bev sniffed. 'She's blonde, obviously dyed, and she was wearing a checked houndstooth coat, beige.'

'Okay, I'll put the word out. If she turns up here, do ring the police because it amounts to harassment,' I said.

'The High Lake police won't care,' Bev said.

'You haven't been arrested or charged with anything,' I argued.

'No, but I will be, I just know it. Tracey's pushing all the blame onto me.'

'Maybe the phone company can check over their logs?' I suggested.

'That's what the police said when I was interviewed, but I don't think they meant it nicely. I think they think it will provide evidence against me.'

'If it shows you trying to get in touch with her, it's got to help your case,' I said. 'I'll go to the chippy now. Then, after tea, you need to get the kids ready for their big holiday at Grandma's house,' I said, hoping she'd take the hint to treat this as an adventure for them.

'I won't half miss them,' Bev said.

'I know, but like you said, it's for the best, and you'll see them every day when you go to do their lessons with them.'

Bev smiled. 'I might allow them a week or two off first.'

Terry came back in. 'Ma says you should come with us.'

'No, Terry, I don't know how bad this will get. Let the kids have some peace. I'll be fine.'

I left them to discuss it while I went to the chip shop.

Chapter Twelve

Work was reasonably distracting from the chaos at home. Derek had taken a call about some kind of disturbance behind Devon Road. I groaned when I went to get my radio and Ray passed it on to me. Mr Paxton at number fifteen was at it again.

'I'll walk out with you,' Andy said. 'I'm on the next beat.'

We stepped out and headed towards our areas.

'You look glum. What's your job?' Andy asked.

'Mr Paxton at 15 Devon Road is one to bear in mind if you ever cover the area. His house backs on to a playing field, but he hates kids and rings up all the time.'

'What was there first: his house or the field?' Andy asked.

'They probably arrived at the same time, but Mr Paxton only moved in a few years ago.'

'Why did he buy a house by a playing field if he hates kids?' Andy wondered.

'My argument exactly. Drunks at night is one thing, but he won't even tolerate the little kids playing. He doesn't like me because I refuse to move them.'

'Can I come with you? I'd like to meet him.' Andy asked.

We weren't supposed to come off our beat areas unless it was to give assistance to someone, but it was only just across from Andy's beat and sometimes a little back-up was not a bad thing. It would be good for Andy to meet Mr Paxton, in company with someone instead of encountering him alone as I had. I'd square it with Shaun. If anything was said, I'd tell him I'd asked Andy to come with me.

'Okay then,' I agreed.

We walked past the playing field and noted that the children playing there were not being disruptive. From there we went on to number fifteen.

I knocked at the door and waited for Mr Paxton to answer.

'He might prefer to speak to you because you're a new face and won't tell him to get lost,' I said to Andy.

Mr Paxton opened the door. 'You!'

'Yes, me again. What's the problem, Mr Paxton?' I asked.

'Those damned kids. Perhaps if you did your job and moved them away, I wouldn't have to keep ringing up.'

'I've told you before: I'm not moving children playing on a playing field. We walked past there and they are not being disruptive.'

Mr Paxton chomped on his dentures. 'So that's it? You won't do as I say?'

'If it means moving children on from an area specifically designed for them, no we will not,' I said.

He looked from me to Andy. 'I fought for this country and when I need assistance, what do I get? An insolent woman and a darkie. You don't belong in uniform, either of you.'

'You watch your mouth!' I exclaimed. 'I don't care if you single-handedly stormed Berlin. You don't insult my friend.' I nodded to Andy and stalked back down Mr Paxton's path. Andy followed.

'I'm lodging a complaint against you,' Mr Paxton shouted after us.

'And I'm going to make sure that your offensive comments feature on our job sheet,' I called back.

Mr Paxton slammed his door. I felt ashamed on Mr Paxton's behalf. Poor Andy didn't deserve to be abused like that. He was a lovely person. I felt as if I had to apologise.

'I'm sorry he used that word,' I said.

'Don't be; I've heard it all before.'

I was still angry. 'It doesn't make it right.'

'No, but I've learnt to pick my battles,' Andy said.

We walked for a couple of minutes.

'Is he married?' Andy sounded as if he was thinking aloud rather than asking a question.

I don't think there is a Mrs Paxton; I've never seen her if there is.' I answered.

'I doubt that he is. He might have something more to think about if he were married.'

'Or maybe she would be a calming influence on him,' I said.

Andy nodded then said, 'Ah well, I'd better get onto my own patch. Have a tranquil one.'

I smiled; he was observing the superstition of never saying the "Q" word lest all manner of chaos descended.

'See you, Andy,' I watched him stroll towards his beat and resumed my own patrol.

*

An hour later, I heard Ray call me.

'4912 go ahead.'

'Sam, Mr Paxton is on about that field again. Be aware, he said he didn't want you but I told him there was nobody else.'

I gritted my teeth. 'Roger, en route.'

I reluctantly made my way to Devon Road and knocked at number fifteen. Mr Paxton answered and looked me up and down and curled his lip.

'Where's your friend?'

Ignoring his question, I asked, 'What's the problem now, Mr Paxton?'

'There's a chinkie woman on the field, but I don't suppose you'll care.'

Normally, I wouldn't have cared but Cathy Chiu was still outstanding. I needed to probe a little deeper.

'A Chinese lady?' I said, hoping he's take the hint that some words were no longer acceptable. 'Is she walking a dog or something, or is she generally hanging about?'

'Hanging around.'

'What drew your attention to her?' I asked.

'We don't have chinks living around here.'

My gentle prompting hadn't had an effect. From his earlier reaction to Andy, I guessed that Mr Paxton disliked a foreigner near his house even more than he disliked the neighbouring children.

'Have you seen her often or just the once?' I wanted to be clear.

'Are you going to see to her?' he asked in a most unpleasant manner.

'First, can you give me a description?' I asked.

'Bloody hell, woman! What description do you need? I just told you; we have no chinks here but there's one on the field. She'll be easy to spot if you bother going there.'

I would check this out but first I needed to head off his inevitable next demand.

'On this occasion, I will check around the field just to make sure all is well with this Chinese woman. Be clear, I will not be moving any children on while I am there unless they are being rowdy.'

'I suppose a half-arsed job is better than nothing,' he grumbled and shut the door.

I walked to the field and surveyed the area. The days were starting to get noticeably longer so it was still light. A couple of children played but there was no sign of any woman.

I walked over to the copse on the far side of the field. There was a small clearing within it with clear evidence that someone had been there recently, but it was often used by teenagers I couldn't be sure someone was staying there. I made a mental note to come back after nightfall, or perhaps a note in the parade book for nights to check it out. I radioed in the results of the job, along with my observations and the parade book request. I didn't want to go back to update Mr Paxton; I didn't doubt he would ring again before long. I resumed patrol. I really hoped it was Cathy Chiu and she was not dead in the sea.

I made hourly visits to the field, but I didn't see a Chinese woman. Before I went off duty, instead of writing off Mr Paxton's call on the job sheet, I completed a suspicious incident form and sent a copy to CID to be attached to the file on Mrs Yang's murder. Mr Paxton would be proud that his call had led to actual paperwork.

*

Back at home, I couldn't settle to anything. I wanted to help Bev so badly, but I had no idea how to help without her—or the CID—seeing it as interference. I could go to the school and try to see who the mysterious photographer might be. Would that be seen as interference? Not if I didn't start questioning people. I'd just hang around and see what I could see and hear what I could hear. I imagined Gary at my shoulder, telling me to be careful and not to butt into another division's investigation, but I pushed the thought aside. If I picked up anything interesting, I would pass it on to High Lake. I had often been told too much information in a case is better than too little.

Next morning, I got up nice and early and drove over to Christopher and Carly's newly ex school. Parents, mostly mothers and a few grandmothers gathered on the pavement waiting for the gate to be opened. I parked a short distance away and walked over to the crowd, choosing to remain on the periphery. I tuned into a couple of conversations around me, which unsurprisingly, were about Beverley. They all agreed on her guilt. I had to bite my tongue to stop myself from shouting at them.

A woman sidled up to me. 'Are you with a paper?' Without waiting for a reply she launched into a monologue, 'I suppose it's about that murdering bitch. It's not right she's wandering around free, mixing with decent folk while that poor little lad is in morgue. It's a shame they got rid of hanging. I know a few of us here would like to pull the lever. I'd love to get her alone for five minutes, she wouldn't hurt anyone else...'

I stared at the woman without speaking and watched as she trailed to silence. Her expression became uncertain. I considered flashing my warrant card and arresting her for something, anything. However, that would definitely be poking my nose into a case that was not from my division. I could see traces of Maureen Clough in her. Not in looks but in her reaction to drama. The wide eyes, the unconsciously upturned mouth. She loved it, she was drawn to it, maybe she even craved it. I think it was Andy Warhol who said that everyone would be famous for fifteen minutes. This woman wanted her fifteen minutes.

I said, 'What's your name?'

'Why? Oh, for the paper.' She grinned. 'It's Mary Lovell. My boy, Darren is in that bitch's son's class.' She pushed forward a boy with greasy, lank hair. 'Darren says he's always been a bit weird. Isn't that right, Darren?'

Darren said nothing. I regarded the unremarkable child who had given my cousin's son a black eye and didn't smile.

'It might be something in the genes.' Mary looked over my shoulder. 'There's one of your lot, over there.'

I turned and saw a woman in a houndstooth check coat fiddling with a camera. I went over to her.

'Do you have a business card I can have?'

She automatically fished a card from her pocket and held it out.

I quickly took the card and read it aloud. '"Anne Leigh. Journalist".' So this was the person who had written that small piece in *The Clarion*.

She eyed me for a moment and I spotted the look of recognition. She knew I was a police officer, but I was not going to confirm it for her.

The children poured through the newly-opened gate and parents started to leave. I moved away from Anne. Mary Lovell came up to me.

'Darren said that Christopher isn't here, so if you're waiting to see that cow, you're out of luck. I know her well, so if you want to come to my house I can give you the low down. For a small fee.' She handed me a scrap of paper with a phone number on it and winked. I put it in my pocket hoping that Anne hadn't overheard. I glanced around but the freelance reporter was nowhere to be seen, so I left too and went straight to Bev's house.

'Do you know Mary Lovell well?' I asked.

'Alky. Rough as a dog's arse,' Bev said. 'We've barely exchanged two words.'

'Well, she's making out you two are best pals and she's happy to dish the dirt, for a fee,' I told her.

'Cow!' Bev spat.

'That aside, that journalist woman was there again. She's called Anne Leigh. She wrote that piece in the paper. I think she's trying to make her name with your case,' I said. 'I'll give High Lake the heads-up. I wish there was more I could do to help you.'

'Thanks, Sam. I appreciate what you do. I especially appreciate that you believe me.'

I squeezed her hand and tried to pass some strength to her telepathically.

I didn't hang around at Bev's; I wanted to contact High Lake with information on Anne Leigh.

I drove straight home and dialled High Lake's number and asked to be put through to the CID office. Once through, I explained about Anne Leigh outside the school.

'So what do you want me to do about it?' the jack asked.

'You could try speaking to her,' I suggested. 'She's harassing a woman and she has intimidated her children.'

'Diddums,' he replied

My jaw dropped. 'I beg your pardon?'

'In case nobody has bothered explaining this to you, it's a free country and it sounds to me as if Anne Leigh is not breaking any laws. She hasn't entered any property or broken anything belonging to Mrs Thompson, or assaulted her or stolen anything from her.'

'She chased a woman and her children. That is plain wrong; it has to be public order offences at least,' I insisted.

'Mrs Thompson is the suspect in a child killing,' he replied.

A suspect? I had thought that by now the report would have confirmed that Jonathan had died as a result of an accident. What other evidence did the jacks have that made Bev a suspect?

'That is irrelevant,' I said. 'It is not okay for a freelance journalist to terrorise children. If Mrs Thompson is a suspect, so's Tracey Quinn, but I don't see reporters harassing her.'

'Mrs Quinn is not a suspect,' he said. 'The injury happened when she was at work.'

And there it was. They, and probably all of High Lake, believed Tracey's story. The investigation was centred wholly on Beverley. This was not good.

'Mrs Thompson is a suspect, not the offender, and is entitled to go about her life without harassment,' I insisted.

'All evidence we have so far indicates that she is culpable,' he said.

'Then charge her,' I challenged. I paused for a moment. 'Your evidence isn't good enough. That's it, isn't it? The PM report supports that Jonathan had a terrible accident, doesn't it? You don't have anything apart from Tracey Quinn pointing a finger and deflecting blame from herself. You're hoping that if you lay on enough pressure, Beverley Thompson will cough. I bet it hasn't even been crimed. And, what the hell are you doing revealing any information on the phone? I could be anyone, I could even be a reporter, or are you also leaking info to the media?'

'I know you're in the job from the way you talk. What's your interest in this?' he demanded.

He'd picked up on my use of jargon, which was now my normal mode of speech. I would have preferred him not to know

I was a police officer. I wondered if I should admit that Beverley was my cousin. No, not yet, even though Tracey had probably shouted it from the rooftops.

'I thought you would want to know that Mrs Thompson is being harassed by a reporter and you might not want the media sticking their oar into an ongoing investigation just yet, but I guess you're just too lazy and incompetent to give a toss.' I slammed the phone down.

'Bloody wazzer!' I shouted. My heart was racing. I went into the kitchen and made tea to calm me down.

Chapter Thirteen

A couple of days later, the phone woke me up. I fell out of bed and staggered to the hall. I must get around to seeing about getting a bedroom extension.

'Bev's been arrested! Properly arrested. On suspicion of manslaughter. They asked her to go to the station and we thought it was to tell her there'd be no further action, but they arrested her,' Terry said.

This was my fault. I shouldn't have goaded the jack at High Lake when I phoned. I felt a big parcel of guilt to put on my pile. I had joined the police to make things better, to help people, but here I had just made things worse.

'Okay, they don't have sufficient evidence to charge her with murder but she is the current main suspect.'

'Is that supposed to be comforting?' Terry snapped.

He was stressed so I didn't take offence, but I was stressed too. I had convinced myself that Bev would hear no more.

'I'm just telling you what I know about situations like this, Terry. She'll be kept in custody and questioned again. They can keep her for twenty-four hours. As long as she's not charged, she will probably be bailed. More enquiries will be made. Then the decision will be made whether to charge her or not.'

'Bloody hell. This is a nightmare. Bev is innocent,' he said.

'I believe she is too.'

'Is there anything you can do?' Terry asked.

'Sorry, it's not my division, and even if it was, I wouldn't be allowed near this.'

'Like doctors,' Terry murmured. 'I've a good mind to go around to see Judith and tell her what's happened. She needs to accept that Jonathan's death was a tragic accident.'

I gasped. 'Terry, no! Promise me you won't go near Jonathan's family. It could be seen as witness intimidation. You'll end up with a criminal record and you'll make things more difficult for Bev.'

'I won't intimidate her, I only want to talk to her,' Terry said.

'No, Terry. You mustn't go near. Believe me, it's a bad idea. You'll end up getting arrested yourself.'

Terry remained quiet for a moment, then said, 'I suppose. Okay.'

I was relieved. 'We just have to let things run their course, however hard that is.'

'Okay. What do I tell the kids?' I knew he wasn't really asking me what to do, he just had a million things whizzing around his head. I looked at the clock and saw it was almost teatime, or breakfast time for me.

'Tell them a half truth, that Bev is helping the police find out how Jonathan got hurt. Give them a chippy tea, maybe a run in the park.'

'That's a good idea,' Terry said.

'They won't notice that Bev's not home while you're all staying with your mum. They'll think she's still in the house. Do you need me to come around?'

'No thanks, Sam. Thanks for talking.' Terry rang off.

I let the handset dangle in my hands. This was a bad development and I was responsible. I also had to let my boss know. Also, I should start following my own advice and stay away from witnesses and potential witnesses.

*

That evening, as I walked across the foyer of our flats on my way to my car, I could see Anne Leigh hanging around the car park.

How had she found my home address? My first instinct was to turn around and go back upstairs, but I needed to get to work. I pushed open the door and she immediately ran over and let off her damned camera in my face. The flash almost blinded me.

'Stop that!' I snapped.

'Do you have anything to say about your cousin being arrested for murder?' Anne demanded.

'My cousin has not been arrested for murder,' I replied whilst walking briskly to my car.

'I have information that she has been arrested for killing Jonathan Cox.'

'I have nothing to do with that incident,' I replied. 'And I have nothing to say to you. Excuse me.'

'Is it true you're using your influence to affect the outcome of the investigation?' Anne asked.

'What influence?! I'm a lowly constable and I work in a different division. I have no influence.' I opened my car and got in.

Anne stood in front of me, blocking my way. 'You warned me off at the school gate. You tried to intimidate me.'

'No I didn't,' I argued, but when I thought about it, I could see that the encounter could be easily spun. Dammit, another bad move on my part.

'It felt like it,' Anne said. 'I have a witness to it.'

I could recognise a veiled threat when I heard it.

Anne's tone turned placatory. 'Why are you so obstructive? I'm just trying to earn a living. It's only a few questions. Don't you think it would be beneficial to get your family's side of things logged?'

'If my family need anything to be logged, they'll do it through the police and hospital, not you,' I closed the door. As far as I was concerned, she could go earn her living on the docks.

Anne's eyes flashed a touch of anger. 'A complaint has previously been made about Mrs Thompson; why didn't the police act on it?'

I wound down my window. 'The police have never received any complaints about Mrs Thompson. Now get out of my way.'

Anne didn't move. 'How many children is your cousin registered for? Does she regularly over mind? Do the social services know that she slapped a minded child?'

That was a new one. Despite knowing she was fishing, I needed to know more.

'What are you talking about?'

Anne smiled a nasty smile. 'She was witnessed slapping a minded child.'

'Rubbish!' I exclaimed. I knew Bev didn't even slap her own children.

'I have been reliably informed that she was seen slapping a small child in her care. Why didn't the police act on a blatant assault?'

'No such complaint has been received and I suggest that you review your sources.' I wasn't going to answer any more questions. I gently revved my engine as a hint to move. Anne reluctantly moved over.

'You think I'm bad. It won't be any time before the nationals latch on, and I will make sure they are aware of the family connections.' Anne smiled like a crocodile.

I stuck my nose in the air and drove to the gate. I saw Tracey standing at her door, grinning. Now I knew where Anne was getting her information—her wrong information—from, and I'd bet my pension that she had lied to Anne about Bev slapping a child. I turned onto the road and headed for Wyre Hall.

I arrived at work with little memory of the drive there. I stalked into the station and prepared for parade. I wasn't in a good mood and I didn't want to join in Andy's prattling with Ken. I had all sorts of scenarios running around my head and every one of them ended with Bev in prison and/or me losing my job.

'Only days left as a single man. Are you getting nervous?' Andy asked.

'No, I can't wait,' Ken said.

I smiled despite my inner turmoil. Ken was a future Phil for some lucky sprog. I hoped he wouldn't leave it as long as Phil did before sitting his promotion exams.

Bert, Benno and Shaun came in and we all stood up.

*

After giving out the duties, Bert handed out the paperwork. He tossed a small sheet over to me.

'What's that?' Andy whispered.

'A court warning. You'll start getting them soon,' I whispered back. It was a Crown Court warning no less. I checked the name and gave an involuntary exclamation.

'Problem?' Shaun asked. They didn't like us to interrupt parade.

'Sorry, Sarge,' I said. 'I just saw the name on this court warning. Maureen Clough. I can't believe she's going not guilty.'

Benno grimaced. 'I got one too, and I heard they're calling Dr McKay and Sister Lomas too.'

'At least they can offer medical evidence, sir. What can I say apart from telling them we attended and got information about the child and dealt with the kick-off afterwards?'

'Is that that kiddie that overdosed on heroin?' Trevor asked. I nodded. 'At least when she's found guilty, the Crown Court will be able to give a harsher sentence,' he said.

'*If* she's found guilty.' I couldn't see how she'd get out of this one, but sometimes the wheels of justice didn't turn the way we hoped.

Bert coughed. 'Let's get on and discuss this some other time.'

'Sorry, Sarge,' Trevor and I said in unison.

I bent over my pocketbook and forced myself to concentrate.

After parade, I did my test call then waited for everyone to clear out of the control room.

'Ray, I need to go and speak to the Inspector. Would you

show me as not available for half-an-hour, please?'

Ray jotted a note on the shift sheet and I went upstairs.

Unlike Gary, Inspector Benjamin kept the door closed. I knocked and went in when he called.

'Sam, how can I help you?' He pointed to the chair I had sat in so often. 'Is this about Shane Clough?'

I sat down and folded my hands onto my lap. 'No, sir. I need to tell you something because I'm not sure how it affects me being in the job.'

'Sounds serious. Just spill it and we can decide how to progress from there.' He settled back and lit a cigarette. He didn't smoke as much as Ray, but with the door shut, the room was starting to get a bit smelly. The Inspectors from the other blocks wouldn't be impressed. It wasn't my place to comment, so I took a deep breath and plunged in.

'My cousin, Beverley Thompson, is a childminder. She has been accused of killing one of the children in her care and has been arrested on suspicion of manslaughter.'

Benno leant back in his seat and picked a bit of paper from his lip. 'I heard about that. Odinsby division isn't it?'

'Yes. High Lake, sub-division,' I confirmed. 'I have to tell you that I do not believe the allegations.'

'Not our division.' He leant on his elbows and exhaled smoke as he thought. 'I'm not sure this will impact you,' he said. 'Does anyone relevant know you are related to her?'

'Therein lies my problem,' I admitted. 'The child's aunt, who is mentally unstable, knows I am a police officer and knows that I am related to Bev. She has made vague threats to me, which I have so far ignored because I don't want to become involved with the case.'

'A wise move,' the boss said.

'This evening, a freelance journalist called Anne Leigh turned up at my home,' I said. 'She ambushed me, took a photograph and shot questions at me. She thinks Beverley has been arrested for murder. She blocked my car and I had to tell her to get out of the way. She made indirect threats to me that she would report me for intimidation if I did not answer her questions. I did not comply. As I left the car park, I saw Tracey Quinn, the aunt, laughing on her doorstep.'

'The aunt lives by you?' Benno asked.

'Yes, the houses opposite The Crags. She's convinced that the entire police force is somehow protecting Bev because of me. I believe, she's feeding false information—no, they're blatant lies—to the journalist, sir.'

'Has something happened that would warrant a complaint of intimidation?' Benno asked.

I squirmed a little. 'I saw Anne Leigh outside my cousin's children's school.'

The Inspector's jaw sagged slightly. 'You warned her off?'

'No, I didn't! However, tonight, she suggested that I did. Also, I never identified myself as a police officer and I never told her I was related to Bev and I certainly didn't give her my address. Tracey must have told her all that.'

'Did your cousin say anything to her by the school?' Inspector Benjamin asked.

'She wasn't there,' I admitted.

'Then why were you there?' The boss didn't look happy.

'There was a mention of the case in the newspaper, coincidentally written by Anne Leigh. It didn't name Bev but it wasn't difficult for someone local to identity her. Her children have been bullied and she was shunned. I wanted to hear what the other parents were saying about her. I wanted to help her and I thought I might be able to get some information she could use.'

'You interacted with the other parents?'

'Not intentionally. I was just going to eavesdrop. One mother thought I was a reporter and pointed out Anne Leigh. I asked her for a business card and that was it.'

Benno closed his eyes. 'Feet first again, Sally,' he murmured, using the name I had used when we worked together previously.

Maybe he was doing with my name what I was doing with his.

'So, let's get this straight. Your cousin has been accused of killing one of the children in her care and has been arrested. You went to the school to eavesdrop on other parents to get evidence that your cousin could use. They believed you were a reporter so pointed out another reporter. You approach this reporter and engage with her.'

'That's not quite right—' I began.

The boss ploughed on. 'That reporter turns up at your home, takes your photograph and asks questions. As you leave you see the aunt by her door, laughing.'

'Pretty much, sir,' I mumbled.

'Have you had anything to do with the deceased child's mother?'

'No, sir. I've no idea what she thinks about all this, or even if she's aware. She's been incredibly quiet about it if she is aware.'

Inspector Benjamin stubbed the remains of his cigarette into the ash tray. 'I'm sure I don't have to tell you not to broadcast this information. I'll take it to the Superintendent, it's only polite to keep him in the loop. If Anne Leigh makes a complaint, it will have to be investigated.'

'I understand, sir, but I think Anne Leigh and Tracey Quinn will back each other up, which leaves me at a disadvantage,' I said.

'Unfortunately, it does. Continue as normal for now. If anything else unfolds, we'll take it from there. Would you be able to go and stay somewhere for a few days to stay out of the way?'

'I could go back to my parents' house,' I said.

Benno nodded. 'It might be an idea if you're being stalked by the press.'

'Yes, sir.'

'I won't ask you to stay away from your family, but you must stay away from the school. Stay away from your neighbour or anyone else connected. Hopefully, this will blow over. Dismissed.'

I left the office and went downstairs. As usual, Ray was on the radio and Derek was answering a phone call.

'Ray, I'm going out now, can you update the sheet that I'm available, please.'

Ray marked the sheet and I went out, not feeling especially comforted by my chat with Benno.

Chapter Fourteen

Next day, I got up just after lunchtime and drove over to Bev's house. She would have to be released later today unless they applied for an extension—and without further evidence on the case coming in. I couldn't see that being approved—but I stopped off at her house to get a change of clothes for her, just in case. I would drop them off at High Lake. It wasn't much but it would let her know we were thinking of her.

Bev and I had swapped keys ages back. It was useful for us to hold each other's spares. I got the key out as I approached the front door. It was a decent neighbourhood, but someone had expressed their displeasure by leaving dog poo in the centre of the doorstep. I was actually relieved that this was all that had happened to the house. I had been to some houses where the windows had been smashed and obscenities had been scrawled on the walls. People around here were more subtle.

I pushed the door open and found more excrement had been pushed through the letterbox and had spread across the carpet as I opened the door. I cleaned up the mess and washed the carpet and the doorstep, then I gathered spare clothes for Bev. She wouldn't need much. I also packed her toothbrush and toothpaste. Our bridewell had a limited supply of personal care items, but High Lake was smaller and I didn't know if they would.

Once I was happy I had done as much as I could, I checked around the garden to make sure there were no more little surprises lying around, then locked up and left for High Lake. From there,

I went to my parents' house as the boss had suggested. Dad was back from the rig, so I was looking forward to spending some time with him, despite the dire circumstances.

As it happened, the clothes I left for Bev were not needed as she was released without charge. Terry went to fetch her and phoned us once she was home. Despite Bev's insistence that he stayed with his mother, he stayed that night with Bev to make sure she was all right.

Mum wanted to go around there, but Dad pointed out that, after such an upsetting event, perhaps it would be tactful to leave Terry and Bev alone until the morning. He was thoughtful like that.

Later that evening, as we ate tea, Dad coughed to draw our attention. Mum and I stopped shovelling sausages into our faces and looked at him.

'I've been thinking,' Dad said.

Mum glanced at me then turned back to Dad. 'Is it what we spoke about on the phone the other day?'

I looked between Mum and Dad. Had something being going on and, yet again, I had been oblivious?

'Sort of,' Dad said. 'You know I'm finding the commute to Aberdeen a bit of a pain?' He paused for an answer. I had none, but I had never thought about flying to Aberdeen then going on a helicopter to the rig as commuting, but when I did think of it, I suppose it was. Mum nodded.

'Now Sam's settled in Gary's flat with a steady job, let's move north.'

'What?!' I exclaimed and almost choked on a piece of sausage.

'What?!' Mum exclaimed.

'Think about it,' Dad said. 'It makes sense. I make more money on the rig than being land-based, but I spend more on air fares and taxis getting to and from home. If we live in Aberdeen, or even outside of Aberdeen, I'd get home sooner and spend less doing it. Lots of oil workers' families live around Aberdeen.'

It did make sense, but my parents would be hundreds of

miles away. I needed time to process it.

'What about my mother? She's getting on now,' Mum said.

'She can come with us. We can look for somewhere with a granny flat so she still has her independence.'

Mum's mouth flapped as she looked at me then looked back at Dad. 'What if Sam needs me?'

Dad smiled at me but said, 'We'll always be there for her, but Sam is all grown up now. Isn't that right, Sam?'

I nodded but still couldn't speak.

'Sam lives her own life now and, when Gary gets back, she'll be getting married. Have a think, Liz, we can talk more about this before I go back, but I think if we decide not to move, I'm going to look for something closer to home. It won't pay as well, but I don't want to continue travelling so much for work.'

Mum pushed her plate away. 'It's so far. And what about my job?'

'You won't have to work, but if you did want to find a job, I'm sure there will be secretarial work up there,' Dad said.

I found my voice. 'I think Dad has a point. I could stay with you just as well in Aberdeen as I can here, and I can phone every day. If Nan goes with you I don't see a problem. Actually, even if she doesn't, I'll still be around to see to her.'

It almost killed me to say that, but Dad was right; I was supposedly independent now and it was time my parents thought of themselves.

'No, no, no, you have enough on your plate without worrying about your nan,' Mum said. She turned to Dad. 'What if Mum won't come with us?'

'Then we need to have a frank talk with her,' Dad replied. He paused. 'You haven't said no.'

'I need time to think. Let's talk about it some more tomorrow,' Mum said. I knew that meant when I wasn't around.

Dad started to eat again, so did I, but Mum pushed food around her plate. I wondered how this would pan out.

Anne got her revenge for the car park incident a few days later. Another article hit the local rag. Bigger this time.

"Childminder arrested in baby death."

"A thirty year old woman has been arrested following the death of a toddler…"

Bev had not been charged so information should still be limited but I didn't trust Anne Leigh not to add a few embellishments. I wasn't wrong, as I read on there was speculation on Bev's ability to mind children, and on her sentence when she was found guilty. When, mind you, not if.

"Mothers at the local primary school told me how the childminder was regularly seen with a number of children apart from her own…"

Bev was a registered childminder, of course she had more than her own kids but she never took more than her registration allowed; however, the inference here was plain.

'I have learnt from my sources that the childminder was witnessed slapping a small child in her care, but no complaint was made to the police as a result of that attack.'

That was an out-and-out lie, but now there was a better than even's chance the High Lake jacks would include that in their investigation. The article went on to describe how Anne had tried to get an interview with an unnamed relative, who happened to be in the police force. The story was far from truthful.

'…the constable swept past me and got into her car. I followed to ask another question but she drove at me, forcing me to leap out of the way. Mrs Tracey Quinn, witnessed the incident.'

'It was terrifying. I heard an engine revving and looked out. I saw a woman standing in the car park opposite. Suddenly a car drove at her and she threw herself to one side to escape. Then the car screeched on to the road and drove away.'"

There was a picture of Tracey pointing at the car park. Great! The immediate neighbours knew Tracey was strange in manner, but now everyone could see the flats without that insight. How long before I got unwanted visitors?

"I have made a complaint to the police about this incident, as has Mrs Quinn."

The lying, conniving pair of bitches, but if that wasn't bad enough, later on, I was dismayed to hear the regional television news programme report on Bev's arrest. They didn't give her name, but it was an escalation we could do without.

I wasn't surprised when Benno called me to his office before parade. I knew this would be a follow up on our talk.

'The Superintendent is a bit nervous about you being outside, so he wants you to be moved to an indoor post. After seeing the write-up in the paper, I think it would be a good idea.'

He didn't mention the regional news. Perhaps he hadn't seen it. Perhaps it didn't matter.

Inspector Benjamin continued. 'I've had a chat with Irene Kildea. She's been saying for a while that she needs an assistant. Starting tomorrow, you're it. Come in for eight and she will give you your shifts from then on.'

Collator's assistant. That didn't sound too bad. I liked Irene and I would enjoy working with her, but I hoped this wouldn't turn into a permanent posting.

'Right!' Inspector Benjamin looked at the clock. 'Parade is about to start. I'll give you a two minute head start.'

I left the office and scarpered to the parade room.

'I wondered where you were,' Ken said.

'The boss wanted to see me. I'm going to be the collator's assistant from tomorrow.'

Ken wrinkled his nose. 'I don't think I'd like that.'

'It'll be interesting. Better than a secondment to the admin unit,' I replied.

The inspector, Bert and Shaun came in and we all stopped talking and stood up.

*

The following day, I arrived at Irene's office in good time, but she wasn't there. I set up another chair at the desk and sat down to read the overnight arrests. Irene did a daily bulletin sheet and the arrests featured on there.

Irene came in, bang on eight. 'Hi, Sam.'

'Hi Irene. I wasn't sure what you needed me to do so I've gone through the overnight arrests. There's nothing of note there.'

'Great. Can you go to the telex room and pick up any messages there, then can you put the kettle on? I'll make a start on the basket. Here's my mug.' Irene unlocked the top drawer and took out a mug. I placed it beside the kettle, which she had tucked into a tight corner beside the filing cabinets. Most offices had a little nook for their kettles.

I went into the control room. It seemed strange to see someone other than Ray at the radio and Derek at the phones. The radio operator was Geoff. I tried but failed to remember the name of the phone handler.

'Bloody hell, it's the B Block shit magnet!' Geoff said to his oppo, who laughed.

'Plain old Sam will do, thank you,' I retorted.

'They've finally had enough and offloaded you?'

I wasn't sure he was joking. 'Not at all. I'm the collator's assistant for a while.'

'I suppose even you couldn't get into mischief there.'

'Very funny. I've come to collect any messages. Irene needs them for the bulletin.'

'In there.' He waved a hand towards the telex room and turned back to the radio.

I actually knew where to find the messages, but I thanked him and went to get them then returned to the collator's office.

'What times do you want me to work?' I asked Irene as I made our teas.

'Anytime between seven and ten. I don't care as long as you do eight hours. If I need you in at a particular time, I'll let you know,' Irene said. 'If you need a midweek rest day, you have to work the Saturday. We don't work Sundays unless we're needed for an operation.'

One of the many things I liked about working shifts was the midweek rest days. Everywhere was less crowded. I wished I could work weekends and have two midweek rest days; however, Irene knew what worked best so I'd follow her instructions, with one proviso.

'I can tell you now that I will never voluntarily come in at seven.' The early shift was the one thing I disliked about working shifts.

Irene laughed. 'Not my favourite time of day either.' The phone rang. 'And so it starts,'

The day went quite quickly. The filing was tedious, as always, but the snippets of information and gossip were sometimes interesting and often funny. I transferred everything onto cards, while Irene typed up the bulletin and rang around other collators for information that she had requested or they had requested. She then did searches as requested from our departments. She also appeared to be planning something involving maps, info sheets and so on. She was a bit secretive about that. I wasn't offended; a lot of stuff happened that I had no idea about and didn't need to know about. I left her to it and concentrated on the routine things so she could get on.

'No sign of Cathy Chiu yet,' I commented when we took ten minutes for a tea break.

'No. Sad isn't it,' Irene replied.

'Frank Morton reckons she jumped into the river,' I said.

'She wouldn't be the first or the last if she has.'

'I wonder if it was Cathy that Mr Paxton saw on the field behind Devon Road?' I had put a card in the system, relaying Mr Paxton's call.

'We can't be certain until that woman has been found and spoken to,' Irene said.

Our conversation petered out. Neither of us mentioned Beverley, the reason I was working there, and Irene gave no sign that she had seen the article in the newspaper. I was grateful for that; it allowed me to pretend that everything was normal. But it wasn't normal and probably wouldn't be normal ever again.

Due to the seriousness of Anne and Tracey's complaints, I knew that the Complaints and Discipline department would have to consider charges against me. Actual criminal charges, not just disciplinary charges. I shuddered at the thought. This was something that could follow me throughout my service even if it didn't result in my dismissal. Steve had once been arrested and, although he had been exonerated, some people—not B Block, but some people—still gave him sidelong looks as if he'd got away with something. I felt that I was holding my breath waiting for the axe to land on my neck. I didn't have to wait too long.

C and D—Complaints and Discipline—did come to see me a few days later. Two men—one sergeant and one constable, both wearing dark suits—introduced themselves. All very friendly, but I asked Irene to stay with me. I could have had a federation rep, but I wanted someone I knew and who knew me.

It was a bit crowded in Irene's office, so we moved to the interview room. Now I sat on the wrong side of the table. For the first time I realised how depressing and even scary that room was. I was trapped behind the table with possibly hostile police officers between me and the only door. Although I believed that I had nothing to hide, I felt my heart rate increase, even though Irene sat beside me. They settled themselves down. A large, brown envelope lay on the table between them.

The sergeant kicked off by cautioning me. He wound it up by saying, 'We're investigating a complaint that you deliberately endangered the life of a woman by driving at her.'

'I did not,' I replied.

'Anne Leigh has complained that you drove at her in a car park. This was witnessed by a Tracey Quinn, who has also lodged a complaint. You understand that, if this allegation is found to be credible, it will lead to criminal charges against you?'

'I understand that, but it didn't happen that way,' I said.

'Why don't you tell us your version,' the constable said.

'First I'll tell you who's who,' I said. 'Tracey Quinn is a regular caller and well known for making unfounded complaints. Check with the collators at Odinsby and High Lake.'

'Or me,' Irene cut in.

I gave her a little smile and continued. 'Tracey Quinn is also the aunt of Jonathan Cox, who died following an accident. Tracey insists that my cousin, Beverley Thompson is to blame. Tracey is a bit paranoid and is convinced there's a big police conspiracy to protect Beverley.'

The sergeant nodded as he jotted something down.

I continued, 'Anne Leigh is a freelance journalist who, I believe, is trying to make her name on the back of Jonathan Cox's death. I believe that Anne is getting all her information from Tracey Quinn. Not all of it is accurate.'

The constable said. 'Now can you tell us what happened when you drove at Anne Leigh?'

'Constable Barrie has already stated that she did not drive at Anne Leigh. Please do not refer to something as a fact when we are still trying to establish the truth,' Irene said.

The sergeant nodded. 'Quite right, Sergeant Kildea.'

'It's pronounced Kil-day,' Irene snapped.

'I apologise, Sergeant Kildea,' the sergeant said.

'As do I,' the constable added.

I don't think I had ever seen any two people look less sincere. I was angry but there was no point in losing my temper and shouting about it all. That's how they get you. Let you drop your guard then you're more likely to let slip something they can use. I deliberately kept my voice even, but I felt my cheeks glow.

'I was leaving for work when I was confronted by Anne Leigh as I walked to my car.'

'Were you parked on the road?' the sergeant asked.

'No, it was the resident's car park. She flashed her camera into my face and was asking me questions—'

'What sort of questions?' The constable cut in.

'What did I think of my cousin's arrest for murder. Was I influencing the enquiry? I got into my car and she stood in front of me, deliberately blocking my way. She refused to move despite repeated requests.' I wondered whether to mention Anne's threats, but then I thought it best not to volunteer information.

'Did you rev your engine?' the sergeant asked.

'Yes, only a little to encourage her to move.' Oh, that sounded bad. 'I was in neutral and there was no danger of me moving the car at that point. It was a hint.'

'Did you drive at her?' the constable asked.

'Absolutely not. She moved out of the way, very reluctantly and slowly I might add, and I drove out of the car park, at a normal speed, and left for work. As I turned onto the road, I saw Tracey Quinn in her doorway, laughing.'

'So you admit you revved the car and drove off?' the sergeant said.

'That's just the bare bones of it. It wasn't like that. I revved gently whilst in neutral, I drove at a normal speed and I never drove at her,' I said.

'You also intimidated her outside a school,' the constable said.

Anne Leigh had made good on her threat.

'Is this also part of the investigation?' Irene asked.

'Intimidating witnesses is a crime, Sergeant Kildea,' the sergeant said.

'But I didn't,' I insisted. 'She is alleging that because I wouldn't give her an interview outside my home. She all but told me that she would make a complaint if I refused to speak to her.'

'Anne Leigh states that you approached her outside the school and warned her off. Many parents witnessed this.' He pulled a statement from the brown envelope. 'We have a statement here confirming that you approached her.'

He put the statement down. My upside-down reading skills were good and I noted that the name was Mary Lovell. I could imagine she would be revelling in the attention.

'May I see that statement?' Irene asked.

The constable pushed it towards her and she laid it out so we both could read it.

It wasn't long. Mary embellished a couple of places and declared that she had had me sussed from the beginning.

'Is this accurate?' Irene asked me.

'Not entirely,' I replied. 'I did not approach Mary Lovell or try to engage her in conversation, she approached me. She assumed that I was a reporter and offered to dish the dirt about Beverley, for a fee. Even if I had taken her up on her offer, it would have been lies because Beverley told me that she and Mary Lovell haven't exchanged more than a couple of words at the school gates. Mary's the one who pointed out Anne to me. I did not storm over to confront Anne. I went over and asked for a business card, and that was all.'

Irene pushed the statement back across the table. 'Your witness is unreliable. Mary Lovell is an alcoholic and a known attention-seeker. She has done this type of thing before. She will stand witness to anything if you pay her, and there is nothing she likes better than to be at the centre of some drama. She caused a case to be kicked out of court last year. DI Webb will corroborate what I am telling you. You are welcome to visit my office and search the systems.'

The constable and the sergeant looked at each other and then at me. I hadn't heard of any of this either, so I couldn't add anything. I remained quiet. I loved Irene.

The sergeant shook his head slightly. 'That won't be necessary. Thank you, Sergeant Kildea.'

The constable took a photograph out of the envelope and pushed it towards us.

'That's me, leaving Bev's house,' I said. 'Who took this?'

Ignoring my question, the sergeant asked, 'Why were you there?'

'I was getting Bev a change of clothes. She was in custody. I dropped them off at High Lake for her.'

The constable took another photograph out. Me outside

Bev's house with a mop. 'Why were you washing the step and the front door?'

'Someone had left dog dirt there. They posted it through the letterbox too,' I replied.

'It's been suggested that you were clearing evidence,' the constable said.

And I could guess who had suggested it and who had taken the photo. I hadn't seen them at all.

'It takes talent to make cleaning up dog poo seem dodgy,' I remarked.

'I think Constable Barrie has the right to be informed of the evidence to which you are referring,' she said.

The constable's ears reddened slightly and he made no attempt to specify any evidence. Meantime, my brain was whirring.

'You got this photo either from Anne Leigh or Tracey Quinn. Probably Anne Leigh. She suggested that I was disposing of evidence, didn't she? In fact, she must have taken the other photo too, and who knows how many more. She must have been spying on the house. So, who gave her Bev's address? It'll be Tracey Quinn! Tracey is giving out personal addresses of suspects and their family.' I was furious and didn't try to hide it.

'It could have been one of the mums at school,' Irene suggested. 'Maybe that Mary Lovell.'

'Possibly,' I reluctantly agreed, 'But Mary Lovell doesn't know where I live; Tracey knows both addresses.'

'Is any part of this enquiry about Constable Barrie supposedly disposing of evidence, or were you just shaking the tree to see what you got?' Irene demanded. 'Has anyone questioned Anne Leigh about why she is following Constable Barrie, or has Tracey Quinn been spoken to about giving confidential information to a reporter?'

'That is not important,' the sergeant said. '

'I think it is,' I retorted. 'I'd like to know.'

He fixed me with a stare. 'Let's go back to the incident in the flats. Apart from Tracey Quinn, did anyone else witness this?'

'Not that I know of,' I admitted.

The constable sighed and gathered up the photos and statements. 'I'm sorry, Constable Barrie, but you're suspended while this investigation is ongoing. I have to say, it looks like Anne has a convincing case. Nothing you have said convinces me that you are not guilty.'

'Hang on, the onus is on you to prove me guilty, not for me to prove my innocence.'

The constable gave a nasty little smile. 'First, this is not a court of law. Second, we have witness statements from different people corroborating Anne Leigh's version of events at the school and at the car park. You can't prove anything that you say happened, actually did happen.'

The air left my lungs in a big rush.

'The onus is not on Constable Barrie,' Irene insisted.

'As I said, this is not a court, it is an enquiry,' the constable snapped back. 'Balance of probability is sufficient for our needs. Also, I don't think we'll have to work too hard to find the proof we need for the courts.'

'If you can think of anything you can add to the enquiry, you know where to reach us,' the sergeant added.

They shepherded us out of the interview room, and Irene and I returned to her office.

'I'm being stitched up by two of the biggest lying bitches on the planet!' I was almost hysterical. I had no idea what to do.

'Sit down Sam, and take a few deep breaths.' Irene sat at her desk and tapped a finger on the wood. 'I'd ask Eamon to go and speak to Mary Lovell, but I'd prefer not to involve him.'

'I wouldn't expect you to do that.' I stood up and gathered my things. 'I'll go home and have a think about what to do about Tracey and Anne.'

'Is there anything you can think of that might be useful?' Irene asked.

I shook my head. 'I've got a photo of Tracey Quinn creeping around the car park photographing my car, but that's all.'

'Why was she photographing your car?' Irene asked,

'I don't know, but it won't be for anything good,' I replied.

'Can I have your photo,' Irene asked. 'It might be useful.'

'I'll drop it off sometime.' I ran my fingers through my hair. 'I can understand Anne Leigh trying to speak to me because she's a reporter and I am related to a suspect. I don't like it but I can understand it. I don't understand why she's lied about me. Also, Tracey isn't a suspect so why is she coming after me?'

Irene hugged me. 'Anne is just responding to information she is getting from Tracey, and Tracey's bonkers. I know it's all tosh.'

'Thanks, Irene.' I kept back my tears until I reached the car, then let them flow.

Chapter Fifteen

I lay low for a few days, licking my wounds. I wasn't sure if my block would even be aware of my suspension. A couple of friends from training school invited me to a nightclub in the city with them, but I couldn't face anyone. Even though I wasn't in the wrong, I felt ashamed and embarrassed.

I thought about my upcoming court dates. I was still a police officer and I would still be able to give evidence as long as it was nothing to with my suspension and as long as I was a primary witness and not just back-up. With the Clough case in the Crown Court, Inspector Benjamin was also giving evidence and so I wouldn't be called, but I still worried about the outcome if I were to be called. A jury would assume suspension was the first step to dismissal and the defence teams were bound to use it to attack my integrity. It would weaken my evidence. What if they found Maureen Clough not guilty because of it? Little Shane would be returned to her, and anyone with half an eye could see how that would turn out.

When I was in a logical mood, I knew I was catastrophising, but without Gary to calm me I lost a lot of sleep. When I did sleep, I had horrible dreams; I even started to dream of the past, something I thought I had put aside. I would wake up convinced I was trapped in a van. In desperation, I contacted my counsellor, but I couldn't get an appointment for weeks. I didn't tell anyone because I didn't want them to think I was unstable. I worried that it might get back to C and D who might use it against me.

Gary would have held me tight and made the madness go

away. Despite that, I was glad Gary hadn't phoned; I didn't know what to tell him, or even if I would tell him until I had no choice. I should just resign and follow Gary to Hong Kong, but even as I thought it, I knew that would not happen. I had to trust the system to find the truth, and for me—and Beverley—to be cleared of wrongdoing.

Gradually I calmed down and returned to what now passed for real life. I visited my nan. I went to the shops. I even went out for tea and cakes with Mum one afternoon. It seemed normal but didn't feel it. There was a huge axe hanging over Bev and me, and I was just waiting for it to fall.

The phone woke me up, again. I looked at the clock and was shocked to see it was gone nine. I was sleeping a lot more these days. I staggered to the phone and picked it up.

'Sam?' I heard Irene's voice.

'Yeah,' I croaked. I needed a cup of tea, stat.

'You sound like shit. Are you okay?' Irene asked.

'Yeah, I just woke up.'

'Oh, sorry. Anyway, I did a bit of digging and guess what?'

I wasn't in the mood for guessing games. 'I don't know. What?'

'You don't want to play? Okay then, Anne Leigh was sacked from *The Town Crier* for misconduct.'

I thought for a moment. 'What has that got to do with anything?'

'Quite a bit, I'd say,' Irene said. 'They sacked her for misconduct. They received a lot of complaints about her methods. She crashed police incidents after monitoring our radio. She would hang around the hospital, then talk people into making complaints and allowing her to interview them. She would embellish stories and suggest wrongdoing, even where there was none. There's other stuff, but it just corroborates her unprofessionalism.'

'Where did you hear that?' I asked.

'Contacts,' Irene answered. I knew better than to ask who it was. Most bobbies had someone who would pass on information.

The CID took it to another level with paid informants.

'I thought she was trying to make a name for herself by hounding Bev and me,' I said.

'Not necessarily,' Irene said. 'I would say that she hasn't been able to get another job in the media because of her reputation. She's either trying to make a name to reintegrate herself or she's given up and has gone completely freelance to make a living. It doesn't seem she's learnt her lesson about gathering information.'

'That's interesting, but I don't see how I can use that,' I said.

'If she is attacking your character, you can counter her so-called evidence with proof that she is not to be trusted. She is so untrustworthy, her newspaper sacked her.'

'That might be useful,' I agreed.

'Keep that card up your sleeve for now. You'll know when to use it,' Irene said. I heard a voice in the background. 'Got to go,' Irene said to me and the line went dead.

I padded off to the kitchen to boil the kettle. I had assumed that Tracey had contacted Anne, but what if Anne had been at the hospital and had targeted Tracey? Why Tracey and not Judith, Jonathan's mother? I suspected the latter would be because Judith has been silent on events and probably hadn't been up for talking to Anne. Tracey however… It must have been like manna from Heaven to Anne.

I drove over to Bev's house, dodged the pile of dog dirt on the doorstep, and let myself in to find Bev sitting in the kitchen. She leapt up when she saw me.

'Sam! I was wondering when you'd come around. Auntie Liz told me about the complaint. Pair of bitches they are. I didn't like to disturb you. I know how it feels when you just want to bury yourself under your blankets and cry. I was going to give you two more days, then phone.'

I felt bad. Beverley had so much going on but she was worrying about me.

'Thanks, Bev. I think I'm okay now.' Then I cried, again. I couldn't stop it. Tears were always just under the surface. Between sobs, I told her about the interview, including the photographs.

'Photos of my house?' Bev exclaimed.

I nodded. 'I was washing dog poo off the doorstep and they made out I was clearing evidence.'

'Right, I'm going to pass that on to my solicitor,' Bev said.

'What good will that do?' I asked.

'I don't know, but it won't do any harm. I don't want photographs of my house in the hands of the media.' She picked up the phone and dialled a number. How many people knew their solicitor's number by heart? It was a testament to the many conversations she had had with the firm.

I ended up staying and having my lunch with her. We both enjoyed the company and the distraction. Eventually I had to go home, but I had a thought.

'Are you definitely not going to use that answering machine?' I asked.

'I don't think so. Terry was going to look at it but he was always busy, then Jonathan…' Bev swallowed and took a deep breath. 'I shoved it into my bedside cabinet. Why?'

'I'd like to buy it off you. I think it's time I started to screen my calls,' I said. 'I want to go back to the flat soon, but if they know my address, it won't be any time before Cowface Quinn or her pet gutter-rat reporter get my number too.'

Bev laughed. 'Cowface Quinn, love it!' Then she stopped laughing. 'I do feel sorry for Judith and I would love to be able to contact her and tell her how much I miss Jonathan. I hate that she'll believe that I caused his injury. I hate even more that she will believe it when Tracey tells her I'm heartless and the police are protecting me.'

'It's interesting that Judith hasn't appeared in any of the articles. Nor has she spoken out in support of Anne Leigh,' I said.

Bev thought for a moment. 'You're right, she hasn't.'

'Perhaps she isn't so blind to her sister,' I said.

'She hasn't spoken out against her either,' Bev said. 'Mind

you, she has other things on her mind.'

We remained silent for a minute, contemplating what Judith's silence could mean, if anything.

'You can have the *Ansafone* for free,' Beverley offered.

'It cost a fortune, you must let me pay for it,' I said.

We argued for a while and eventually agreed on a fiver and a nice present for Christopher and Carly. Bev went upstairs and brought it down.

'I think that's everything it came with. The tape's still in it. There's a spare tape in the space where the wire goes.' She placed it on the coffee table.

'That's great, thanks.' I picked it up and carried it to the door.

'Careful where you put your feet when you leave,' Bev said.

Good advice. I sidestepped the dog dirt, waved to Bev, and drove to my parents' house. I loved my parents, but their house was starting to feel less like home, especially now they were thinking of moving to Scotland. The flat was now home and I wanted to return there.

'What's that?' Mum asked when I carried the *Ansafone* in.

'I bought Bev's answering machine to screen calls after I go home. Can I set it up here to make sure it's working?'

Mum sat on the bottom stair while I fiddled with the telephone socket. 'All this new technology. Where will it end?'

'We'll probably have home computers and be able to see who is calling eventually,' I replied. Mum laughed.

I connected the *Ansafone* and a red light came on. Good, that meant power was reaching the machine. Now what?

'Where's Dad?' I asked. He normally helped me with complicated stuff.

'He nipped out, he'll be back a bit later,' Mum replied.

Oh well. I pressed a few buttons just to see what happened. Suddenly, the tape started rolling and a voice came from the speakers.

'Hello. Hello,'

'That sounds like Beverley,' Mum said.

Another voice came onto the tape. 'It's Tracey, you keep ringing me at work. I thought you'd have answered more quickly than this. Were you busy with the baby?'

I heard Beverley exhale, but instead of responding to the jibe, she said, 'Jonathan isn't well, Tracey, I think he needs to see a doctor.' No chit-chat, just straight to business. Not like Bev. How often had she phoned before Tracey had called back?

'I can't come right now, I'm busy,' Tracey said.

'Tracey, he needs a doctor, he's drowsy and he's been sick. Was he ill last night? Is there something I should know?'

'I'll tell you if I need you to know something,' Tracey said.

I disliked her more than ever.

'I told the woman I spoke to that I was worried and for you to collect him as soon as possible. Did she pass it on?' I head the exasperation in Bev's voice.

'Yes, but as I said, I'm busy. Not everyone has the luxury of sitting at home drinking tea and watching children play. Judith pays you well enough, so can't you deal with him or can't you cope?'

I heard Bev's intake of breath.

'Who's that talking?' Mum asked. 'I don't like the sound of her.'

I put my fingers to my lips. I wanted to hear what was being said.

Bev spoke. 'You've never quite understood that Judith is not my employer have you, Tracey. I'm not a nanny. Jonathan is ill and needs to see a doctor. If you won't come, tell me where Judith is and I'll contact her.'

'You can't, she'll be travelling back now. She'll collect him at the normal time, as arranged.'

'Then you need to come, Tracey, or I'll have to ring an ambulance.'

Tracey sighed. 'Oh very well, I'll speak to my boss.' The call terminated and I wasn't sure who had put the phone down.

'What was that?' Mum asked.

'Bev asking Tracey to get Jonathan. We didn't think the machine was working. Terry was going to look at it. Thank God he didn't.'

'That's evidence isn't it?'

'It could be, Mum. It's a bit vague but it's proof that Bev did ask Tracey to get Jonathan. That will help if they try to go for an act of omission to prove their case,' I said.

The tape stopped, then started rolling again. I heard Bev's voice. I shushed Mum and listened.

'Hello.'

'It's Tracey. You took your time answering again.'

'Where are you, Tracey? It's been over an hour.'

'I had something I needed to finish off,' Tracey replied.

'How much longer will you be?'

'Maybe another hour,' Tracey said.

'Tracey, if you don't come and take this child to the doctor right now, I'm going to ring an ambulance. It could be meningitis,' Bev said.

'Does he have a rash?' Tracey asked.

'No,' Bev replied.

'Then it's unlikely to be meningitis. I'll get there as soon as I can.' Again the call ended, and I got the distinct impression it was Tracey who had terminated the call.

Again, the tape stopped and restarted, I heard Bev's voice again.

'Hello.'

'Beverley, stop ringing my workplace or I'll tell switchboard to block your calls. I'll get to you when I finish.'

'Tracey, I'm ringing an ambulance for Jonathan.'

'Don't you think you're overacting?' Tracey said. 'I wouldn't have brought him to you if he hadn't been fine—'

I caught the abrupt finish. Tracey had let something slip. Beverley noticed it too.

'Hadn't been fine? Fine after what? Is there something I should tell the doctors?' I heard a touch of panic in Bev's voice.

Tracey remained silent for a moment. 'He bumped his head this morning, but he was fine.'

'You'd better tell me what happened so I can tell the doctor,' Bev insisted.

Tracey sighed. 'He slipped on the stairs and bumped his head this morning. He wasn't hurt.'

'And you still brought him to me?! I wouldn't have waited this long before calling an ambulance if I'd known that. Bloody hell, Tracey!'

The call ended and I knew it was Bev who had put the phone down, just before ringing 999.

The implications of the phone exchanges crashed in on me. If Tracey had told Bev about Jonathan's fall he would have received treatment sooner and might have lived. It was beyond tragic.

'Tracey *did* tell Beverley that Jonathan had fallen,' Mum said.

'Did you ever doubt it?' I took a breath. 'Sorry Mum, but this is huge. This tape is proof of Bev's innocence. Bev can't even be criticised for failing to seek help for him; she had tried to get Tracey to come for him and had specifically told her that he needed to see a doctor. This tape is precious.'

Mum wrapped her arms around her knees. 'You should tell Bev, then take the tapes to High Lake.'

I remembered the High Lake jack almost telling me that Bev deserved any harassment because he assumed her guilt. I had been in the job long enough now to know that not everyone was as straight as Webby and his crew. I might be wronging that detective, but I wanted to create an audit trail.

'I'll take it to Wyre Hall. It will go through the system to High Lake,' I said.

'Will they let you in?' Mum asked.

I paused. 'I suppose so. Only one way to find out.' I wondered about keeping it from Bev but she needed some good news. Also, knowing Mum, she might let it slip anyway. 'I'll go to Wyre Hall and you let Bev know. Don't let her get her hopes up too much, and it would be best she doesn't contact High Lake.

I suppose she can let her solicitor know.' I took the tape out; it was one of the mini cassettes like the ones we used in dictation devices at the station, I could use one of the players to listen to the tape there.

I drove over to Wyre Hall and pulled into the car park. As Eamon once told me, act normally and everyone will think you belong there. Nobody challenged me as I went up the stairs to the CID office. I wasn't familiar with the jacks on duty when I got there. Mike, Eamon and the others B Block normally worked with, were all on rest day; however, I spotted DI Webb in his office, so I went over and knocked on the open door.

'What are you doing here, Sam?' he asked.

'I've found evidence in Jonathan Cox's case.' I held up the *Ansafone* tape.

DI Webb pursed his lips. 'Sam, you can't get involved in this. It's not our division, and you're Beverley Thompson's family, and you're suspended. I should throw you out.'

'I know, sir, but I thought this was too important and I wanted to make sure it wasn't lost. I bought my cousin's answering machine from her to screen messages. When I plugged it in, the tape started and played the messages between her and Jonathan's aunt.'

DI Webb paused for a moment. I think he understood my reason for bringing it to Wyre Hall. 'Why wasn't this seized by High Lake?'

Good point. 'I don't know. Maybe because it was in her bedside cabinet, out of reach of the kiddies and she didn't think to tell them about it?' I left out that we had struggled to get it going so she had abandoned it. It was irrelevant and it wouldn't affect the tape's evidential value. Whether it was connected by chance or by design, the calls were taped and there was no arguing with that.

'Still, they should have taken it.' DI Webb took the tape from me and plugged in a tape player. 'Let's see if there's anything worthwhile on here.' DI Webb put the tape into the machine and pressed play. Nothing happened.

'Why isn't it playing?' I asked.

'It is, but there's nothing,' he replied.

I must have somehow deleted it when I took it out of the machine. I pressed my face into my hands. I'd ruined Beverley's chance of freedom.

'Hang on,' DI Webb said. 'He pressed another button and to my utter relief, I heard Bev's voice.

We listened until the messages ended. DI Webb remained silent for a minute.

'What do you think, sir?' I asked.

'That final call is the clincher. Are you certain that it's Jonathan's aunt who is speaking on the tape?'

'Certain,' I replied. 'I'd stand up in Crown Court and swear it.'

'Right. I'll have to pass this on to High Lake, but I'll call them to let them know we have it. First though, I think we should make a copy for our own records.' DI Webb said.

I wasn't sure how to do that, but DI Webb simply set up a cassette tape recorder and replayed the mini tape. When it had ended, he played back the cassette. It was a little faint but clear. There was still no doubt that it was Tracey talking.

'That should be okay,' he said. 'Now I'll ring High Lake.'

I went to leave but he waved me back. 'Sit down. This won't take long.' He yelled through to nearby CID aide to fetch two teas, then picked up the phone and dialled. 'Jerry? Norman here. That childminder job you have. Your lads missed something. I have a tape here that I think proves the childminder didn't injure the child; in fact, she tried desperately to get the child's aunt to take him to the doctor.' He grinned at me as Jerry, presumably DI Webb's equivalent at High Lake, replied. I could hear the indignant tone even though I couldn't hear the words. 'Well, I'm sorry Jerry, but when you hear the tape you'll have to agree... No, no, don't worry about that. It's in our property system now. It'll reach you through the usual channels. Speak later.'

The aide brought in two teas and put them on the desk. DI Webb took the tapes out of the machines. 'Here, lad, book these into property. I need separate reference numbers but link them both. The big cassette must remain in our system but I want the little one back here ASAP, so go now and come straight back.'

The aide took the tapes and left.

'Could I make an observation, sir?' I asked.

'Go ahead.'

'Bev has had all this hanging over her for ages. The tape could take a couple more days to reach High Lake the usual route. Is there some way we could speed things up so Bev can have some peace of mind?'

'I suppose I can get the aide to drive it over, but I want a trail,' he said.

That suited me; I wanted a trail too. 'Thank you, sir.'

DI Webb picked up his tea and leant back on his chair. 'That was a good find, Sam.'

'Thank you, sir.' I took a drink from my mug. I wasn't used to drinking tea with DIs so I wasn't really relaxed, even though I had known DI Webb for some time.

'You've finished your probation now, haven't you?'

'In February,' I confirmed.

'Have you decided what's next?'

'I was hoping for my driving course next, but with this suspension… I don't know.'

Di Webb just gave a little smile. He knew how that could pan out.

I continued. 'If I survive this, I might go for the promotion exams later in the year, but even if they ignore a recent suspension on my record, I don't think I have enough experience yet for promotion or to move into a department.'

'You're probably right, but there's no harm in getting your exams out of the way, and an aide's course under your belt,' DI Webb said.

No harm at all. The six month attachment to CID as an aide

was the first step to becoming a jack, but wasn't a commitment to that path. I was getting married when Gary's posting ended in just under three years, but that didn't mean I could just kick back and coast along. I wanted a career and I wanted to progress. I couldn't see that changing even after I was married. I really should discuss this in more depth with Gary.

'I think I will apply for my aide's course,' I said.

DI Webb slurped his tea and nodded his approval. 'I'll endorse that. Being an aide doesn't mean that you can go off and cause mayhem, though. You will still need to do as you're told.'

And make tea and do the filing and all the boring stuff. 'I understand, sir.'

'I think you'll do well here,' DI Webb said.

'Thank you, sir.' I finished my tea and put the mug on his desk.

The aide returned and handed DI Webb the small tape with the property reference number attached to it.

'Thanks, lad. What are you doing now?'

The aide glanced at me. I guessed he had heard of my current predicament and was uncertain whether he could trust me.

'I'm getting information DS Finlay requested for when he's back on duty, sir.'

'Will it wait? I need you to drive this over to High Lake.'

'I can do that at once, sir,' the aide said.

'Good lad. Make sure you don't hand it over to anyone until someone signs for it,' DI Webb said. 'If nobody wants to sign for it, bring it back here.'

He was as mistrustful as me. The aide left and DI Webb said, 'He's a good lad. From D Block. He's fitting in well here and he's keen. He takes all the little, shitty jobs without complaining. I think we'll keep him.'

I recognised that DI Webb was giving me the heads up on what he expected of me if I became an aide.

'Go on then, bugger off and let me get on,' DI Webb said.

I didn't take offence because I knew him well enough to know that no offence was meant. It was just the way he spoke.

I stood up. 'Thank you, sir.'

He smiled. 'You did good, kid,' he drawled in a fake Humphrey Bogart accent.

I wasn't sure that Jerry would share that view, but, as I had heard so often, not my division and therefore not my problem.

Chapter Sixteen

Ken's wedding day was sunny but not too warm. I wore my light grey skirt suit and a white blouse with an embroidered summer hat and matching shoes, which suited the weather. I had wondered if I should miss the wedding, given the circumstances. I was still smarting over my suspension and I wasn't sure how I'd be received. Then I figured that I had not done anything wrong and I had no reason to hide away. Still, I arrived at the church with only about fifteen minutes to go before the service started, so I could keep out of the way and slip into the back if necessary.

I needn't have worried. Steve and Emma were already there in the churchyard, chatting to Phil and Jo and Andy. They waved and I gratefully went over to join them. I was a little surprised that Irene and Eamon were not there, but then Ken didn't have the same level of friendship with her that I enjoyed, and he had said that he and Gaynor hadn't been able to invite everyone.

'You look nice,' Jo said.

'Thank you, so do you,' I replied. 'Is Ken inside?'

'He is, he's inside talking to the vicar,' Steve said.

'I wonder what they're talking about?' Emma said.

'Probably the football results,' Andy said.

'Oh, I'm sure they're talking about more important things, like the meaning of life,' Emma said.

I laughed. 'I'm with Andy. It'll be the football.'

'Ladies and Gentlemen, would you please take your places,' called someone. 'Best man, your presence is required.'

'See you later,' Steve said to Emma.

'I'll look after her while you're busy,' Andy called after him.

We all filed into the church and I sat on the groom's side, next to Emma who twisted in her seat in her eagerness to look around the admittedly impressive architecture.

'I'd like to marry in a church,' said Emma.

'Blooming heck, it's early days yet,' I replied.

She laughed. 'Silly, I don't mean anytime soon. But when I do marry, I'd like it to be in a church. What about you?'

'I haven't given it a lot of thought,' I said. I should give it some thought; after all, I was engaged but with everything else that was happening, I really hadn't had time to worry about it.

Ken fidgeted next to Steve, then the organ began and we all stood up.

'Just like parade,' quipped Andy, making us all giggle.

Ken and Steve shuffled into the aisle and turned to watch Gaynor take her last steps as a single woman.

Gaynor looked a picture as she walked down the aisle in a lace-trimmed, Empire Line dress that nicely disguised her tiny bump. She carried a bouquet of small, pink roses and baby's breath in her left hand, and linked onto her father's arm with her right hand. Behind her, holding the long veil aloft, walked two little bridesmaids clad in pink, knee length dresses with white ankle socks and white shoes. Each had a flower circlet on her head. The smallest pageboy I had ever seen, aged two or three and dressed in a tiny, pink waistcoat that matched the bridesmaids dresses, toddled behind them with his thumb in his mouth. He held hands with his mother, Gaynor's sister and matron of honour, who wore a full length version of the bridesmaids' outfits, minus the ankle socks. It might be what my dad termed a shotgun wedding, but they had still pulled all the stops out. Ken would never have to worry about not giving Gaynor a spectacular wedding.

'Doesn't she look gorgeous,' Emma whispered to me.

I nodded. As Phil said: long dress, fancy hair and flowers. He was right, I did want that.

A dark thought wriggled to the front of my mind. What if things went wrong, and the complaint Anne Leigh had made was proved. I would be charged with endangering her life. I wasn't sure what the exact charge would be, with the incident happening on a private car park rather than a public road, but I was certain that I would be sacked. I deliberately pushed the thought aside. If that happened, I would fly out and join Gary in Hong Kong. There would be no reason to delay our wedding and I would have Christopher and Carly follow me down the aisle.

If he still wants to marry you. I again pushed the thought aside, with a little more force this time. Of course he would still want to marry me, and I refused to allow these insidious little thoughts spoil this lovely day. I focused on Ken and Gaynor, who were exchanging their vows. In three years that could be Gary and me. I felt the corners of my mouth lift into a big smile. Things will be okay.

*

I didn't get back until late, so I was surprised when the phone rang.

I snatched it up before it could wake Mum. 'Hello?'

I could tell it was Gary before he spoke because of the crackling on the line.

'What time is it there?' he asked.

'Gone midnight,' I whispered. 'Mum's in bed.'

'Apologise to Liz for me,' he said. 'How was the wedding?'

'It was lovely. The weather was good, Gaynor looked wonderful.'

Gary laughed. 'All brides look wonderful.'

'She looked especially wonderful. It was a wonderful day.'

'Did Steve try to kiss you again?' Gary asked.

I laughed. 'No, he was with his new girlfriend, Emma. A nurse he met in hospital.'

'Good, I can relax now.'

I tried to laugh quietly but Mum peered over the landing. 'Who is that?'

'Gary. Sorry to disturb you, Mum,' I said.

'Sorry, Liz,' Gary called into my ear.

Mum went back to bed and left us to whisper to each other in the dark.

*

The following day I returned home to the flat but I didn't want Tracey to waylay me, or Anne Leigh, which made me think of Complaints and Discipline. I told myself I should hear something from C and D over the next couple of days, It wasn't as if I had had a lot of evidence to offer so, basically, it was about whether they believed me or chose to take the word of Anne, Tracey and perhaps Mary Lovell, despite her past form. Judging by my interview, I suspected that it would be three against one, and I would lose. This time next month, or even next week, I might no longer be in the police.

The car park was clear of reporters or Tracey when I arrived, so I pulled in, making sure to leave my car where I could see it from our flat. Then I scuttled in. I still assumed that Tracey would be looking out for me to inflict more torment.

The caretaker came out of his flat as I crossed the communal foyer. I smiled and nodded a greeting. He smiled back.

'I gave the film to your boss.'

'I think you must have the wrong person,' I said.

'No,' he insisted. 'Tall, good looking woman, dark hair, a bit on the scrawny side. She came to see you yesterday but you've been away and we got chatting.'

It sounded like Irene, but I still was a bit confused.

'I've been staying with my mother,' I said. 'What film?'

'The film of the car park...' He paused, 'Oh, of course, you won't know about it. She told me she was investigating a complaint about a woman almost getting knocked over in the car park.'

'We don't have cameras in the car park, but I think it would be a good idea if we did,' I said.

He shuffled his feet. 'You know we sometimes get kids messing around up here, I suppose it's because we're so close to the beach and the fairground isn't that far.' I nodded. He continued, 'After you said you saw someone by your car that time, I started to worry, so I set up a camera in my window to keep a watch on my car. Just my car you understand, I'm not allowed to film everyone else's without permission and I'd have to put up notices.'

I understood what he was saying and I silently blessed him for it.

'I suppose it's unavoidable that your camera picks up things in the background,' I said.

He looked relieved. 'Yes, yes, exactly. I don't deliberately film the car park, but it's unavoidable. Your car is next to mine now, so I might get your car in the shot too.'

That seemed like a good thing to me. I made a mental note to park next to the caretaker's car as often as possible.

The caretaker continued, 'When your boss told me about the woman having to throw herself out of the way, I wondered why nobody had mentioned it to me. I should have been informed. I am the one who looks after these flats after all.'

I nodded sympathetically. 'Yes, you should be kept informed.'

Professional pride mollified, he continued. 'I checked back to the date and time she told me and I saw what happened.'

This was brilliant! 'What did you see?' I asked.

'You, walking across the car park with a woman following you. There's no sound so I don't know what you were talking about. I saw her stand in front of the car and you saying something out of the window. Probably telling her to get lost.' He grinned.

'Something like that,' I admitted.

'Then she stepped aside and you were able to drive away. She didn't have to jump at all. Then she walked out of shot. I thought this was just the type of thing your boss wanted. She'd given me her number, so I rang her and she came to collect it earlier on.'

I could have hugged him. 'I'm sure she appreciated the trouble you took. Clifford, isn't it? Thank you.'

Clifford preened and went back to his flat.

I almost didn't need a lift to get to our flat, I was so elated, I could have flown there. I did a happy dance in the lift, then let myself into the flat and did a happy dance in the hall then another in the living room. If the film was a clear as he described, I was home and free. I gathered the mail, most of which was junk, and went into the living room to sort it. Then I remembered the photo in the kitchen drawer, I'd promised to give it to Irene. I went and got it before I forgot, put it in my handbag and went back to the living room to continue my sorting.

About an hour later, someone knocked at the door. I answered it and found Clifford the caretaker in an agitated state.

'That woman who lives opposite has just deliberately scratched your car,' he blurted out.

'What?!' I was already reaching for my keys.

'I saw her come into the car park, she looked around then ran something along your car and ran off.'

This was too much. I'd been back for an hour and she'd spotted me. Somehow, my mere presence had angered her enough to damage my car. She really wasn't normal.

'Would you be willing to stand as witness to that if I make an official complaint?'

He nodded. 'They can have the film too.'

Of course, his camera. 'I bet you're glad your car is being filmed,' I said as we went downstairs. 'It's lucky I parked next to you.'

He nodded grimly. 'I'm going to petition the owners for a proper security system.'

'I'll support that,' I said. 'I bet most people here would. You should do some leaflets and get votes on it.'

'Yeah, good idea.'

Downstairs, I went to my car and groaned when I saw the long scratch, the full length of one side.

Clifford sucked his teeth. 'Two wings and two doors. That's going to cost you.'

'Thanks to you, we know who did it. I'm going to contact the police, I expect they'll want to speak to you,' I said.

'No problem, I'll get the film ready,' he said and hurried off inside.

*

Once I had phoned the police, who promised to send someone, I phoned Irene.

'Clifford the caretaker tells me you have a film,' I said.

She cackled. 'Not anymore. C and D have it, but it's well logged into our system so it can't be "mislaid". Let them wriggle out of that one.'

'Thanks, Irene. And I do mean that most sincerely.'

'It's fine.' She paused. 'I don't think you have to worry anymore about the rest of it, either. I participated in the incident where Mary Lovell cost Webby a case last year. So I spoke to him and told him it looked as if she was doing the same thing again. He leapt at the opportunity to teach her a lesson and authorised me to get someone to speak to her. Once it was official, I asked Eamon to go to her house and to tell her he was double checking on her statement because it was so vital to the investigation.'

'She'd have loved that,' I said.

'She did and wouldn't stop talking. Long story short, her statement had more holes than a colander. Eamon seized on it and finally she admitted it might be a bit exaggerated. She also didn't think it right that police could interview her for free because, get this, Anne Leigh had given her a tenner for her interview! Mary also said that Anne suggested that you had intimidated her by the school and she wondered if Mary had noticed. Of course, Mary said she had noticed and it was only fair that she went as witness for Anne.'

'You're joking,' I said. 'Anne Leigh has bribed a witness?'

'Yes. Then Mary asked Eamon for a bottle of vodka in exchange for more information. Eamon suggested strongly that she gave that information in exchange for him not arresting her for obstructing an investigation.'

'Anne will argue that it was only lawful payment for her own interview,' I said.

'Yes, but when Eamon asked, there was no receipt or anything. With Mary's form, any lawyer worth his salary will be able to convince a court that Anne bribed her to bear false witness,' Irene said.

Anne Leigh had bribed a witness! Oh, this was so good. Irene was officially my favourite person in the world.

'Unfortunately, Anne also told Mary that you were related to Beverley,' Irene said.

'That was to be expected,' I said.

'Anyway, enough chit-chat, what else is happening?' Irene asked.

'I've got that photograph. I meant to give it to you. Also, Tracey has scratched my car, but she's on film, courtesy of Clifford, the caretaker. I'm waiting for the local police to come.'

Irene laughed loudly. 'Sorry, I'm not laughing at the damage to your car, but are these people thick?'

'Nobody knows there is a camera,' I said.

'It'll be interesting to see how she copes with being arrested for criminal damage,' Irene said.

'The big news is that I found a tape of Beverley talking to Tracey on the phone.'

'Webby told me,' Irene said.

Of course he did. Nothing happened in that station that Irene didn't hear about.

'It's all falling into place,' Irene said.

'None of it will bring that little boy back,' I whispered, but

Irene heard me.

'No, but you and Beverley are victims too.'

The doorbell rang. 'Here's the police, got to go. Thanks again, Irene.' I went to the door and let in a policewoman. Similar age to me and from her number, a similar amount of service. I didn't recognise her from training school, so perhaps an intake or two behind me.

'Hi, I'm Constable Taylor. Petra. You reported criminal damage to your car? May I call you Samantha?'

'Sam. Thank you for coming, Petra.' I didn't mention the Blue Peter dog who had died the previous year. She would have heard all the jokes anyway. I brought her in and offered her a cup of tea. I always appreciated a little hospitality at jobs so I was happy to offer it to a fellow officer.

'I had a quick glance at the scratch on the car as I came in,' she said as we settled with our drinks. 'Are you sure it was the woman opposite?'

'Positive. Our caretaker has caught her on film,' I said. I went to my handbag and got the photograph of Tracey photographing my car. I passed it to the policewoman. 'It's not the first time she's targeted me. This is from a little while ago.'

Petra peered at the photo. 'Why was she photographing your car?'

'No idea.'

'May I keep this?' Petra asked.

I thought for a moment. That photo would be more use in Irene's hands. 'Sorry, but I'm subject of a disciplinary enquiry at the moment. I need that photograph as proof of her malicious intent.' I was surprised how much it hurt to say that.

Petra didn't seem disturbed by this admission and handed the photo back. 'No problem. It's useful to know if there's some background. Which division are you from?'

'Egilsby, Wyre Hall subdivision.' There wasn't much more to say. 'Should I introduce you to Clifford? He's the caretaker and he's got the film.'

'That would be good.' Petra finished her tea then we went downstairs. I tapped on Clifford's door.

Clifford opened the door. 'Oh, hello again. Do you want that film?'

'Yes please, Clifford,' I said. 'This is Constable Taylor.'

'Pleased to meet you. I'm the caretaker, I look after this building.'

'Pleased to meet you, Clifford,' Petra said. 'I'd like to look around the car park.'

'No problem, go wherever you wish.' Clifford threw out his arm as if giving her the keys to the kingdom. I guessed that in his eyes, he was.

Petra and I went outside and she closely examined my car. 'This will need more than a rub down with *T-Cut*, it's gone right through to the metal.'

'I hope my insurance will cover it,' I said.

Clifford came out to join us. 'Did you tell her that I saw her doing it?'

'Yes, I did,' I replied.

Petra looked around. 'Where are the cameras?'

'There are none,' Clifford said.

I stepped in. 'Clifford has a camera in his flat on his own car.' I pointed to the window of the ground floor flat that was closest to our cars. 'We've had kids messing around in here. I'm lucky that I happened to park next to him.'

Clifford nodded vigorously.

'Right. May I see this film?' Petra asked.

Clifford showed us both into his flat, shouted instructions to his wife to get everyone a cup of tea, then set up a projector and ran the film. There was just enough of his own car in the shot that Clifford would be able to maintain that it was for his personal security, but there was a fair bit of the car park also visible, including the area where my confrontation with Anne Leigh had taken place. No wonder Irene was so pleased with it.

The film was unequivocal. Tracey stood by my car, looked

around and then ran something sharp, along the length.

'Would you be able to give me a copy of that?' the policewoman asked Clifford.

'I copy all my films if they show anything noteworthy,' Clifford said. 'In case the police ever need them. I don't mind going to court if necessary.'

'That's very helpful, thank you,' Petra said.

Unlike Mary Lovell, who craved attention, Clifford's eagerness to help was entirely benign. This building was his to care for, and he took his duties very seriously. I was grateful.

Petra and I finished our tea, shouted our thanks to Clifford's wife, then went to my flat, where she completed a crime report. Then she called for a car to assist in transporting a prisoner. I wouldn't be able to see the arrest from my windows, and I didn't want Tracey to see me gawking from the car park, but I would make sure I saw a copy of the report. Irene would sort that for me when I returned to work. If I returned to work.

*

Much later on, I got a phone call from Petra.

'Mrs Quinn denied everything despite the film; however she's been bailed on condition she does not set foot in the car park or the flats themselves. If you or Clifford see her, please call us because she'll be breaching bail. In fact, report any incidents that occur. She's odd. She seems to say whatever comes into her head in response to a question, even if it contradicts something she's already said. It's like dealing with a child who can't think beyond the next five minutes.'

'She has gone through a distressing experience; her nephew died,' I said. I didn't think for one minute that that had any bearing on her behaviour but I wanted to sound reasonable.

'I believe so, but that does not give her the right to go around damaging other people's property.'

I thanked Petra and hung up. I was going to enjoy this and,

with Tracey excluded from the flats, I felt safe to return home full time.

Chapter Seventeen

A week later, there I was, in uniform but still suspended, waiting to give evidence in the magistrates court. It was a straightforward case; the defendant was just trying it on by pleading not guilty, but I was still nervous. On my way into the building, I had spotted Anne Leigh. Reporters often sat in on court cases to find something for their paper, or in the case of freelancers, something juicy they could sell. I couldn't object because courts were open to the public unless specifically held in camera, or private, which was practically unheard of in a magistrates court. I just hoped that she hadn't seen me.

I heard the usher call my defendant into court and waited for my turn. I would go in after the plaintiff had given evidence. When the call came, I entered the wood panelled room and made my way around the pew-like seats to the witness box. I stepped up and faced the magistrates. Two men and one woman. They looked nice enough people, each dressed in the usual smart business outfits. The woman gave me a small smile, which I returned and waited for the questions.

The first couple of minutes went without hitch, I confirmed my identity and rank to the prosecution. Then I saw Anne Leigh come in and sit in the public gallery. Dammit! I tried to ignore her and concentrate on the questions. The evidence was overwhelming and I felt confident of a conviction.

Then, when the prosecution had finished, the defence solicitor stood up.

'Constable Barrie is it true that you are suspended from duty at the moment?' he asked.

I looked at the public gallery; Anne Leigh looked back with a smirk. Bitch! She must have told the defence about me. There was no way they could have known otherwise. She must have seen me and looked up what court I was appearing in then found the defence solicitor. She had deliberately tried to undermine me.

I reminded myself that I had nothing to hide and pushed out my chin.

'Yes, it's true,' I stated.

'Would you mind telling the court the reason for your suspension?' the defence solicitor asked.

It had nothing to do with this case. However, I didn't want him to accuse me of being difficult or evasive, so I declared, 'I have been the victim of a malicious complaint…'

I became aware that the magistrates were talking together and not paying any attention to me. I stopped speaking. I felt the knot in my stomach tighten. Were they about to dismiss the case? This was the very thing I had been dreading. If it could happen here it could happen in the Crown Court and the consequences would not be good.

'Madam Clerk?' the chairman said.

The legal advisor stood and faced the bench. 'Can I be of assistance, your worships?'

They beckoned her over and they talked together, too quietly for me to hear. The legal advisor was exactly that: she advised on legal matters within the court and held a lot of sway. I wondered why they would need her counsel in the middle of my giving evidence. Finally they seemed to agree on something and the legal advisor returned to her seat.

'Does your line of questioning have any relevance to the case we are hearing?' The chairman asked the defence solicitor.

'Not directly, but I wish to demonstrate that the constable—'

I wanted to shout at him, but that was not the done thing in court. Best to show the dispassion I was not feeling to disguise the anguish I was feeling.

The chairman cut across him. 'Was the constable under suspension when the defendant was arrested for the offence?'

'I. No...' The defence solicitor's voice trailed away.

The chairman addressed me. 'Constable Barrie, were you under suspension when you arrested the defendant?'

'No, your worship. I was suspended later when I was falsely—'

The chair turned away abruptly. 'The constable's duty status is irrelevant here. Do you have any questions relevant to the case?'

The defence solicitor visibly deflated. 'I have no further questions, your worships.' He bowed to the bench and sat down.

I looked across to Anne Leigh. She looked satisfyingly disappointed.

'Thank you,' the chairman said. 'Constable, you may leave.'

'Thank you, your worships.' Even though the chairman was the one doing the talking, Alan had drummed into me that it was important to address the whole bench. I stepped down from the box and, instead of leaving the room, I sat behind the solicitors. Now I had given my evidence, I was free to listen to the outcome of the case.

Finally, my defendant got his moment in the spotlight. Instead of rolling over and admitting that he had no defence for the offence, which he hadn't, he puffed out his chest and dramatically pointed in my direction as if he were Perry Mason.

'My lord, I want to say that I object to the evidence of a corrupt police officer being taken seriously.'

Oh great! I didn't believe that the defendant had first heard about my suspension just when I had given evidence. It was more likely that the solicitor had shared what Anne had told him with his client before the case. I would be the talk of the town before tomorrow. Also, I was not a corrupt!

'I'm not...' I began but shut up. Engaging in public arguments would just play into a certain journalist's hands. She was already leaning forward, eager to hear what the defendant had to say. I had to allow the evidence to speak for itself.

The legal advisor stood up. 'Your worships, we have no

evidence that Constable Barrie is corrupt or that we should not trust her evidence. We have heard in this court that she is currently suspended but I remind you that, in law, suspension is a neutral act during an investigation. This offence predates the start of her suspension by several weeks. Also, for the defendant's information, this is a magistrates court and he should address the bench as your worships.'

The defendant wasn't backing down. 'Then why was she suspended, eh? They don't do that for nothing do they? What's she been up to, eh? She had to have been up to something dodgy while she was out arresting people. That's not right.'

The chairman homed in on the defence solicitor. 'Please advise your client to hold his tongue.'

The defendant ignored his solicitor's pleas.

'Even if you convict me today, I'm appealing because her evidence is unreliable. I bet she's been taking backhanders or sleeping with informants.' He jabbed a finger towards the bench. 'And you lot will have your noses in the trough too.'

That was too much. The woman magistrate audibly gasped, even the solicitor put his head in his hands.

'How dare you—' I began.

The chairman cut in. 'Another word and I will hold you in contempt of court. Constable Barrie, to avoid further upset, it would be politic for you to leave the court at this point.'

He was right, I needed to be away from there for the case to continue. I was torn between outrage at the allegations and gratitude that the magistrates were having none of it.

I stood up and bowed to the bench. 'Yes, of course, your worships, and thank you.' I went to the waiting room, shaking with tension. This was just magistrates court; how bad would it be if I got to Crown Court?

A few minutes later, my defendant slammed out of court, closely followed by his solicitor and an usher. I stepped back out of sight behind a pillar, but I could hear him as he went down the grand stairway to the exit.

'Fucking wankers! You said that they'd throw out the case because that fucking copper was bent,' he shouted at the solicitor. 'You said her evidence would be declared suspect.'

'I said it might be, not would be. I didn't promise anything,' the solicitor argued.

'You didn't deliver anything either. A fucking big fine and a record, that's all. What was I paying for, eh?'

The solicitor lost his temper and shouted back, 'Don't forget, you came here expecting a conviction. I only found out about her suspension today when that journo spoke to me, and I only used the information because it was your only chance.'

I wished I had a voice recorder that picked that last bit up. He had admitted in public that a journalist had told him about me.

'Out, the pair of you before I call security,' the usher said.

'You can fuck off as well,' the defendant shouted.

'I'm so sorry,' the solicitor said to the usher.

I saw security gather at the foot of the stairs. The usher gave the slightest shake of his head, so they allowed the men to pass by into the street.

I descended the staircase and approached the usher, who was on his way back up. He grinned at me and shook his head. I had the feeling this was an almost daily occurrence for him.

'Lucky for him that it was just the magistrates. If that had been the Stipe, he'd be in the cells by now, he has no time for people like that,' the usher said.

'Yeah, lucky,' I agreed. The Stipe, or stipendiary judge, was, unlike the magistrates, legally trained and salaried. He did not need a legal adviser in his court and could hold the court by himself. Our current Stipe was known to have a short fuse and a dislike of drama in his court. 'Did you hear him say a journalist had told him I was bent?'

'Yeah.' The usher stopped right by me. 'Want me to make a note of it in case it's needed in future? Their worships are unhappy too.'

'I might not need it, but would you note it please?'

'No problem.'

I thanked him then headed back home. I would seek advice on today's events. I was fairly sure that the solicitor had breached some rule, even if Anne hadn't.

*

Anne struck again when the local rag next came out. In the courts section of the paper, that normally reported on people convicted of things that the paper thought interesting, or things that were less interesting if there was little news that week, Anne had managed to get a bit of column space for my court case.

"Man found guilty following court argument."

'...found guilty despite objecting to evidence given by a police officer who is currently suspended from duty. Constable Samantha Barrie of Wyre Hall police station gave evidence despite being suspended pending an investigation into her conduct. An argument broke out when the defendant objected to the officer, which resulted in Constable Barrie being ordered to leave the court..."

I was incandescent with rage. Anne certainly knew how to spin a story. It was technically correct but it hadn't been like that at all. It wasn't an argument, the defendant was on a rant, and I hadn't been ordered out, the magistrate quite reasonably had asked me to leave to calm the situation.

I was furious with Anne Leigh and I was disappointed that there had been no incursions by Tracey for me to report; however, I did receive a couple of letters in the post: one from the Open University and one from the Complaints and Discipline department. I recognised the envelope. This would either be a summons to a disciplinary hearing in front of the Chief Constable, which would almost certainly lead to the sack, or confirmation that I was in the clear.

I carried them into the living room and opened the OU letter first. It was all the information I needed to choose a course and enrol. Something to look at when I was able to concentrate. That left the C and D letter. I held it in a shaking hand for a good five minutes trying to pluck up courage to open it. Finally, I threw it down and went into the kitchen to make myself a cup of tea. I carried my drink into the living room and put my mug on the coffee table. I was putting off opening the letter but, eventually, I ran out of excuses. I snatched the letter up and ripped open the envelope.

Inside the envelope was a letter informing me that the investigation against me had ended and they had concluded that there was no case to answer. No apology, no information about my suspension or whether Anne or Tracey were facing charges, just bald facts. I was off the hook.

I drank my tea whilst rereading the letter several times, just to make sure I had not misunderstood anything. Then the relief kicked in and I had to rush to the bathroom, where I puked my tea into the toilet. I returned to the sofa and sat staring out across the grey water of the Irish Sea. I was relieved but irked at the coldness. C and D didn't care about the suffering I had endured; I was just another number to them. They didn't care about the upset in the court, they didn't care about the worry, the potentially lost friendships. I was aware that I had had few phone calls, but that was par for the course in cases like mine; people were tied up with their own lives and, even if they thought of me, they would keep their distance. Then I thought, was it fair to blame C and D for doing their job? I was innocent, but I knew there were actual corrupt police out there. I would want them to go to town on cases like that. I accepted that, although generally unpopular, C and D were necessary. However, I would not ever be applying to join their ranks.

So, what now? Did I just return next shift as if nothing had happened? Did I have to go through some kind of induction to ease me back in? B Block were on duty so I phoned the inspector's office and managed to catch Benno. I explained the contents of the letter to him.

'Am I still suspended, sir?' I asked.

'I don't see how they can keep you on suspension if there's no case to answer,' he replied.

'Should I just come back tomorrow? Am I still the collator's assistant? Do I rejoin the block?'

'Let me speak to the brass and I'll get back to you.'

I ended the call to let the inspector make his phone calls. Meanwhile, I phoned Mum to let her know I was no longer out in the cold. If Gary phoned me tonight, I would tell him about it, briefly. I wouldn't mention how it had affected me. No point in going on about something that was now in the past. If only Beverley could have a positive outcome too, I would be completely happy.

Chapter Eighteen

There was no great fanfare when I returned to Wyre Hall. No induction, no formalities, I simply reappeared on the rota, turned up when told to and continued where I had left off as Irene's assistant. Because Bev's case was still ongoing, the boss thought it best I remained off the streets. I didn't expect anything different. Nothing much had changed. I was disappointed to read that Cathy Chiu was still outstanding despite regular calls from Mr Paxton about the Chinese woman on the field. It seemed as if Frank was right and she was in the river.

B Block were on duty when I went to collect the messages. I hadn't seen anyone since Ken's wedding and I was keen to catch up with the news. I popped into the enquiry office to see how Steve was getting on. He was sitting at the desk but stood up when I came in.

'Sam, I'm sorry I didn't call…'

I patted his arm. 'It's okay. You had to look after your own career.'

'I know, but you came to see me when I was arrested. It's just…' his voice trailed away.

'It doesn't matter. With an arrest in your past, it might have looked bad if you had been in contact with me while I was under investigation.' I understood. Nobody wanted C and D to take an interest in them as well. 'How are things going with Emma?' I asked to change the subject.

He blushed. 'Pretty good actually. Mum likes her almost as much as she likes you.'

'That's great.' I was pleased for him.

'Sam, stop nattering. I need those messages,' Irene called from her office door.

'Sorry, on my way,' I called back. 'Speak later,' I said to Steve and trotted off to the collator's office.

*

After scoff, Inspector Benjamin came into the collator's office.

'Bad news, Irene,' he said. 'You're losing your assistant. The Superintendent has decided that Sam needs to get back outside.'

'I need an assistant,' Irene argued.

'He suggests that one of the typists is moved to your office. It's proved a popular suggestion in the typing pool,' Benno said.

'A civvy, in here?' Irene huffed. 'I'm not comfortable with the idea of a civilian seeing some of the stuff that passes through here.'

'They see a fair bit of stuff upstairs,' Benno pointed out.

'Completed reports. Some of the stuff in here isn't even verified, it's rumour and hearsay. I help plan operations in here. I'd prefer another police officer.'

The inspector shook his head. 'Not going to happen I'm afraid.'

Irene snorted. 'Fine. They'll need to sign a confidentiality agreement then.'

'They've already signed the Official Secrets Act the same as us, what more do you want?' Benno argued.

'They haven't been through the same training. They might not understand how vitally important confidentiality is in here. They won't even be able to talk about some stuff in the station.'

'I'm sure you'll train them well.' Benno grinned.

'You're not going to win this, Irene,' I said.

'Fine! But I get the final say on who comes here.'

'Agreed.' Benno said. 'Denise Dawson, Annie Turner and Debbie Rowlands have all expressed an interest.'

'Not Debbie, I wouldn't trust her,' Irene said. 'She's known for being over-fond of the nightclub scene and there are whispers that she dabbles in illegal substances. I've heard people talking about the state of her on Monday mornings. If she gets a G & T inside her, she can't hold her own water, never mind keep secrets. She's hanging on by her fingernails as it is.'

'Not Debbie then,' Benno agreed.

'Annie is a part-timer. Would she be willing to increase her hours and work the occasional weekend?' Irene asked.

'I'm not sure; we'd have to make sure she understands your requirements,' Benno said.

'Civvies get to work part time?' I was surprised. Police officers didn't get that option.

'Typists aren't considered as vital to the force as police officers,' Irene replied.

'That leaves Denise,' I said. Denise was a twenty-seven year old redhead with a dry sense of humour and an impressive repertoire of rebuffs for the many policemen who showed interest in her.

'Denise would be okay,' Irene admitted.

'Good. She starts at eight tomorrow.' Benno turned to me. 'Back with B Block tomorrow.'

'Yes, sir,' I said.

Irene thumped the desk after the inspector left. 'Bloody hell! He had that planned all along.'

I hadn't got to work with Irene for very long but I was happy to be going out again. I wanted to feel that things were normal even if true normality would take a little while longer.

*

Next day, I was given a town centre beat. Bert's plan to mix up the patrols must still be ongoing. I knew the town centre pretty well but I hadn't worked there apart from riding in Phil's car before I went solo. Walking the beat there would be different. If I needed help or a ride back to the station with a prisoner, I was pleased it would be Phil.

I got two shoplifters, which were straightforward and only took up a couple of hours each. Overall, it was a peaceful day from my perspective. I walked along at a sedate pace, window shopping as I went. Waldman's had some nice material that would make good curtains. Not that curtains were a priority for the flat, apart from the bedroom to block out the light following a night shift. We were high enough that passers-by couldn't see in, but the voyeuristic seagulls could be a pest. From there I meandered past the chicken shop, relishing the aroma of roasting bird. There were worse ways to spend time.

An hour from knocking-off time, I began to move towards the station. I couldn't go in yet but there was no harm in sticking to the edge of my beat, so I had a shorter walk in when it was time. My route took me past Chiu's chip shop. I paused, remembering Eric's smile and enthusiastic greeting for his customers, Cathy's quiet bustling by the fryers as her belly grew, then Mrs Yang's unsmiling presence. This had been such a busy place, now it looked desolate and bleak. The note about being closed for bereavement was still attached to the door, though a little ragged around the edges now. A *"For Sale"* sign drooped overhead.

'You'll have to find somewhere else for your chips, love,' said a passing woman.

I turned around and she grinned at me. She seemed friendly so I grinned back.

'A prize spot like this and a station full of hungry bobbies practically around the corner. I bet this is snapped up in no time,' I said.

The woman chuckled. 'I suppose so. Tragic what happened though, wasn't it? Who'd have thought the baby blues could get so bad.'

'Yeah,' I agreed.

The woman walked on.

As I was about to resume patrol, I thought I caught a movement in the back. I pressed a hand against the glass to block the light and peered in but there was nothing. I stepped back and listened. Nothing. I couldn't shake the feeling that something was not right. I went to the entry behind the shops and crept along to the rear of the chippy. The big gate was locked.

I was about to go over the wall to investigate, when I remembered that I should let people know where I was and what I was doing. I had been pulled up enough times for rushing into situations.

I moved away from the gate but kept it in sight. '4912 to control.'

'Go ahead,' Ray replied at once.

'I'm behind Chiu's chippy. I think there is someone in there. I'm going to investigate.'

'Negative!' Ray snapped back. 'Wait for assistance.'

At once I heard him directing Phil in Mike Two to my location and then acknowledging Mike Sierra Two—Shaun—who must have volunteered.

A few seconds later I heard someone running towards my location. Andy came racing around the corner into the entry and bounced off the opposite wall in his haste. Rubbing his shoulder, he hurried towards me. I put my finger to my lips to warn him to remain silent. We peered through the side gap of the gate but couldn't see anything. Then I heard distinct shuffling.

Andy was taller and fitter than me, and he was wearing trousers, so he was up and over the wall in a second. I hitched my skirt and reached to pull myself up, but the gate opened.

'It was only held shut by a latch and bolt,' Andy said.

'Let's leave it open for the others,' I said and gratefully walked into the yard. '4912 to control,' I transmitted.

'Go ahead,' Ray ricocheted back.

'Constable Broad is with me. We can hear movement so we're going inside,' I said. 'The rear gate is now open for access.'

'Roger,' Ray replied. 'Mike Two, ETA?'

I heard the beeping as Phil replied.

'Roger,' said Ray. '4912, Mike Two is two minutes away.'

'Roger.'

Andy and I crept to the building and listened at the door. Definitely movement. Andy tried the door handle. It wasn't locked. He threw the door open and stepped back in case of missiles or offenders waiting with blunt instruments.

'Police!' he shouted and went through the door.

I heard a small cry of alarm. I pushed in front of him and saw Cathy cowering in a corner of the kitchen, half-hidden by cooking oil boxes. She raised her hands and I could see blood running down one arm. A long kitchen knife lay at her feet.

'Cathy, what have you done?' I wasn't just talking about the cut on her wrist. I slowly moved forward, grabbing a tea towel as I passed the sink. 'Let me see your arm.'

She held out her arm and I crouched beside her, making sure I slid the knife towards Andy. Not that I didn't trust her, but I had been to enough jobs now to know that things could take a downward turn in a second. The wound was little more than a scratch. The thin skin had parted but she hadn't severed anything important. I gently bound it with the tea towel.

'You'll have to go to hospital with this,' I said.

'No!' Cathy shouted and tried to stand up.

'No argument! This needs to be seen by a doctor,' I insisted. Also said doctor could get her admitted for her mental health problems, which she probably realised.

She sank back down and allowed me to finish wrapping the tea towel around the wound to stem the blood. She was so thin, bedraggled, and grubby. She looked and smelt like she hadn't washed in a long time.

'Where have you been?' I asked.

'Around,' she replied.

'Where did you sleep?'

'Anywhere.'

'Devon Road field?' I asked.

'Sometimes, but boys came and shouted at me. I was in their place.' A tear ran down her cheek.

Mr Paxton really had seen her, but somehow she had avoided us when we went to check the field. She would have had no problem hiding in the smallest places. Had I not glimpsed movement, I would have walked straight past the shop and she would have remained on our *misper* list.

I sat back on my heels and tried to appear as non-threatening as possible.

'Cathy, tell me about Yang Hui Ping.'

I heard Andy draw closer to listen.

Cathy rubbed her good hand across her face. 'She killed my baby.'

'No, Cathy. We spoke about this, Mrs Yang didn't murder Rose,' I said softly.

'I believed you. Everybody said that Rose was not murdered, but I heard Eric and his mother arguing. She said that he should put me in a mental hospital, sell the shop and go back to Hong Kong. Forget about me and Rose. He should start again.' She looked from me to Andy. 'She said she had had to do the same when she fled to Hong Kong. She left her husband and took Eric.'

'It was a different time then. She had to make some tough decisions,' I said.

'She allowed her baby to be killed. Did she tell you that? Her baby girl was imperfect, like Rose, and her family didn't want to waste food on her. Eric was angry. I have never seen him so angry.' Cathy allowed her head to fall back. 'Living through those times has affected her. So many people died, she thinks life is cheap now. You arrested her, but she fooled you and you let her go.'

I dropped my chin to my chest. I recalled Mrs Yang's interview with DI Webb, but I didn't see any value in revealing all that to Cathy. I said, 'Cathy, we didn't arrest Mrs Yang, we simply questioned her because of your allegations. We are satisfied that she didn't kill Rose. I thought you understood that. There was an inquest. The coroner has ruled that Rose died of natural causes.

It was a cot death.'

'You're trying to trick me. She's sent you to get me. She'll kill me too for being a bad wife.' Cathy staggered to her feet so I stood up too.

'Cathy, Eric's mother is dead.' Had she really forgotten that Yang Hui Ping was dead?

Cathy staggered a little. 'She is dead?'

'Yes,' I replied. 'You put a pillow over her face. Did you mean for her to die?'

Cathy shook her head and opened her mouth to answer just as Phil and Shaun ran into the building. Cathy screamed and pushed past me. Andy tried to stop her, but she ducked under his arm and ran towards the shop part of the building.

I ran after her. 'Cathy, wait. These are my friends; they won't harm you.'

Cathy was too lost in her paranoia to listen to me. She snatched up a huge cleaver from the worktop and held it in front of her. I stopped—we all stopped—and watched her back up into the area behind the fryers.

'Cathy, you're not helping matters,' I said. 'Put down the cleaver.'

'I want to be with Rose,' she wailed.

I heard Shaun on the radio asking for more back-up and an ambulance. Yes, Cathy needed urgent psychiatric help, but I wasn't sure that more policemen would be helpful.

'Lads, I think Cathy is feeling overwhelmed. It would be better if you stepped away,' I said. *And stayed out of sight,* I thought.

'Andy, get outside and direct the ambulance to the rear,' Shaun said.

Andy didn't need telling twice. I wondered if Shaun was getting him out of harm's way without wounding his honour. I had often been sent out on some errand when I had been a sprog and it had taken months for me to click on to what was really happening.

193

Meanwhile, I hadn't taken my eyes from Cathy, not while she was waving a cleaver around.

'Cathy, you know me. I want to help you. Put down the cleaver and let me help you.'

I took a step closer, but she raised the cleaver with both hands as if she would throw it. I immediately stepped backwards ready to duck. Phil and Shaun dodged behind the wall. Cathy's bony hands shook from the weight of the cleaver. If she did throw it, her aim would be poor and it could go anywhere. Something niggled at the back of my mind. I had learnt not to ignore my niggles.

'Sam, get back here. Let us deal with this,' Shaun called, disrupting my thoughts. I could imagine how they would rush Cathy to get the weapon from her. A cornered animal was at their most dangerous, and it was the same for humans. Cathy had backed herself against the wall and had nowhere to go so to escape, she had to fight. If they mistimed it, they or Cathy could be severely injured.

'I think she's listening to me,' I said. 'Let's give it another minute.'

Cathy still held the cleaver up, so I remained out of arm's reach, just in case, and smiled at her.

'See, I don't want to hurt you and my friends are loud but they only want to help,' I said.

Cathy looked at me and, for the first time since I had arrived, she looked as if she was present in the moment. 'My baby is gone and now I will go to prison.'

'I think you're not well and you need to go to hospital,' I said. 'I'm sure the court will agree.'

Cathy threw her head back and repeatedly banged it hard against the wall.

'Stop it, Cathy! You'll hurt yourself,' I cried.

'I am crazy! I can't go to hospital. Who will help Eric with the shop? I want to be with Rose.' She gave a loud scream and released the handle and the cleaver fell to the floor. I sprang forward and hoofed it backwards towards Shaun and Phil. I didn't see what they did with it. I knelt beside Cathy and put my arm around her shoulder. I could feel every bone, every sinew. How could she have had the strength to suffocate Mrs Yang? I once read somewhere that stress can sometimes give someone superhuman strength, but even if that was the case, wouldn't Cathy have had wounds: scratches or something? Mrs Yang would not have remained still as she was suffocated, she would have fought for her life. It had been a while, so superficial wounds might have healed but Mrs Yang was heavier than Cathy and, even if she had not been able to overwhelm Cathy, she would have inflicted some deep scratches that would scar. All I could see were the self-inflicted wounds to Cathy's wrist. My niggle began to coalesce into a firm thought.

'Cathy, when you heard Eric and his mother arguing, what did you do?' I asked.

'I ran away and hid. She was shouting at Eric.' Cathy wiped a tear from her face with the back of her hand.

Cathy ran while Mrs Yang was still alive, so who could have killed her? Could Cathy have crept back later?

'Did you go back later on?' I asked.

'No—' Cathy began.

'Ambulance is here, Sam,' Shaun called, cutting off Cathy's voice.

'Let's go outside,' I said to Cathy.

'No!' She looked around in panic as the ambulance crew came in. 'Don't let them take me!'

I recognised one of the ambos, Clem. Our paths often crossed at incidents. He nodded a greeting to me and knelt down beside us.

'Cathy, these are ambulance men, this one is called Clem. I know him. He's a kind man and he won't let anyone hurt you. They will take you to the hospital. I'll come with you if you want,' I offered.

'Yes, come with me.' Cathy held my hand but allowed the

195

ambos to examine her arm.

'You'll need a stitch or two in that,' Clem said.

I helped Cathy to her feet and put my arm around her skinny shoulders. Shaun and Phil followed us and we walked through the yard to the waiting ambulance.

Ken and Andy stood by the gate with their staffs drawn and discreetly held tight against their legs. Spider hovered in the entry, looking with distaste at the discarded chip papers and dog dirt, and trying not to touch anything.

I called over to her. 'Charlotte, help me get Cathy into the ambulance.'

Spider came over and grabbed Cathy's arm. 'God, she stinks.'

'So would you if you'd been living rough for weeks,' I said. 'She's being cooperative so be gentle even if you can't be tactful.'

Spider and I guided Cathy into the ambulance and onto a trolley. Clem wrapped a blanket around the trembling woman. Spider exited as soon as possible.

'Clem, I need to speak to the sarge before we go. It won't take a minute.' I reassured Cathy that I wasn't leaving her and hopped down the step. 'Shaun!' I shouted.

Shaun came over to me. 'What's up?'

I walked him a few steps from the ambulance. 'I don't think Cathy killed Mrs Yang.'

'What are you talking about? She's off her head and Eric said she did it,' Shaun said.

'Look at her, Shaun. I've seen more substance in a glass of water. How did a scrawny, sick girl like that hold down a woman who is twice her weight? Mrs Yang must have fought back, so where are the marks? Cathy told me she ran and hid when she heard Eric and his mother arguing.' I lowered my voice. 'I think the only one strong enough to have done it is Eric.'

There. I'd said it. I thought Eric had killed his mother. Shaun had been a DC before his promotion; he knew I was talking sense.

'Okay, we need to speak to CID, but first we need to get this girl some help at hospital. She's a suspect and flight risk. She's already run away once, so you need to remain with her. I'll get someone to relieve you when I can.'

I climbed back into the ambulance and sat on the bench opposite Cathy. She held my hand as we left for the general hospital.

Dr McKay was the duty doctor at casualty. She recognised me and came over.

'Hello again. It's a bit quieter than last time you were here.'

'Hello, Dr McKay. I'm glad to hear it, but I have a woman who's been living rough for a few weeks. I have to stay because she's a suspect in a murder.'

'I see.' Dr McKay threw back the curtain and surveyed Cathy, who had curled up like a foetus on the bed. 'She's malnourished, certainly anaemic. I believe that lesion on her upper arm is scabies, and she's got nits.' Dr McKay turned to me. 'I need to give this woman a proper examination. Go to the pharmacy desk, tell them I sent you and they'll give you something with which to wash your hair. You'll have to send your uniform for cleaning as well.'

Whilst I was impressed with the doctors ability to diagnose so much from a distance, I was less impressed to find that Cathy had probably given me nits and possibly passed on scabies. However, I did as I was told and went to the desk. The woman was very helpful when I explained the situation and I came back a short time later with a bottle of hair wash, body wash and cream in case of scabies. Strictly speaking, I probably shouldn't have left her, but Dr McKay was with her and I didn't think she'd stand any nonsense, even if Cathy had the strength to try to escape.

Dr McKay had taken blood from Cathy and had given her a thorough once over.

'It's as I said: scabies, nits, near starvation. Bloodwork will confirm anaemia, I'm sure, and I'll have to stitch her wrist. I'm concerned about her mental state. I've asked a colleague who specialises in mental health to come and assess her.'

'She has been suffering from post-natal depression. Her daughter died at just a few weeks' old. Cot death. The doctor gave Cathy some tablets. I don't know what but I'm sure she won't have been taking them while she was living rough,' I said.

Dr McKay pursed her lips. 'She needs more than just tablets. I'll wait to see what my colleague says, but I think the psychiatric unit would be the best place for her.'

'I need to remain here for now, and I expect another officer will take over when I'm off duty,' I said.

'I'll ask one of the nurses to bring you a cup of tea.' Dr McKay said. 'I'll arrange for something to eat for Cathy too.'

This was very civilised. I pulled up a chair and parked myself next to the cubicle. I gratefully accepted tea and a biscuit from a nurse and prepared for a long wait.

*

Later on, way past knocking off time, when Cathy had been stitched, sedated and lay safely in bed in the psychiatric wing of the hospital, my relief finally arrived. I returned to Wyre Hall. I was bone-tired despite sitting for much of the time at the hospital. I suspected that weeks of stress were taking their toll.

Geoff was on the radio again. He turned in his chair when I came in to return my radio.

'It's the B Block shit magnet again. Only you could get yourself into mischief in the collator's office.'

'What do you mean by that?' I snapped.

'C and D coming to see you and you getting suspended,' Geoff said.

I really wasn't in the mood. I wanted to go home, have a hot bath and use my new lotions and potions, and then sleep forever.

'I did not get myself into shit, I was the victim of a malicious complaint.'

'You must have done something dodgy to get suspended,' Geoff insisted.

I was reaching the end of my tether. He was only voicing what a lot of other people were thinking, but it stung. 'What part of "malicious complaint" do you not understand? I didn't do anything. They investigated and there was no case to answer.'

Geoff laughed. 'If you say so, shit magnet.'

I overshot the end of my tether and screeched sideways into a cold, cold rage.

'If I hear you call me "shit magnet" or speculate on my conduct once more, I'm putting in an official grievance against you. It's bad enough knowing that there are members of the public who think it's okay to jeopardise your job, your freedom even, without having to deal with ignorant, fat, ugly buffoons inside the station.'

I didn't swear much, but occasionally I felt the need for a hearty swear word or two. In places I could not let rip with profanity, I always resorted to petty insults.

'Bloody hell, keep your hair on; it's only a bit of banter,' Geoff said.

'Keep your banter to yourself. I've had a tough time and I'm tired of it all.' I felt close to tears, because I knew this was how every other block saw me. I was the B Block shit magnet who had somehow got away with something. I didn't like it. It wasn't right and it wasn't fair.

'Anyway, Mike Finlay wants to speak to you,' Geoff said. 'He's in the bridewell. I advise you to wind in the attitude before you speak to him.'

'Get stuffed!' I left before Geoff could say anything more and went to the bridewell.

Mike was hunched over a charge sheet in the charge office. He looked up and grinned when he saw me. 'All right, Sam?'

I forced a smile back. I felt a bit fragile but that didn't give me the right to snarl at everyone. I wasn't angry with Mike. To be honest, even Geoff wouldn't have annoyed me half so much normally. He'd just been the final straw. I should apologise to him, or maybe he deserved it and he should keep his stupid opinions and banter to himself. I'd decide later.

'All right, Mike. Cathy has been moved to the psychiatric unit.'

He nodded. 'Good, good.' He put down the sheet. 'Tell me, what exactly did Cathy tell you?'

'The full story is in my statement, which I'll submit before going off duty,' I replied. 'In a nutshell, she told me that she had overheard Eric and his mother arguing about the time Mrs Yang had had to flee to Hong Kong during a famine. Cathy got scared and ran away. She's been living rough in the area.'

Mike pursed his lips. 'I suppose you're too young to have heard much about that famine. I was at school but I remember hearing terrible stories about people resorting to cannibalism, though that might have been exaggerated.'

I had done some reading about it since Mrs Yang's interview. 'It was man-made, wasn't it?'

'Caused by the agricultural policies of the time. I think the government there like to keep it quiet.' Mike rubbed his hands together. 'Anyway, that's all in the past. What's this about you thinking Eric killed his mother?'

'Cathy has always been thin, but now she's skeletal. I don't think she was ever strong enough to have killed Yang Hui Ping. Mrs Yang was much heavier than Cathy. The only person I can think of who might be strong enough to have killed Mrs Yang by suffocation is Eric.'

'A reasonable assumption. We'd need to get him in for interview before making any decision on how to proceed,' Mike said.

'Yes, Sarge,' I said. I knew they wouldn't include me with that, which irked me. It was time to put in an application for my CID aide's course. If I didn't like it, I could always try something different when my six months was up. 'I'll make a start on the paperwork. I'd like to get home before the start of my next shift.'

Mike laughed and turned back to his charge sheet.

The station sergeant headed me off as I made my way to the

report writing room.

'What's happened between you and Geoff? He's complained about you.'

My heart rate doubled at least. 'He made out that I have somehow got away with illegal activity. He called me an offensive name. He called me "shit magnet." I'm hurt and I want to complain about him.' Geoff wasn't the only one who could lodge a grievance.

The sergeant sighed. 'Come with me. Let's sort this out.' He walked into the control room.

'I have nothing to say to him,' I said from the corridor.

'I've got nothing to say to her,' Geoff said from inside the control room.

'Shut up the pair of you before I knock your heads together,' the sergeant said. 'Sam, get in here.'

I reluctantly entered the control room and glowered at Geoff, who glowered back.

'Right. Geoff, you said Sam overreacted to a bit of banter. Sam, you say Geoff hurt your feelings by an accusation that you have got away with wrongdoing.'

We both agreed.

'Sam, did you call Geoff an "ignorant, ugly, fat baboon"?' the sergeant asked.

'No, it was "ignorant, ugly, fat buffoon",' I clarified. 'But baboon will suffice.'

'See?!' Geoff cried.

The station sergeant scowled at me. 'Geoff, did you call Sam a "shit magnet" and imply she had been dishonest or misbehaved in some way?'

Geoff exhaled. 'Yes, but it—'

The sergeant cut across him. 'Do you two really want me to go ahead and lodge grievances? Neither of you will look good in it.'

We glared at each other for a full minute before Geoff mumbled. 'No.'

The sergeant turned to me. 'Samantha?'

I was tempted to insist on a grievance. I had that right but, if I did go ahead, Geoff would only insist on his grievance being lodged and neither would go anywhere because it was just claim and counter-claim. I also declined.

'Let this be an end to it.' The station sergeant went back to his office.

Geoff and I glared at each other some more before he muttered. 'Sorry.'

I gave an equally grudging apology and went to the report writing room. Open warfare had been averted, but we would never be friends and I wouldn't ever trust him.

Chapter Nineteen

I was feeling emotionally bruised with everything that had happened so, a few days later, I went to see Irene for a chat. She always managed to straighten me out.

I waited for Denise to be out of the way and tapped on the glass panel. Irene waved me in.

'Hi, Sam.'

'Hi.' I didn't want to dive right in with my problems. I looked around. Nothing much had changed since Denise had arrived. 'How's Denise settling in?' I sat on the chair nearest the door.

'We had a few "full and frank exchanges of views", as politicians and bosses like to say, but she's settling.' Irene air-drew the inverted commas. 'Hey, remember Maureen Clough?' she asked.

'How could I forget her. Shane Clough is still in hospital with possible brain damage.'

'He's been released into care.' Irene grinned at me.

'He's recovered?'

Irene waggled her hand. 'Not entirely. He might never recover entirely; there's some issues but nothing that would stop him living a full life. He's gone into foster care.'

'That's the best thing that could happen for that little lad,' I said.

At last, something good was happening. Now was a suitable time to speak about my feelings.

'Irene, do you ever get… Do you…?' I didn't know how to say what I was thinking. Irene watched me without expression. I tried again. 'Do you ever regret joining the police?'

'It wouldn't be normal if I didn't from time to time,' Irene said. 'I don't get that so much now, but when I was on patrol there were times I hated people. I think anyone who works with the public feels that way sometimes.'

'Yes! That's it. I hate the public! I hate that some person can ruin your life by lies and not face any consequences. It makes you distrust everyone.'

'You could take legal action against them if you chose,' Irene said.

'Civil action, and even if there is some criminality, the job wouldn't support you because it's so much trouble for such a little inconvenience.' I declared. 'But it's not a little inconvenience. It's devastating, and the wait for a decision is agony. Even if we did decide to take civil action, the person would just counter with another complaint so we'd go around in circles. Also, I hate having to defend the organisation when it's dragging its feet unnecessarily over a decision on a case.'

'Okay, okay. Take a breath,' Irene said. 'I take it Beverley hasn't heard anything yet?'

'Nothing. They have a tape of the phone calls; how much more evidence do they need?' I was panting after my outburst.

'There's nothing we can do there, Sam. Sometimes you just have to sit on your hands and wait.'

'Like we waited to speak to the Jacksons that time,' I snapped. 'That went well, didn't it?'

'You don't still feel bad about that, do you?' Irene asked.

'Yes! No. Sort of. Not personally, but I do think of them and I get angry that it could all have been avoided with a phone call.'

'A phone call that could only have been made when it was clear they were no longer considered part of the case,' Irene argued. 'Do you think Beverley is a danger to herself?'

'No. She's low but not suicidal. It's not fair though,' I said. 'I'm not sure if I even want to be in the police anymore.'

'No, it isn't fair,' Irene agreed. 'You're not the only one who feels overwhelmed and angry at times. It takes a gritty person to weather these storms; not everyone can. You've come through so much; it would be a shame for you to give up now. Remember, as some Russian bloke said, everything passes. There's a bit more to it than that, but—good, bad or indifferent—it all passes. Something good will happen soon that will restore your faith in people and you'll feel differently. Why not contact your counsellor?'

'I already did.' My breathing was slowing, as was my heart rate. Getting things off my chest had helped.

'Good. Think hard before acting, Sam. If you rush off and resign, it won't address the problems you are experiencing. Sometimes, it's best to remain and tackle what is bothering you from the inside. Be it inside the organisation or inside your own head. If all else fails, find yourself a nice little place in admin. They work permanent days and don't interact much with the general public.'

'I wouldn't like that,' I said.

'There you go then; you have your answer. You like being operational and you don't hate the public; you're just going through a troubled time. It will pass,' Irene said.

Irene was right, I didn't hate *all* the public and I did *mostly* like being a policewoman. I was reacting to events. Anyone who had been exposed to the stuff I had experienced over the last few months would feel edgy and demoralised.

We had been warned in training school not to become too emotionally involved in cases. Beverley was different; that was family and I couldn't help but become emotionally involved, but what sort of police officer would I be if I didn't care at least a little bit about the rest of it? No, I wouldn't resign, nor would I dwell on things I couldn't change.

'Thanks, Irene,' I said. 'You always manage to put my head back on.'

'No problem. Sam. We all need someone to talk to sometimes.'

Denise came back in and clocked Irene and me. 'Should I

leave?'

Irene looked at me.

'No, it's fine.' I stood up. 'Thanks again, Irene.'

I left them to it.

'Sam!' Bert called from the sergeants' office as I walked past.

'Yes, Sarge?' I went into the office, where Bert and Shaun were poring over a shift rota.

'You start your driving course on the 31st of July.' Bert said.

'Yes!' I had been waiting for this. Just as Irene had said, the bad times would pass and something good would happen that would alter my whole mood.

I could drive but police driving was something else. As far as the driving school were concerned, I was currently classed as Level 4—that is, I had passed my DoT test—but I would be Level 3 at the end of my course, equivalent to the DoT advanced driver, and able to drive the panda cars and small vans, provided I passed the practical assessment and the exams. I would be taught safe pursuit (whether there was such a thing was hotly debated), I would be taught how to cut through traffic using the blues and twos—the lights and two-tone sirens—I would be driving at very high speed. If I did well, I would have the option to go on to the class for Levels two or one. Level two was police advanced driver status and required for anyone wanting to go into the traffic department. It was not just safe pursuit, but aggressive, offensive pursuit and a whole lot more, with very powerful vehicles. With a level one, I could drive anything anywhere (apart from HGVs, they required a different test). I couldn't wait.

'We're going to be a bit short,' Shaun commented.

'It's only for a month,' Bert replied.

I almost skipped out of the office. I stopped off at the enquiry office to speak to Steve.

'I got my driving course,' I said.

'Great! There'll be no stopping you after that,' Steve said.

It occurred to me that I might be being insensitive, since Steve's own course had been postponed until he was back up to fitness.

'Sorry, Steve, I didn't think. You're still waiting for yours. Have you heard anything about it yet?'

'I'm going for a medical next week, if I pass I'm coming back onto normal duties,' Steve said. 'I'll probably get the course after yours.'

That was good news, but I hoped Bert wouldn't put me back into the office once Steve was back out.

'Isn't it time you were back out, Sam?' Shaun called from the sergeants' office.

'Just on my way, Sarge,' I called. 'Got to go,' I said to Steve and hurried out to face the public.

*

As the following day's parade wound up, Inspector Benjamin said, 'Finally, many congratulations to Phil Torrens, who is leaving us next month to take his place as the patrol sergeant on A block at High Lake.'

Spontaneous applause broke out. Phil stood up and gave a little bow. I clapped as hard as anyone, but I didn't want him to go. He was my rock, my go-to in times of trouble. I envied A block at High Lake. I wondered if I could arrange a transfer, but then I would miss B Block.

'John, you will take over Mike Two,' the boss said.

John Batt was our spare driver. He looked up from his book, startled at first but then settled into a wide smile.

'Yes, sir.'

'Are you having a do, Phil?' Trevor asked.

'I might have a scoop or two at the police club,' Phil replied.

We all took that as a definite yes.

Parade ended and we went to collect our radios. I stopped off in the front office to speak to Steve again.

'Phil's going to High Lake.' I was bereft.

'He told me before parade.' Steve eyed me. 'We'll be among

the experienced ones now. The sprogs might come to us for advice.'

'Imagine that.' I worried that, if they did, I might not know the answer. 'Who do we go to?' I had finally voiced my concern. Yes, there were other more experienced officers on the block, but I didn't feel I could talk to them the way I could talk to Phil. I didn't trust Trevor not to spread everything around the station, and I didn't feel I could talk to Frank Morton or some others at all.

'We'll have to rely on ourselves and each other. Failing that, there's always Ray and Derek and the sergeants,' Steve said.

'Self-reliance is overrated,' I grumbled.

'But necessary. If we're promoted, how can we expect to lead a block if we're still seeking regular reassurance. We have the training; we just need the confidence.'

I knew Steve was using "we" in place of "you". He was right, I needed to cut the umbilical and start trusting myself. When did Steve get so wise? Come to think of it, when *did* Steve get so wise?

'What have you done with Steve Patton?' I asked. 'Should I take you to our leader?'

He laughed. 'I've had a lot of time to think.' Then Steve grew serious. 'I could have died, Sam, and what would I have left behind me? What have I accomplished? Apart from family pictures, would there be anything left to show I've been here?'

I gaped; Steve never spoke like this. He never expressed such profound thoughts.

'At our age, can any of us say we've done much?' I asked.

'You overcame something that few people experience, and you are using your experience to help other people. I've done little that counts for anything. I even joined the police to avoid following Dad and Richard into the Marines,' Steve said. 'One day, I'd like my own family. I want to be able to tell them stories about my life. While I was off sick, I decided it was time to stop messing around and get serious about my career.'

'I liked the old Steve. I didn't always like his tricks, but I liked him,' I said.

'I'm still here, but we all have to mature, Sam. Can you imagine Andy still bouncing around like an untrained puppy when he's forty?'

'I suppose not,' I reluctantly agreed.

'Or forty-year-old me walking into a hospital ward dressed as a pirate?'

I giggled as I remembered that episode. 'Actually, I can imagine that.'

'We can still have fun,' Steve said. 'But in a couple of years, if we're not already in the departments, they'll call on us to mentor sprogs. I want to do a decent job of it.'

Gary was in Hong Kong, Phil was leaving on promotion, Alan had retired. Steve would go off to the traffic department or some other department, but had already changed. Gaynor's pregnancy was distracting Ken. One by one, I was losing those I was closest to at work. I still had Ray and Irene to talk to, but everything was changing. Even my parents were talking about going to Scotland. Steve was right; I had to embrace self-sufficiency.

Bluntly, I had to grow up. I had come a long way from when I had first arrived at Wyre Hall, but I still had a long way to go. I needed to trust myself to deal with stuff and seek advice only when necessary.

'Sam, are you still here?' Irene called from the door to the collator's office.

'Here,' I replied and went to see her.

'I thought you would like to know that Tracey Quinn is now pleading guilty to damaging your car.'

'So I no longer have to appear in court?'

Irene nodded. 'Spot on. You'll get official notification shortly.'

What about the rest of it? The lies she told, the anguish she caused to me and to Beverley through that damned reporter. I would have to have a think about that.

'Thanks, Irene,' I said and went out to begin my patrol.

Chapter Twenty

A couple of days later, I dropped by the collator's office to see Irene again. I hadn't spoken to Mike or Eamon and I wanted to see if my hunch about Eric Chiu had been correct. Irene wasn't there; however, Denise was.

'Can I help you?' she asked.

'Hi, Denise, I came to see Irene,' I replied.

'She's upstairs speaking to DI Webb,' Denise replied.

'Not to worry.' I went towards the drawers to check on Eric.

Denise stood up and blocked me. 'What are you looking for?'

'A card on Eric Chiu,' I replied, a little miffed at Denise's officious demeanour.

'For what reason?' Denise asked.

'I've been dealing with his incident. I need to see what we have on him. What has that got to do with you, Denise?'

Denise stood very straight. 'I'm the collator's assistant. I can get you the information you require. Just let me know and I can have it ready for you when you get back from patrol.'

'Or I can do what I have always done and go and look for myself right now,' I snapped.

'We have to be careful. There is confidential information in there, some of it not even verified…'

It sounded as if Irene had had another talk with her about expectations.

'…you might be checking on your neighbours or your own family, which wouldn't be appropriate, especially in light of your recent suspension.'

'I take exception to that! The complaint was a malicious lie. If the brass have decided I can be trusted to keep the streets safe, I think I can be trusted to look at a blooming card.'

'What's going on?' Irene asked as she came in.

'Constable Barrie is trying to get information from the cards and refuses to tell me why she needs it,' Denise said.

At the same time, I said, 'Tell her we're all on the same side and I am not a criminal, will you? In fact, remind her which department provides most of your information.'

Irene rolled her eyes. 'Sam, get what you need. Denise we need to talk again.'

I got the card I wanted and scanned it quickly. Nothing of note. Just to prove a point, I also checked the cards on Cathy Chiu and the chip shop. Nothing much new there apart from Cathy still being in hospital.

'Irene, do you know what's happening with Eric Chiu? There's extraordinarily little on the card and nothing at all for the last month.'

'The CID are dealing with that,' Denise said.

Irene's eyes flicked to Denise. 'I believe DS Finlay is dealing with that. I expect he'll update it when he has a moment,' she replied.

'Has Eric been interviewed yet?' I asked.

'DS Finlay—' Denise began.

Irene interrupted. 'Yes, there has been an initial interview but he hasn't been charged with anything.'

'Okay, thanks.' I shot a look at Denise and left.

As I closed the door, I heard Irene say, 'I've told you before, I need an assistant, not a gatekeeper. We don't just work for CID...'

I trotted off to the control room to speak to Ray and Derek. 'What's going on in there? I practically had to fight Denise to look at a card. I used to get on okay with her.'

Derek laughed. 'We're taking bets on how long it'll be, before Irene throws her out. I say give it another two weeks.'

'No. End of this week,' Ray said.

'What's happened?' I asked.

'Denise thinks she is queen of the castle since she moved out of the typing pool,' Ray said.

'Mind you, she always thought herself a bit superior because she used to take the Chief Inspector's work,' Derek said.

'Maybe that's why she's funny about letting people look at the cards,' Ray said. 'The brass wouldn't want their communications to be public knowledge.'

'I wondered if it's because of my suspension. She insisted that I should tell her what I wanted and why and she'd get it for me, but you know how sometimes one thing leads to another and you end up with a pile of cards. Individual requests just slow everything down,' I said.

'It's not just you,' Derek said. 'She says that she's part of the CID now and only CID should have full access for their investigations.'

'Rubbish! Collators are for everyone,' I said.

Steve came in from the enquiry office. 'That's not the best of it. Irene has had to work late most days this week because when she left at her normal time, Denise locked the office to keep people out when she and Irene weren't there.'

'That's what they do in the typists' office,' Ray said. 'It stops basket-ratting in the wee hours.'

Basket-ratting was a time honoured tradition where some bobbies, not all, would risk a fizzer by entering the offices of admin and senior officers to go through the paper waste before the morning cleaners could empty the bins. Apparently, it was a good way to glean any information that might be useful. Trevor was strongly suspected of being a basket-rat because he always knew what was happening upstairs. I always wondered if the brass had set up cameras in their offices, so I didn't risk it.

'That meant that nobody on nights, or the last half of lates, could have got the information they might have needed!' I was shocked.

'Or the first hour or two of earlies,' Steve said.

'What about the info basket?' The basket where bobbies left information, intelligence, whispers and rumours for Irene to add to the system. An integral part of the collator's role and provider of many pieces of the jigsaw that was an investigation.

'Denise has been taking the information personally. If you need to update a card, she insists you tell her what you need to say and then you have to trust that she tells Irene, then updates the correct card with the correct information,' Steve said.

That might be the reason for the paucity of recent information on the cards. Maybe some people were not bothering rather than pass information to Denise.

'Irene went ballistic when she found out,' Steve said.

Derek chuckled. 'We could hear her shouting from here. In the end, the boss went in.'

'We couldn't hear that though,' Ray added.

'Maybe Denise just needs time to adjust,' I said. I'd get Irene alone at some point and get the full inside story.

Denise came out of the collator's office holding a sheet of paper and glanced our way. Her cheeks were deep pink. It looked like Irene had torn a strip off her. We all stopped talking as she came towards us, so she had to have known she'd been the topic of our gossip. Nobody cared.

She stopped by the door. 'Sergeant Kildea needs me to send a message on the telex.'

Derek held out his hand. 'Give it to me, I'll sort it.'

Denise hesitated then held out the sheet. 'It's important it goes at once.'

'I'll sort it,' Derek repeated and placed the sheet on the desk but made no move towards the tiny telex room.

Denise's lips thinned. She remained by the door for another few seconds then turned away without another word.

Derek grinned, picked up the sheet and went to the telex office to send the message. He'd sent his own message to Denise, loud and clear.

'I'm off out,' I said.

I cut through the enquiry office and headed towards the door. Denise was just going back into the collator's office. I pretended I hadn't seen her but she called out to me.

'Constable Barrie. Samantha.'

I turned back but remained silent. Let her do the talking.

She took a couple of steps towards me. 'I'm sorry if I came across as being a bit fussy.'

'You came across as being downright rude and obstructive,' I said.

Denise swallowed. 'I'm sorry. Upstairs, I dealt with the senior officers and I was under strict instructions to keep their work separate from the rest of the work that came in. If the Chief Inspector needed something, he would ask for it and I would get it for him.' She preened a little. 'I was more of a secretary than a typist.'

The Superintendent had a secretary but I supposed if the CI wanted to use a typist as a secretary, then that was nothing to do with me.

'So you thought that that was how a collator's office ran too?' I asked.

She nodded. 'I thought that by volunteering as Sergeant Kildea's assistant, I could move properly into admin and secretarial work. It's better paid than typing.'

'And you thought the collator was just there for the jacks? Do you have any idea how a police station actually works? I don't mean the hierarchy, I mean the everyday workings, the departments, all of them. How we all fit together.'

'You uniforms attend the jobs and the CID do the investigating,' Denise said.

'You think CID are the centre of the hub?' I asked.

'Aren't they?'

'Some will tell you they are but there is much more to it than that,' I responded. 'You might think that we plods are bottom of the heap, but let me tell you, we are the foundation upon which the entire force rests.' I could hear myself getting preachy, but I needed to say it. 'Without response officers, nobody would attend incidents, no work would come to the other departments, Without our interaction with the public, very little information would come in and trust would be lost. Without us patrolling, there would be no visible presence and no deterrent to the criminals. Traffic, Mounted, Dogs, Communications, CID, and all the rest of the departments are important, but without us, there is no policing as the public like to see it, and as a force, it's the public that has to come first. The upshot is, we uniforms need access to the collator's files as much as CID or anyone else does.'

Denise chewed her lip as she considered my words. 'Can we start again?'

I hesitated for a moment, but she looked sincere, hopeful even.

'Sure.' I nodded towards the control room. 'May I suggest that you offer to make that lot a cup of tea. That would go a long way to rebuilding bridges.'

She smiled. 'Thanks.'

I left her to it and went out.

*

After work, I called off to visit Bev. The nights were definitely lighter, so perhaps I shouldn't have been so surprised at the absence of dog dirt. The offender wouldn't want anyone to see them.

As usual, Bev and I perched at the breakfast bar, drank tea and chatted about everything, except for the accusations that were hanging over her.

I heard a movement by the front door. 'Did you hear that?' I asked.

Bev shook her head. 'Nothing.'

I heard another scuffle against the door.

'If that's another dollop of poo…' I leapt of my seat and raced to the door to catch the phantom poo dropper. Bev followed close behind me. I wrenched the door open and saw a woman standing on the step. There was no dog dirt around and, as far as I could see, no suspicious bags or bulges in her clothing.

'You shouldn't be here!' Bev cried.

'Who is this?' I demanded.

'I'm Judith,' the woman said.

What was Jonathan's mother doing here?

'Bev's right, you shouldn't be here. You need to leave,' I said.

Judith looked past me to Bev. 'Please can I come in? I'd like to speak to you.'

Bev considered Judith for a minute, then said, 'Okay then, but Sam's staying with me.'

Judith stepped inside. I could see that Bev was torn, but she didn't offer her a cup of tea. I stood with my arms folded. Bev indicated for her to sit down. I sat opposite and fixed Judith with a cool look. I was suspicious of this visit. What was Tracey up to now?

'I wanted to speak about what happened,' Judith began. 'I should have come sooner but I wasn't in the right frame of mind. It's been hard since Jonathan…'

Bev opened her mouth to say something, but I frowned. She remained silent. Let Judith say her piece. We'd then find out soon enough what was going on.

'Does Tracey know you're here?' I asked. 'Do the police?'

Judith shook her head. 'I haven't told anyone, not even my husband, but the police have visited me, which is why I decided I had to come and talk to you.'

'Why now?' I demanded. 'The police must have spoken to you more than once since all this began. You had to have been aware that they were considering charges against Bev.'

Judith's cheeks reddened. 'Yes, but it all fitted in with what Tracey had told me.'

'Okay then, we don't want to jeopardise the enquiry, so I

217

think you should say what you came to say, then leave. People might get the wrong idea,' I said.

'Let her speak, Sam,' Bev said.

I reluctantly backed off and left Bev and Judith to it.

Judith started. 'Tracey and I haven't spoken in a while. She has always been... difficult, and I couldn't cope with her dramatics after losing Jonathan.'

Oh boo hoo, I thought. I know it was uncharitable but I was still hurting after all the problems Bev and I had endured.

'I just want you to know that I know you wouldn't have hurt Jonathan deliberately. I did tell the police that, but Tracey insisted that you had been neglectful if not abusive.'

'I didn't hurt him at all,' Bev snapped. 'Tracey told me that he'd fallen at her house before she brought him. I begged her to get him when he became ill, but she wouldn't come.'

I so wanted to tell her about the tape, but I remained quiet.

Judith considered Bev's words. 'That's not what she told us and that's not what she told the doctors or the journalist at the hospital.'

'I spoke to the doctor when I arrived there with Jonathan,' Bev said.

'Tracey told them you had lied.' Judith couldn't meet Bev's eyes. 'They had no choice but to call the police.'

'I guessed as much,' Bev said.

'Which journalist?' I asked.

'I don't know. She was in the waiting room. Tracey had got herself into a tizz when the doctors came to talk to us about how Jonathan had received his injury. I explained to them that my husband and I had been away and Tracey had been looking after him. I had to rely on her account of things. She lost her temper and said that they were trying to blame her. She caused a bit of a scene and then accused the doctors of not trying hard enough to save him. It's what she does when she gets into one of her states; she invents stories as she goes along and gets ideas that might or might not be true. She doesn't seem to care if she's caught out later on. She just can't tolerate being in the wrong. It's one of the reasons her marriage didn't last long. I think she sometimes actually believes what she says…' Judith let her voice trail away and gazed into her lap. 'It was after that the journalist came over.'

'Can you describe this journalist?' I asked.

Judith rattled off a near perfect description of Anne Leigh. I was getting an insight into why Tracey had pushed the blame onto Bev.

Judith continued. 'She made comments about negligent staff. My husband and I told her to get lost. The doctors had just told us that our son was unlikely to survive, and we couldn't be doing with her questions. Tracey was keen to talk though, especially when the journalist mentioned cases of abusive childminders.'

That was interesting. Anne Leigh seemed to have a knack of feeding into Tracey's mindset. Maybe, it was she who gave Tracey the idea of blaming Bev. I raised an eyebrow to Bev who gave an almost imperceptible shrug back.

'Why have you stopped speaking to Tracey?' Bev asked.

Good question. I waited for the answer.

'She overstepped the mark during Jonathan's funeral and told relatives we were always gallivanting off and leaving him with her, which wasn't true. She and my husband have never got on, but he'd had enough this time and threw her out. She called the police and told them he'd punched her. Luckily, many relatives had seen what had happened so nothing came of it. She then said that losing Jonathan was our punishment for treating her so badly.'

'Wow.' Bev shook her head.

I said nothing; this was typical Tracey. However, I wondered why nobody had ever suggested that she had something wrong with her. To lie, to cause ructions the way she did, even among family, was not normal.

Judith stood up. 'I'll go now. I don't blame you for Jonathan. Accidents happen. I tried to stop proceedings but the police told me it was too far gone to stop and they had to follow up all allegations.'

Bev replied, 'I know you think you are being fair, but Jonathan didn't have an accident, or any harm come to him in my care. That is another fabrication from Tracey. I want you to know that I don't blame you for the actions of your sister, despite the devastating consequences. Thank you for trying to call off the dogs.' She paused, then said. 'I wish I could have attended the funeral, to say goodbye. He was a lovely boy and I miss him. Perhaps I could visit his grave and put down some flowers or something?'

I could see the uncertainty in Judith's eyes; however, she recognised the truth in Bev's words. Judith nodded then left. I saw her to the door. She had barely stepped onto the path before I shut the door on her.

Bev was staring out of the window after Judith when I returned to the living room.

'Why are the police taking Tracey so seriously whilst ignoring the child's actual mother?' she said so quietly, I wondered if she was talking to herself.

'Because the parents were away and Tracey was here,' I responded.

Bev nodded. 'I suppose that makes sense.'

'You should mention Judith's visit to your solicitor, just in case someone tried to use it against you,' I advised. 'You're bound to get some news soon and you'll be able to put all this behind you,' I said.

Bev pointed to the sky. 'Oh look, there goes another pig at thirty thousand feet.'

Chapter Twenty-One

Finally, my day in Crown Court arrived. We were on lates, so Benno and I had had to come on duty a couple of hours early to be at the court for 1:45pm. The building looked impressive and intimidating, exactly as designed. The Inspector and I booked in and went to find out which court Maureen Clough was appearing in. Once we had settled that, we went to the waiting area and hung around with other police officers who were waiting for their own cases to be called. Some had their pocketbooks out and were rehearsing replies in anticipation of the questions. Somewhere in the mass of people outside the courts would be Dr McKay and Sister Lomas. I looked out for them but I couldn't see them.

Sometimes, it could be a long wait, but today we were quite lucky and they called for Dr McKay just after two. I saw her enter the court.

"This shouldn't take too long,' the boss said.

It didn't. About fifteen minutes later, Dr McKay came out. She saw us but didn't come over. She couldn't speak to us before we had given evidence.

Sister Lomas was only in there five minutes, then they called for Inspector Benjamin.

About five minutes in, I heard shouting from the court. Everyone nearby stopped what they were doing and turned towards the noise. I saw an usher and a security officer slip into the court. I didn't even try; I was a witness who had yet to give evidence, I would have been kicked out at once.

A couple of reporters decided that our court was more interesting than the cases they had initially chosen and followed the usher into court. Things quietened down and the security officer came back out. I would have to ask the boss what had happened later on.

Inspector Benjamin was in there for a long time. My fellow officers were called to their own courts one by one until there were only three of us left. I was becoming anxious; what could they be talking about? Eventually, the usher came out and called my name. The boss must have parked himself behind the solicitors to hear the outcome of the case.

I entered the court. The jury were sitting in two rows along one wall facing the witness box. Maureen was standing in the dock flanked by white-shirted bridewell staff. Behind her were the steps leading down to the cells.

I looked over to the public gallery, which had the reporters sitting in it. I spotted Anne Leigh and inwardly groaned. What mischief was she planning now?

I whispered to the usher, 'That reporter up there, she has printed untruths about me in the paper. Can I ask for her to be removed?'

'Sorry, love. It's a public arena and we're not in camera,' he said.

Unless the judge decreed the case was to be heard in private, there was nothing I could do. Okay then, let Anne Leigh do her worst. I had already lodged a formal complaint with the paper for accepting her work. I didn't expect to hear any more, but they might speak to her about her about it. With luck, they might decide not to use her again.

I walked around to the witness box, nodding at the boss, who had indeed installed himself behind the solicitors, then mounted the stairs to the box. I bowed my head to the judge.

'Oh here she is,' Maureen shouted to the jury. 'This one is worse than the last lying pig. Baby snatcher. Bloody hypocrite.'

I was surprised to hear a word like that from Maureen. Her

vocabulary was normally much more basic.

I swore in and waited for the first question.

'Could you identify yourself?' the judge asked.

'I am Constable 4912 Barrie, stationed at Wyre Hall in Egilsby division, your Honour,' I replied.

'She's not a pig no more,' Maureen shouted.

I turned to her and saw her smirk.

'You thought I wouldn't know, did you? I told you I'd remember your name. I seen you in the paper. You're sacked. You got thrown out of court because you kicked off.'

I turned back to the judge to await his comments. Maureen continued to shout.

'Your evidence is worth nowt, you're bent.'

The judge looked at me, raised one eyebrow then looked back at Maureen.

'We spoke about his earlier, Mrs Clough. You will be quiet or I'll have you removed.' He turned to the jury. 'The jury will disregard any comments the defendant has made.'

'She's the problem,' Maureen said.

'Last warning,' the judge said to her.

One of the bridewell officers moved closer. Maureen shut up.

'Do you have any comment, Constable Barrie?' the judge asked.

'Your Honour, I am an operational police officer. I am not corrupt and I have never kicked off in a court. The incident the defendant is referring to is when my presence incensed another defendant and he became verbally abusive. I happily left to avoid further upset.' I decided to have a little fun. I pointed to the public gallery. 'Ask that reporter up there. She was present at the time. She reported on it. In fact, she's reported on a lot of my recent activities, including a discredited complaint.'

Anne's cheeks reddened as everyone turned to her.

Maureen shouted at Anne. 'You want to report on her for stealing my baby for no good reason.'

'This is the small child that we have heard was left unsupervised with a bag of heroin?' the judge asked.

I suppressed a smile, as did some of the jury. Anne drew back into the shadow.

'That wasn't my fault, he shouldn't have climbed up,' Maureen said. 'And I was there, I was just asleep.'

'Shall we continue or are you going to interrupt again?' the judge said.

Maureen remained quiet and I was able to give my evidence. I wasn't needed for much. I only corroborated what the boss had already said and described how Maureen had struck him across the face with a chair leg causing an injury that needed stitches.

Afterwards, Inspector Benjamin and I went into the waiting area while the jury went out to deliberate.

'Do you want to wait for the verdicts?' he asked.

'No, sir. I think it's a foregone conclusion and she'll only scream at me again. I'd just as soon go back to the station. They'll send the results over anyway.'

So that's what we did.

*

A couple of hours later, I was on my break. Unusually, the boss had instructed us not to go back out afterwards as he wanted to speak to us and second break all together. It was a bit risky to leave the streets unattended, so it had to be something really important.

We stayed put in the refs room and waited for second refs to meet us. I noticed that Trevor, who normally ate with us, was no longer in the room.

Inspector Benjamin came in with Bert and we all stood up.

'Thank you. In case you're wondering where Trevor is, I've already spoken to him and he's out covering for a few minutes with Shaun. I didn't want to do this over the radio because, as you all know, some people can monitor our frequencies and I don't want them to know what I'm about to tell you yet. I'll come straight to the point so you first reffers can get out quickly. Maureen Clough has escaped from Crown Court and is at large. You all know her; she's wearing jeans and a blue blouse.'

'How did that drug-addled wreck manage that?!' I exclaimed. I realised that I had spoken out of turn. 'Sorry, boss.'

He didn't seem to mind on this occasion. 'There was a kick-off amongst other prisoners as they were boarding prison transport. It got quite nasty by all accounts, and everyone waded in to sort it out. While everybody was distracted, she somehow slipped away.'

'Blooming heck, heads are going to roll for that one,' Ken said.

'Was it planned, Boss?' Phil asked.

'It seems more opportunistic. Needless to say, a warrant has been issued, not backed for bail.' The Inspector grinned. 'One good thing from our perspective: the prison officers had taken over custody so it's not our mistake. I believe a sacking or two is in the offing, not least because they had unlocked the gate before all the prisoners had been boarded and secured. Anyway, you all know what she looks like. Everyone be aware.'

'Her little boy is in care. Has anyone informed the social services or warned the foster parents, boss?' I asked.

'Good thinking. I'll ask the control room to make a few phone calls to make sure it's done.'

'Do we know where the foster parents live?' Ken asked.

'No. Social services will deal with that though,' the Inspector said.

'Is she handcuffed?' Steve asked. 'She won't get far if she's handcuffed.'

'We assume so because she was troublesome in court and then she was waiting to go onto the prisoner transport. It's unlikely she will have found someone to get them off her,' the boss replied.

That was unusual; females were considered weaker and so weren't normally handcuffed in court. She had to have been really bad if they had decided to use 'cuffs on her.

'Right, that's it for now. First reffers go out now. I'll update you all when I get more.'

I went out and walked slowly to my beat. The Crown Court was a fair distance away so it was unlikely that Maureen would be in our area yet, even if she was heading this way. Even so, I concentrated my patrol nearer to the Ship Streets, just in case I spotted Maureen returning home.

Chapter Twenty-Two

I was just contemplating quickly visiting on my friend Karen Fitzroy, who lived near the dock, to scrounge a cuppa, when Ray transmitted, 'Mike One from control.'

The radio beeped as Mike One answered.

'Please make number 47 Thatcher Road, report of a disturbance.'

The radio beeped, then continued to beep for a couple of minutes.

'Mikes Two and Four also making,' Ray said.

Thatcher Road was on the other side of town, practically in the next division. It was a nice road of semi-detached houses, built about ten years ago. Each road in the area had been named after some profession or craft: cooper, fletcher and so on, but so far the area had not been given a nickname. Disturbances there were unheard of.

I was too far to be of help, so I didn't call up.

Ten minutes later, Ray called up again. 'All patrols stand by for observations.' Ray broadcast. 'Observations please for Maureen Clough.'

I thought the boss had been concerned about the radio hams that monitored our calls. What had caused the change of mind? I got my answer a second later.

'She has abducted her two-year-old son, who is currently in foster care. The child is wearing a green pullover and brown trousers. He has blond hair and grey eyes. Maureen is wearing jeans and a blue blouse. She might still have handcuffs on.

She is in an unstable frame of mind and there are concerns for the child's safety. Any sightings, call in for assistance before approaching her. Control out.'

Thatcher Road must be where Shane's foster parents lived. The question was, how did Maureen know where to go? I wondered where I would go if I were Maureen. Not back home, that was for sure. It would be an obvious starting point for the search, but Maureen might not think of that. Maybe she would try to take him back to her own house. I couldn't help at Thatcher Road but I could look out in my own area. Tea forgotten, I started out towards Clipper Street.

As I passed the dock gates, I saw a woman walking towards Quay Five with a toddler. Quay Five was the deepest and largest dock, intended for the biggest ships. Sometimes, local mothers would take their children to look at the ships that were in. The Port Police didn't like it because it wasn't safe. The worrying thing here was, there were no ships in that particular dock at this time and, from where I was, the woman looked like Maureen. Also, the toddler was wearing brown trousers and a green pullover.

'Maureen!' I called. She didn't stop so I hurried after her. I called into control to ask for back up but I didn't want to let her out of my sight.

She stopped by Quay Five and stood with the child, looking into the water. I was worried about her proximity to the edge. It was low tide, but still deep and if she fell in, it would be hard to climb out up the slimy, sheer sides. At least the nights were lighter although I estimated we only had about an hour of daylight left.

I slowed down and called out again.

'Maureen!'

She turned to me and I saw she still had her handcuffs on.

She awkwardly picked Shane up. 'You! Fuck off!'

I slowly walked towards her. 'You have to let Shane go. He's settled in his foster home and it's cruel to take him away.'

'Still after my baby? You can't have him.'

I did want her baby: I wanted to take that child and put

him back with his foster parents, where he would be safe and properly cared for.

'I just want him to be safe and for you to get help,' I said.

'I lose him either way.' She rested her cheek against Shane's head and held him closely. Shane seemed quite settled and sucked his thumb. In that moment, I believed that in her own inadequate way, Maureen loved Shane but heroin had befuddled her brain, rendering her incapable of thinking much beyond her next fix.

'How did you find him, Maureen?' I asked.

She smirked. 'Her next door tried to visit him. They wouldn't let her in but she saw him leave with the social worker and heard them mention the road. She told me when she visited. I went there and knocked on some doors until I found what house he was in.'

I held out my arms. 'Let me have Shane. Get clean, then you can think about access again.'

I could hear sirens: back up was on the way. Unfortunately, Maureen heard them too. I should have thought to ask for a silent approach.

'If I can't have him, nobody can,' Maureen shouted. She swung around and hurled Shane into the water. The child screamed, as did I, then he disappeared underwater.

Without thinking, I leapt into the water and frantically reached out with every limb to feel for the toddler. Nothing. I came up, took a gulp of air then ducked under again. I opened my eyes but the water was filthy and clouded and I couldn't see an inch ahead of me. I came up for another gulp of air and caught a glimpse of movement a few feet away. I struck out towards it just as it disappeared. I again dived down and my fingertips brushed against something. I grabbed hold and pulled it to the surface with me and I was elated to find it was Shane. He took a huge breath then screamed and clawed his way up my arm to cling around my neck. I manoeuvred him onto my back. It was surprisingly difficult. I had to kick like crazy to keep us above water. I lost a shoe forever.

'Keep a tight hold and we'll have a little swim to the side.' I knew I wouldn't be able to get a grip on the slimy stones but I had to try something. Some of the docks had built-in ladders attached to the side: I would try to find a rung to grab. Even if I couldn't get us out of the water, it would stop us from sinking.

There was no sign of his mother but Phil and Ken appeared at the side, along with some Ports Police officers.

'Hold on, Sam,' Phil called.

'There's no life belt!' Ken shouted. 'Some little scrote must have cut it off.'

Didn't they realise that there were lifebelts around the docks for good reasons? Shane's and my imminent drownings being one of them.

I was getting very tired and cold, Shane was worryingly quiet, but still had hold of me. An ambulance arrived and the crew also peered down at us. A Ports Police officer arrived with a lifebelt, undoubtedly filched from another dock. They really needed to keep on top of the lifebelt situation.

Keeping hold of the rope, he threw the ring into the water and I gratefully took hold. My arms shook with a mixture of cold and exertion.

'Come on Shane, let's have a sing-song,' I panted. 'The wheels on the bus go round and round…'

Shane wasn't joining in. I was getting very worried about him.

The Ports Police officer, Phil and Ken hauled us to the side then tried to reach down to us, to no avail.

'You couldn't have done this at high tide?' Phil quipped.

'I know you like a challenge,' I responded. I inhaled filthy water and went into a coughing fit, which made me swallow more water.

There were big chains hanging down the side of the dock wall that disappeared into the water. I had an idea.

'If you get me to those chains, I'll try to pull up then you can grab the baby. Then we can think about getting me out.'

They pulled us to the side then. Ken lay down and started to wriggle, headfirst down the chain as Phil held his feet. I pulled myself up as hard as I could. It was so difficult, but I knew I would only have one or two chances. I was so cold my hands were starting to seize up.

Ken grabbed at Shane and just managed to grip on to his clothing. He hauled him up and a ports policeman grabbed him and almost threw him at the ambulance crew.

'Is he okay?' I shouted.

'He's breathing, so that's good,' they shouted back. They whisked him away.

My turn, but I couldn't pull myself up again. I tried but I was too weak. I lost my grip and slipped back into the water. It wouldn't be long now before I slid underwater and that would be that.

'Get into the ring, Sam, We'll haul you up,' Phil called.

I saw one of the Ports Policemen taking off his helmet and jacket. Evidently preparing to jump in to rescue me. I hoped he wouldn't because then there would be two of us to fish out of the murky dock.

I could have ducked under the ring but I worried about ever resurfacing. Instead I laboriously pulled it over my head and draped my arms over the sides, then I hung like a drowned rat as Phil, Ken and a couple of Ports Police heaved me slowly out of the water. While I was grateful for the rescue, I wondered if they really needed that many. It wasn't good for my ego.

As I got closer to the top, many hands grabbed my clothing and then I felt hard ground beneath me. I slithered out of the ring, got onto my hands and knees and vomited.

'There's all sorts of shit in that water,' said a ports policeman. 'And I do mean that literally. Even fish refuse to swim in there.'

Another ambulance arrived.

'Where's Shane's mother?' I asked.

'Dunno,' Phil said.

'She was right at the side of the dock; you must have seen

her as she made off,' I insisted. 'She's still got the handcuffs on.'

Everyone looked at everyone else.

'I expect we'll pick her up later,' the Ports Policeman said.

I felt like I was missing something, but another wave of nausea distracted me.

The ambos loaded me into the ambulance.

'I don't need to go to hospital, I just need to warm up and get some dry clothes on,' I complained.

The ambulance driver laughed. 'You have just been in some of the dirtiest water on the planet. It's full of oil, bilge, dead animals. As a minimum you need antibiotics.'

I thought about the water I had swallowed and nausea hit again. Luckily, the ambo had anticipated this and held a large bowl in front of me. I wrapped myself around it and spent the journey to the general hospital to hospital emptying my stomach into it.

*

At the hospital, I took the opportunity between bouts of nausea to change out of my soaking, stinking uniform and into a dry hospital gown. Doctors stuck many needles into me. I hoped that at least one of the cocktail of chemicals they were giving me contained something to stop me throwing up. I had to be empty by now, but still I was heaving.

'I think we'll admit you,' the doctor said.

'I want to go home,' I argued.

'And I want to make sure you don't develop typhoid or something equally nasty.' He watched me for a minute. 'Tell you what, if you can stop being sick for twelve hours, I'll let you go as long as you come back if you start to show any symptoms out of the ordinary.'

'That's still tomorrow,' I complained.

'Take it or leave it.'

I took it. I had little choice.

Phil came in to see me. He sat as far away as possible while I heaved into a metal bowl. When I finished, he took it from me and pushed it out of sight while I pulled myself together.

'Have you found Maureen?' I asked when I was able to talk again.

'Yes, she was in the dock with you. She didn't survive,' he replied.

I frowned. 'I didn't see her.'

'You were concentrating on the kiddie. We could see her just below the surface in the far corner. Ports Police were trying to fish her out but it was plain she was already dead. When the Ports Police got her out, they found she'd put a couple of lumps of metal in her pocket, probably off the links from one of those huge chains that they have lying around. Not enough to take her to the bottom, but enough to exhaust her very quickly. She wasn't able to swim because of the handcuffs.'

'Blooming heck. So what about Shane?' I asked.

'He's going back to his foster parents, once everyone is sure he's recovered.'

I smiled despite the growing nausea. Maureen didn't know who Shane's father was, so nobody needed to worry about him suddenly swooping in to take the child. Maureen might have been struggling with addiction, she might have loved Shane, but frankly, he deserved better, and with her out of the way, he would get it. Shane could be adopted and look forward to a better life.

I gestured frantically for the bowl and snatched it from Phil's hands. Just in time. I almost turned myself inside out retching into the bowl.

'There can't be much left in there,' Phil said.

I flopped back onto my pillows, worn out. My stomach hurt, my sides hurt, everything hurt.

Inspector Benjamin put his head around the curtain. 'Is this a bad time?'

I gurgled something incomprehensible at him. Phil stood up and offered him the chair. The boss shook his head.

'I just wanted to let you know that Shane is doing well at the children's hospital. He's got an upset stomach so they're keeping him in for a couple of days, but you did a good job keeping him out of the water.'

A nurse came in and the boss stopped speaking.

'You gentlemen will have to leave now. We're moving the patient to the observation ward.'

The boss and Phil left, and I was put into a wheelchair and pushed through to the observation ward off the casualty unit, where I remained in misery for the next twelve hours.

About an hour into my stay at hospital, Mum arrived. She was not happy.

'I can't believe I had to hear that you were in hospital from Steve's mother,' Mum complained. 'Why wasn't I contacted?'

'Because I'm an adult. I'm not seriously ill,' I replied. 'How did Mrs Patton know I was here?'

'Steve told her, of course. He still speaks to his mother.'

'Stop being so dramatic,' I said.

'She rang to ask about you. Were you just going to go back to the flat alone?' Mum demanded.

'Yes.'

'You're coming back with me,' Mum stated.

'I can hug a toilet just as well at home as I can at your house.' It suddenly struck me that this was the first time I had not referred to my parents' house as "home". I think Mum felt it too. She watched me for a minute before speaking.

'You should have gone to Hong Kong with Gary.'

'Mum, this was a rescue. It's not like the other times,' I said.

'The outcome was the same. You're in hospital. I hate this place. I wish you'd gone into something safer, like bomb disposal.'

I laughed aloud. Mum had finally found her sense of humour. I hadn't seen it for so long, it was nice to be able to laugh with her again.

After a moment, Mum laughed too, then said. 'Come to ours. Just for a couple of days while you recover.'

I nodded. 'Okay, just for a couple of days.'

*

At my parents' house, Mum shepherded me through the front door. Dad came in from the kitchen and hugged me.

'I've put on a nice, rich lamb stew for tea. You need some colour in those cheeks.'

I felt my stomach flip at the mention of food, but I smiled my thanks. Normally I loved Dad's lamb stew.

'You see, Jim, this is why I can't go to Aberdeen,' Mum declared. 'Sam still needs me.'

'What? Hang on, I thought it was pretty well a done deal?' I said.

Dad leant on the door frame. 'Mum's been having cold feet. She worries.'

'If you're having second thoughts, Mum, don't put it on me,' I said.

'I'm not,' Mum said. 'But you do need me.'

I hugged her. 'Mum, I will always need you and Dad, but you cannot live your life around me. I don't see why you should not go if you want to go.'

'Who would take care of you if we went to Scotland? Gary is thousands of miles away,' Mum argued.

'I would take care of me, like a normal adult.'

'I think we need to talk some more, Liz,' Dad said.

'Yeah,' Mum agreed. She seemed flattened. She went into the kitchen and flicked on the kettle.

Dad and I just looked at each other. I noticed for the first time the bags under his eyes and how deep the wrinkles in his forehead had become. He was only just fifty. I could put it down to the harsh life on the rig, but I knew that he worried about me as much as Mum did; however, he was more willing to loosen the leash. I liked being looked after but it caused Mum and Dad unnecessary worry.

Mum and Dad had had a long distance marriage for so long, I hadn't even noticed the toll it must be taking on Dad. I felt slightly ashamed that it had taken me until now to see it. Dad liked his job and the money was good. Moving to Aberdeen was important to him, so I had to encourage Mum to go with him. I realised that this was all part of what Steve had been saying. I had to start being more self-sufficient.

Chapter Twenty-Three

I returned to the flat the following day and went back to work the day after. I must have lost a stone in weight. My waistband was definitely looser, but I wouldn't recommend the bilge water diet to anyone.

At the station, I had to put up with people crossing their fingers at me and shouting 'Unclean, unclean.'

I responded by putting up two fingers to them.

*

Bert gave me the town centre again. I walked towards the shops, passing Chiu's chippy on the way. Someone had added a *"Sale Agreed"* banner to the *"For Sale"* sign. The little hand-written note was now gone from the door. I saw someone in the back. They weren't trying to hide themselves so I wondered if it was the new owners getting ready. Now was as good a time as any to introduce myself. I went around the corner, where a transit van filled the end of the entry that ran behind the shop. I nipped up the entry and peered through the open gate into the yard. Several boxes had been moved out there.

Eric came out of the shop carrying another box. He saw me and put it down with the others.

'Hello.' Eric seemed more like his usual self than I'd seen for a long time.

'Hello, Eric,' I replied. 'I wasn't expecting to see you, I saw movement and thought it might be the new owners.'

'I am moving out some personal items and cleaning ready for the new people to take over.'

Normally, I became wary when I heard of people who have been through something bad, cleaning and organising things, especially since events in Kensington Road a few months back. It can sometimes be a warning of tragedy to come. However, it was reasonable for Eric to be clearing a recently sold property so I tried to relax.

'Have you come to remind me about my appointment?' he asked.

'What appointment?'

'I have to come in to speak to Mr Webb later on. Didn't you know?' Eric asked.

'No. I'm not CID.' Which reminded me, I should get my application for my aide's course in. I'd probably already missed this year's deadline.

'I think they want to talk about Cathy and my mother again.'

'I'm so sorry about what happened,' I said.

'Sometimes fate brings bad things.' Eric looked me squarely in the eyes. 'Do you believe in fate, Constable Barrie?'

That threw me a bit. My religious status was best described as agnostic.

'I'm not sure.'

'Many people are unsure. That's okay. I believe that we reap what we sow. If we do something bad, something bad will happen to us in return.'

'If you do something good, then fate will bring good fortune?' I asked.

Eric nodded. 'Cathy has done nothing wrong, but she is suffering. I believe that good things will come to her in the future.'

I wished I shared his conviction. Life so far had taught me that terrible things happened to good people for no reason and often there was no reward at the end of it. That was why the idea of an idyllic afterlife was so appealing to some.

'My grandmother did something bad and she suffered fate's revenge. My mother did something bad and now she is dead. One day, I will reap what I have sown.'

I felt a tingle at the back of my neck. Was he trying to tell me something?

'Have you done something bad, Eric?' I held my breath waiting for his answer.

A phone rang inside the building. Eric jumped. I lost the moment.

'I need to answer that. It will be the new people asking if I have finished. Perhaps I'll see you later at the police station.' He hurried inside, leaving me frustrated in the yard. I couldn't leave it like this. I followed him into the shop.

Eric had packed everything neatly away. The surfaces gleamed and the shop looked bigger for it.

Eric finished his call and turned to face me.

'We need to talk, Eric,' I said.

Eric remained silent. I had learnt to use silence. I waited and waited. Continents collided. New mountain ranges rose and fell. Eventually he looked at me and said, 'Not doing something can be as bad as doing something.'

'Yes,' I said. 'Eric, what are you trying to tell me?' No more shilly-shallying, we needed to thrash this out.

Eric moved to the preparation area. I remembered that this was where Cathy had got the cleaver so, although there was nothing alarming in sight, I kept my distance. I pressed my transmitter once, just to reassure myself that I could shout for help if necessary.

'My mother and I argued.' Eric stared at the floor.

'Cathy told me, she overheard you,' I told him.

Eric's head jerked up. 'Cathy heard?'

'That's why she ran away,' I said. 'You were angry and she was frightened.'

Eric began babbling in his own language and paced the small area.

239

'Eric, I can't understand you. What are you saying?' I cried.

He stopped pacing and stood stock still. 'I killed my mother.'

I wasn't sure if he was talking literally or figuratively. 'Eric?!'

'She went on and on about sending Rose away. She said she was useless. When Cathy became ill, my mother said I should leave her and go back to Hong Kong.'

I needed to caution him before he told me anything more. I needed to arrest him. To hell with self-sufficiency, I needed someone with me.

'Eric before you say anything else, I need to tell you that I am arresting you on suspicion of the murder of Yang Hui Ping.' Even though I heard him confess, I still had a lot of bureaucracy to wade through, although I had no doubt that CID would take this from my hands. It occurred to me that his mind had also been pushed to the limit and might have tipped over the edge. I had heard false confessions before, usually made by attention seekers or people who truly feel guilty over something but were not responsible for the crime.

Eric stared at me as I recited the caution. I kept an eye on him in case he suddenly acquired a cleaver or a knife, but he didn't move.

'Don't look so upset. I know what my fate is. You must do your duty,' Eric said.

He was comforting me!

'I need to call for a car to collect us,' I told him. He stood quietly as I radioed in and asked Ray for transport, and for him to inform supervision and the CID.

'Tell me about it,' I said when I had my arrangements in place.

The dam wall had broken and Eric was almost eager to talk.

'My mother and I were arguing again about leaving Cathy and moving away. My mother told me her story, the full story she had never told me before. She left my father in Peking during a very troubled time in Chinese history, because he ordered her to hand over her new-born daughter—my sister—to his mother, who killed her.'

'Like you said, it was a difficult time. People had to make challenging decisions to survive. Given the culture in China at that time, I'm not sure Mrs Yang would have had any choice but to obey her husband and mother-in-law,' I said.

Eric continued his story. 'My mother fled with me and told me my father was dead. I was a small child and I don't remember him at all. On the day I... the day she died, she told me that she killed her mother-in-law because of what she did to my sister and that is why she had to escape. I was... shocked.'

I said, 'Also she might have been suffering post-natal depression. We call it the "baby blues" here. It sounds minor but it can be really serious. That is what Cathy had, and Rose's death made it worse.'

'If I had had time to think about it, I might have been able to forgive my mother for what she did all those years ago, but not for what happened to Rose.' He looked around the shop. 'We had so many dreams, such ambition. This was going to be the first of an empire... I told my mother that when Cathy was better, we would start again. My mother told me that my life would be easier without Rose. I was very angry; as I shouted, my mother tried to talk to me. Eventually, I stopped shouting and listened to her.' Eric took a huge breath that came out like a sob. 'She admitted to me that when she checked Rose, she saw that she had stopped breathing. Instead of calling for us or trying to help Rose, she sat down again and left her. We might have been able to save her!'

I couldn't believe what I had heard. Mrs Yang was not so innocent after all.

'We loved Rose so much but my mother said that she took the chance to help me and that it was for the best. That is when I realised that Cathy's suspicion had been right all along. My mother might not have murdered Rose, but not doing something to help is just as bad. I should have listened to Cathy!'

I didn't know what to say, so I allowed Eric to continue.

'I completely lost my temper. I don't remember what I did, but when I became aware again, my mother was dead on the floor with a cushion over her face. I was distraught. Despite everything, I loved her. She had been a good mother to me. I carried her up to her bed and laid her on it. I washed her face and then called for an ambulance.' Eric sank to the floor and wept loudly. 'Our family is cursed.'

For want of something to say, I sat beside him and patted his shoulder. I wasn't condoning what he had done, but somehow, I understood him. Everything he had believed and valued had crashed down around him and the red mist had descended.

I heard footsteps in the yard behind the shop. 'In here,' I shouted.

Inspector Benjamin and Shaun came in, followed by Mike Finlay and Eamon. They took in the scene and once satisfied there was no immediate danger, they relaxed a little.

'Eric has confessed to me that he killed Yang Hui Ping. It was in the heat of the moment when she revealed something distressing to him.' I spotted Mike winding up to arrest him but, sorry, this was my arrest. I had always had to pass on anything serious, but I wanted my name on this. 'I've already cautioned and arrested him. He is fully co-operative.' I knew that that this arrest would still be passed over to CID, but my name would be on it.

The boss gave a small smile. 'Very well. Shaun, you can drive Sam and her prisoner back to the bridewell. Mike, I'll see you and Eamon back at the station.'

I helped Eric to stand up.

'I need to lock up and drop the keys at the estate agent,' Eric said.

'The boss can do that for you,' Mike said.

Mike was getting a little revenge for Benno not handing my prisoner over to him.

Inspector Benjamin smiled, 'Of course.' He held out his hand and Eric gave him the key. 'Which estate agent is it?'

'Harlow's,' Eric said. He then turned to me, almost keen to be off.

We walked through the yard and, without saying anything, the men took up positions to the front, rear and sides of Eric in case he did bolt for it. We got to the car without incident and Shaun drove us back to Wyre Hall.

I booked Eric in and was pleased that my name and number appeared on the charge sheet. Now I would get credit, even though CID would conduct much of the bureaucracy that came with such arrests. This would look good when I finally got around to putting in my aide's application.

Mike and Eamon did the interview. It was a mere formality; Eric confirmed everything he told me. He seemed almost happy, even a little hyper, which is why the bridewell sergeant suggested ringing the police surgeon.

'I'm not saying he's a suicide risk,' he said, 'but the way he is, it's not normal.'

I agreed and phoned to arrange a visit.

Mike and Eamon came out of the interview room. The bridewell officer went in and brought Eric out. He saw me and smiled sadly.

'Harvest time.'

The bridewell officer opened the gate to the male cells and Eric disappeared inside.

'I've arranged for the police surgeon to visit Eric; he seems over-happy, if that makes sense. The sergeant thinks so too. He's put him on half hourly obs.'

'I go along with that; we'd be criticised if he did try to harm himself,' Eamon said. 'Poor Eric, he won't be free anytime soon. He's lost everything. His child, his wife, his mother, his business, his liberty. Everything. Even his memories will be tainted now. He might end up in hospital just as Cathy gets out.'

Mike said, 'Not that Cathy will be getting out of hospital anytime soon. She's terribly ill but at least she won't be facing murder charges when she recovers. I think Eric will have a good chance of playing the mental health card.'

'I don't think I've ever felt sorry for a murderer before,' I said.

Mike sighed. 'Being able to see the person behind the crimes, be it good or bad, makes for a better cop.' He got a mischievous gleam in his eye. 'Anyway, as the arresting officer, you can complete the file. We'll sort the paperwork for the interview, and the pathologist report for Mrs Yang's PM, but you can do the rest. Let us have it ASAP.'

It would take forever! My statement alone would be pages long. I didn't want Mike to see how daunted I felt. I smiled. I had done hundreds of files; this was just a little knottier. I would manage. I should think of it as an opportunity to prove that I would cope in CID.

'Of course. Thanks.' I smiled my fake gratitude for them allowing me to do the file.

Chapter Twenty-Four

Beverley's mental health was suffering as she waited to hear the outcome of the investigation. I had never seen her so low. I didn't think Beverley was a danger to herself, but it was worrying that the accusation was still hanging over her. I couldn't understand how it was taking so long. Anyone could see that Bev was innocent, thanks to that tape.

I called to visit her to try to keep her spirits up. Unusually, there was no dog dirt on the step. It seemed that every time I had been there since this whole mess started, I had had to dodge a pile of poo. As fast as Bev cleared it, more appeared and we had never been able to see who was doing it. Bev still refused to report it to High Lake, convinced they would not care. From my experience, she was probably right.

We sat at the breakfast bar and drinking tea and generally putting the world to rights.

'Mum and Dad have finally decided they are going to Aberdeen,' I told her.

'I'm pleased for them, but I will miss Uncle Jim and Auntie Liz,' Bev said.

'I know, but we can go to visit,' I said. 'Christopher and Carly will love holidays in Scotland.'

'I'm surprised your nan is considering going with them,' Bev commented.

Bev was related to me on my father's side. She didn't have a drop of Welsh in her.

I laughed. 'She was always a feisty old bird. She'll be company for Mum while she settles in and makes new friends. Mum is pleased because she can still keep an eye on her. They're looking at houses handy for amenities, so Nan won't have to worry about getting to the shops or a doctor or the hospital.'

'I hope she never has to go there,' Bev said.

'She's getting older. Statistically, she'll need to visit a hospital more as she ages.'

'So is the house on the market?' Bev asked.

I nodded. 'And Nan's house. They're asking ten thousand for Nan's house and twelve thousand for their house. They'll put the money together and buy a nice place in Aberdeen.'

Bev's eyes grew round. 'Wow! Just think what they can buy with twenty-two thousand pounds.'

'Well, don't forget, Mum's brother in Canada. Nan wants half the money to go to him when her house is sold. That way, when she pops off, Mum and Dad won't have to worry about finding the money to send to him his share of the inheritance. The house will be in Mum and Dad's names so they won't lose anything. It'll all be done properly with solicitors.'

'Still, that's...' Bev quickly did the sum in her head. 'Seventeen thousand. I heard the big, four-bedroomed, detached houses on that new estate near your station are going for fourteen thousand. Property is cheaper in Scotland, isn't it?'

'I think it depends on the area, like here,' I replied. 'Anyway, there will be plenty of room for visitors.'

'There certainly will,' Bev agreed.

'Changing the subject, I finally got around to enrolling in the OU,' I said.

'What are you studying?' Bev asked.

'Basic sociology-type thing as the foundation course. I'm not sure yet what path I'll take, so I thought that was a good base,' I said.

'Criminology would be good for you,' Bev said.

'Or Humanities, or pretty well anything. Someone at work said that any degree opens the door to promotion.'

'So you are planning on making a career in the police?' Bev asked.

Before I could answer, the phone rang. Bev answered it and put the receiver back with a shaking hand.

'That was the CID. They're coming around to speak to me. Now.'

I stood up but Bev grabbed my arm.

'No! don't go. I need someone with me. What if it's bad news?' She paced back and forth wrapping her arms around herself.

'It won't be. They're sure to tell you you're off the hook.' Nobody could argue against that tape. 'You should tell Terry.' God, how I wanted to tell her it would be okay.

'Afterwards. When we know whether I'm going to prison or not.'

'It'll be okay,' I said.

She watched me for a moment. 'You know something. What is it? Am I in the clear? Please, tell me.'

My cheeks grew hot. Oh well, it'll all be in the open shortly. 'I've heard a whisper, but don't count your chickens…'

'Why didn't you tell me?!' Bev cried.

'I can't tell you. Just wait to hear what they have to say,' I replied.

I set out mugs and teabags and boiled the kettle ready to make drinks when the CID arrived. Then we sat chatting for a short while. Bev urged me to confirm what I'd heard, but I couldn't. I'd seen too many things go wrong to tell her for sure. Eventually, our talk petered out and we sat in silence until the doorbell rang.

The colour drained from Bev's face. 'I'd better answer it.'

She showed two people into the living room. A smiling woman and a po-faced man who looked like he'd rather be on the moon than in this house.

'Sam, would you join us?' she called.

I flicked on the kettle went into the living room and saw them perched on the sofa.

'This is my cousin, Sam. I would like her with me,' Bev said to them.

'That's fine. We just want to clarify a few things with you,' the woman said.

'Tea?' I asked.

'Don't bother on our account,' the woman said. 'I'm DS Margaret Tilley, or just Margie if you prefer. This is DC Ellery.'

He grunted a greeting. He offered no first name. Definitely here under protest.

'I'm here to talk about a tape we received of a conversation between you and Tracey Quinn,' Margie said. 'We've all had a listen and it appears pretty conclusive that Jonathan had an accident at his aunt's house on the day he died.'

Bev caught my eye and I gave her my biggest, cheesiest grin.

Margie continued. 'However...'

However?! I hated that word. However what? How could there be any doubt?

'...it was suggested that perhaps Jonathan had a previous accident whilst in your care and we have had to investigate that.'

DC Ellery nodded. I bet he was the snotty git I spoke to when I rang High Lake.

Bev's smile fell. 'He didn't...' Bev buried her face in her hands. 'How can I prove this didn't happen?'

'Who said that? Was it Tracey Quinn?' I demanded.

'She's been harassing my cousin,' Bev said. 'She keyed her car.'

'I am aware of tensions,' Margie said. 'We spoke to Jonathan's mother, Judith Cox. She is understandably distraught, but she confirmed that Jonathan had not been injured in the weeks leading up to his death.'

Bev gave a loud sob. Margie gave a sympathetic smile. 'We know from the post-mortem that Jonathan was a well cared-for child. He had no old injuries and hadn't seen the doctor for weeks before he died. He had a blow to the head that caused a slow bleed, and that bleed killed him. The effects would not have been evident at first, which is possibly why Tracey felt able to drop him off that morning.'

'He'd have lost consciousness surely,' I said.

Margie shrugged. 'I don't know; I'm not a doctor so can only go by the pathologist's report.'

'So…?' Bev couldn't bring herself to ask the question.

'So, I'm pleased to tell you that as far as you're concerned, there will be no further action.'

Bev screamed and leapt to her feet. I stood up and wrapped my arms around her and let her cry out all her fear and frustration of the past weeks.

Margie nudged Ellery. 'Make some tea.'

'Kettle's boiled,' I said over Bev's shoulder.

He stood up without argument and went into the kitchen.

It took a few minutes for Beverley to calm down, but eventually, she wiped her eyes and sank onto the armchair. Ellery, who didn't look so po-faced anymore, put drinks on the coffee table.

'What happens now?' Bev asked.

Margie said, 'Like I said. You're clear and free.'

'Tracey? Her actions afterwards indicate that she knew she'd messed up and she was trying to deflect blame,' Beverley said.

'I agree,' Margie said. 'And I promise you that we are looking at that, but you don't need to worry yourself any further.' Margie said. 'It's up to you whether you decide to seek restitution via civil court.'

'I just want this to go away,' Bev said. She paused. 'What about that awful reporter, Anne Leigh? She made a false allegation about my cousin and put it in the paper and Tracey lied about witnessing it. That's libel or defamation or something.'

'Civil law,' I said. 'I'll speak to my boss about it. Nothing for you to worry about.'

'Unfortunately, we can't stop a free press from mooching around. She'll lose interest in you, now you're no longer a suspect,' Margie said. 'We need to think about heading off any defence Tracey might put up should we decide to charge her. Do you have any proof of when you got the answering machine, Mrs Thompson?'

'I might be able to find a receipt,' Bev replied and went to the drawer where she kept all her papers. After a couple of minutes, she held up a sheet of paper. 'I haven't come across the receipt yet, but I do have a bank statement showing the cheque Terry wrote out. She passed it to Margie who perused the statement. Bev pulled a chequebook from the drawer. 'What's the cheque number?'

Margie recited it and Bev flicked through the cheques. 'Here! The cheque was made out to Tandy.'

Margie sucked her teeth. 'This is okay, but it's challengeable. It's a handwritten stub and there's only a note of the cheque number on the statement. We would have to ask the bank to confirm the payee then we'd have to get Tandy to confirm what was bought. That will take time' She turned to Ellery. 'Get cracking on that tomorrow.'

'Yes, Sarge,' he replied. I guessed at that point that he was an aide.

Bev resumed her rummage in the drawer. 'It's not here! I can't understand why I'd throw it out. We're careful to keep receipts in case there's problems and we have to take things back.'

'Don't worry. If you can't find it, we will just have to contact the bank and the shop,' Margie said.

'Bev, you said Terry wrote the cheque. What would he do with the receipt until he could put it with the other paperwork?' I asked.

'He'd put it in his wallet...' Bev snatched up the phone and dialled a number. 'Hi Ma, it's Beverley. Is Terry there please?' She crossed her fingers towards me and I did the same. 'Terry? Yes, I'm fine, don't worry. It's over Terry, it's all over at last.'

I heard Terry shouting his relief on the phone.

Bev said, 'A strange request, but do you have the receipt from when you bought the answering machine? It's not in the drawer so it might be in your wallet.'

'He's just checking,' Bev whispered to us. I held my breath for the minute it took Terry to come back to the phone.

'Hello? That's wonderful. That paper is gold. Don't lose it, the police want it.' Bev put her thumb up to us.

'I'll go and get it,' I mouthed to her.

'Sam will come and get it now,' she relayed. She paused as Terry spoke. 'He says no, he'll bring it straight over.'

'That's great,' Margie said.

*

Terry came in and looked around us laughing together; even Ellery was smiling.

'Well, I didn't expect to find a party.' He held out a package wrapped in newspaper. 'Someone put another turd on the doorstep. I'll just go and flush it then put the paper in the bin.'

'That wasn't there when we arrived. Is this a regular occurrence?' Margie asked.

Bev nodded. 'Every day. I've never been able to catch them. At least they haven't posted it this time.'

'Why is there no record of this?' Margie asked.

'I don't report it. What's the point? Everyone thought I was guilty so I didn't think police would be interested.' Bev sighed.

'Of course we'd be interested,' Margie declared.

That prat I had got on the phone would not have been in the slightest bit interested. I saw no benefit of bringing that up so I said nothing.

'Oh well, it's all over now. I just hope that the newspaper will say something about it,' Bev said.

'I wouldn't count on it,' I said. I was getting cynical.

'Do you have that receipt?' Bev asked Terry when he came back into the room.

He held it out and Margie took it. 'This is good.'

'Why is it so important?' Terry nodded when Bev mimed tea

drinking to him on her way out to the kitchen.

'This receipt proves that you didn't have the machine until shortly before Jonathan died,' Margie said. 'It means that Tracey can't say the tapes are from another incident.'

Terry's face lit up. 'So those calls prove that Bev tried her best for that little lad and his aunt was negligent? Have you charged her with anything?'

'Whoa,' Margie cautioned. 'It proves that Beverley tried to get help for Jonathan and would have taken him to the hospital sooner had she been aware of the full facts.'

'That little boy died because Tracey kept those facts from Bev then didn't come back when Bev contacted her!' Terry's voice rose has he spoke.

'Calm down, Terry, she's on our side,' I said.

'It also proves that Tracey told Beverley that Jonathan had an accident at her house before he was dropped off here,' Margie said, showing no sign that she had taken any offence.

Terry took a deep breath. 'Sorry, but it's been hard. The kids and me with my mother, and Bev coping with all this alone.'

'I wasn't alone,' Bev said as she brought a tea tray in. 'Sam and Auntie Liz have been great, and I saw you and the kids every day. Ma always made me welcome when I arrived.' She put the tea down. 'Did you tell your work everything's okay now?'

'Not yet. I'll give them a ring and let them know everything is sorted,' Terry said.

Bev put her hand on her hip. 'I'll bet you'll still be the first out if there are ever redundancies.' She turned to Margie. 'Terry's work sent him home, "on leave".' She waggled her fingers to show the quotation marks. 'It's not fair. My whole family have suffered because of this. If Tracey had come clean at the start, none of this would have happened. I bet she wouldn't even have been charged with anything because accidents happen.'

'Perhaps so,' Margie agreed.

'Maybe now the neighbours will stop putting turds on the doorstep,' Terry said.

'It doesn't matter. We're moving,' Bev stated.

'Are we?' Terry asked.

'Yes, I'm not staying here. Mud sticks and so does dog dirt. I couldn't trust any of the neighbours again. We're going to see an estate agent tomorrow.'

Margie stood up. 'I'd better get this receipt back to the station. We don't want anyone to know we have this evidence yet, so keep it quiet.'

Terry saw Margie and Ellery out.

'You can childmind again,' I said. 'You need to let social services know.'

'You are kidding?' Bev retorted.

'I thought you liked your job?' I replied.

'I did enjoy minding, but I would constantly worry about something like this happening again. Even if Alma contacts me, I'm not doing it. I'll find a part time job to fit around school hours.'

Terry came back in.

'Terry, I don't think we can let the kids come back yet. The neighbours don't know I'm in the clear and there might be more trouble,' Bev said.

'That's a thought,' he agreed. 'You don't have to worry about bail conditions now though, do you?'

'I suppose not,' Bev replied.

Terry rubbed his hands together. 'All back to Ma's then, and tonight you can stay over.'

Bev smiled. 'As long as she doesn't mind.'

'You know she loves you to bits,' Terry hugged Bev.

'I'll get off. Give Christopher and Carly a big hug for me.' I left Bev and Terry to discuss their future arrangements.

Chapter Twenty-Five

At our next parade, Bert chucked over a large envelope left for me by Irene. Attached was a note. *'I think this will interest you.'*

I didn't open it straight away, I waited until parade was over then I went into the report writing room and opened it before going out. It was a transcribed interview.

The first part consisted of mundane introductions and instructions. Present had been, Tracey Quinn, Laurence Baker—Tracey Quinn's legal representative—DS Margaret Tilley and DI Jerome Rigby. I smiled when I read his name. Jerry had not been happy when Webby had phoned him about the tape. It was also interesting that Tracey had felt the need to bring legal representation.

Next came the nitty gritty of the interview.

JR: Thank you for coming today, Mrs Quinn. We offer our sincerest condolences on the loss of your nephew, but we have some questions that we need to ask to clarify the circumstances around his death.

TQ: What is there to clarify? Jonathan died because that woman didn't take proper care of him. Ask my sister, Judith Cox.

MT: We have already spoken to Mrs Cox. I'm surprised she didn't tell you that. When did you last speak to your sister?

TQ: I rang her yesterday.

MT: Didn't she put the phone down when she realised it was you?

TQ makes no response.

JR: Tracey Quinn, you are not obliged to say anything unless you wish to do so, but anything you do say may be taken down in writing and given in evidence.

LB: You have just cautioned my client.

JR: Standard procedure in cases like this. You know that, Mr Baker. We have to consider whether bringing charges is appropriate.

TQ: You need to charge that woman. Jonathan died because of her neglect. Maybe it was even deliberate. Beverley Thompson has a temper.

JR: Mrs Quinn, our evidence does not support that Mrs Thompson deliberately hurt Jonathan. You must stop throwing out accusations without basis. You said at the hospital that Jonathan hadn't been hurt at your home.

LB: My client has already explained to various police officers that her nephew had been with the childminder all day, so his injury must have happened there, either accidentally or deliberately.

JR: Thank you, Mr Baker but we are satisfied that Mrs Thompson did not deliberately inflict an injury on Jonathan. Mrs Quinn, what would you say if I told you that we had evidence that the injury did not happen at the childminder's home?

LB: I'd say that the evidence you have is flawed. The child never returned to his home.

TQ became distressed and the interview paused.

That phrase got to me too. Little Jonathan went to stay with his aunt overnight and never went home again. I gulped and continued reading.

Interview resumed.

JR: Mrs Quinn, we have a tape of phone calls that you made to Beverley Thompson when she was trying to get you to collect

Jonathan because she was concerned about his deteriorating condition.

LB: (to TQ) No comment.

TQ: (to LB) She doesn't have an answering machine so they must be lying. Police do lie to get you to confess.

JR: In fact, Mrs Thompson does have an answering machine. Also I am not lying to you.

TQ: Isn't she breaking some law by secretly recording phone calls?

JR: Mrs Thompson has not broken any laws. In fact, by letting us listen to the tape, she has given us a much clearer picture of events.

LB: May my client and I hear those calls?

The log showed a break when Tracey and her legal representative listened to the tape.

Interview resumes.

JR: Do you have anything to say about what you heard on the tapes?'

TQ: Actually, I do remember making those calls. It was ages ago. I did collect Jonathan and he was okay.

JR: Can you give us some idea how long ago that was?

TQ: Oh, about three months ago.

JR: So early February?

TQ: About then.

JR: Before Valentine's Day?

TQ: Yes.

MT: Mrs Thompson has provided proof that they did not buy the answer machine until Saturday the 11th of March. I remind you that you are under caution.

LB: I'd like to confer with my client.

TQ: No need. I'd say that I must have mixed up my dates.

MT: But you were sure the tape was from before Valentine's Day. The fourteenth of February.

TQ: I must be wrong. It must have been in March, after they bought the machine.

MT: So Jonathan was injured twice?

TQ: Yes. It just goes to show how neglectful Beverley Thompson is.

MT: Twice in a few days?

TQ: Yes. No.

MT: Yes or no?

TQ: No.

MT: No, he wasn't injured twice?

JR: Remember, we have proof that Mrs Thompson got that machine just days before Jonathan died.

TQ: Yes, he was injured but it was longer than a few days between accidents.

MT: Then the first accident could not have been recorded at all because Mrs Thompson didn't have the answering machine then. You seem to be a bit unsure about dates.

LB: No comment.

MT: On the first occasion that you say was the one recorded, why would Mrs Thompson ring you instead of his mother?

TQ: I don't know.

MT: She rang you on the second occasion as well?

TQ: Yes.

MT: How come the second occasion wasn't recorded?

TQ: I don't know. Maybe the machine was switched off.

JR: Why did you refer to the second occasion, when Jonathan received the fractured skull, as an accident when you have insisted that Mrs Thompson harmed him?'

LB: No comment.

TQ: Beverley told me what happened when I arrived at the hospital.

JR: Told you that Jonathan had fallen down the stairs by accident?

TQ: Yes. The other children distracted her. It happens a lot. I sent her home.

MT: Why?

TQ: I didn't need her.

MT: Both incidents involved Jonathan falling down the stairs?

TQ: No, yes.

MT: Which?

TQ: You're confusing me. She was negligent. I've read up on it, she is guilty of manslaughter by being reckless. You'd better charge her or I'll make a complaint.

JR: During inspections by the social services, they noted that Mrs Thompson does not allow the children to go upstairs. She keeps a gate on the stairs. How could he have got onto the stairs if there's a gate?

LB: Tracey, you are under caution. Please listen to me and stop answering the questions until we talk.

JR: Mrs Quinn, the tape has clearly recorded you telling Mrs Thompson that Jonathan was fine after he'd fallen down the stairs at your home.

TQ: A little tumble. He couldn't have fractured his skull from that. It had to have happened with Beverley.'

MT: So the answering machine has taped calls from the incident in which Jonathan was fatally injured. That's the second incident. You said it was the first incident on the tape.'

TQ: You're trying to confuse me! Laurence, you said you wouldn't let them bully me. Why aren't you stopping them?'

LB: I have advised you not to answer any further questions but you won't shut up!

JR: Mrs Quinn, Mrs Thompson—far from being negligent or reckless—tried to get you to collect Jonathan for some considerable time. According to the tape, Jonathan had received his injury before you left him with her. The post-mortem report does not mention any recent injuries. The first incident you spoke about could not have happened. You are lying.

TQ: How dare you! It's because she's got a copper in the family, isn't it! You all protect each other. How do I know that tape is genuine? It's something you made to trick me, isn't it! You've fabricated tapes to make me look bad.

LB: Be quiet, Tracey.

TQ (to LB): Don't you dare to speak to me like that! You're fired. I don't want you here anymore.

LB leaves the room.

Interview paused to allow TQ to compose herself.

Interview resumed.

MT: Mrs Quinn, I can assure you the tape is real and it's clear from the tape that Mrs Thompson was worried about Jonathan.

TQ: She didn't say it was so serious. I'd have come at once if I'd known.

JR: Now that's just not true, is it, Mrs Quinn.

TQ: I didn't hurt him.

JR: And I believe that. Jonathan's death was as a result of an accident at your home. Nobody deliberately injured him; it was a tragic accident.

TQ: He slipped on the bottom couple of stairs but he seemed okay. I wouldn't have taken him to the childminder if I'd thought it was bad. I'd have phoned Judith. Oh, Judith, she'll be furious.

JR: She is devastated. Not only has she lost her little boy, but her own sister has lied to her about it. Her husband is considering their position and might seek legal advice. As might Mrs Thompson. I'm sure you wouldn't have deliberately hurt Jonathan, Mrs Quinn. Accidents happen, but your constant, malicious lies to attempt to deflect any blame from yourself have caused distress to many people.

MT: Had you told Mrs Thompson about the accident, she would not have waited before ringing the ambulance when Jonathan's condition deteriorated. You lied and lied. Even today, you lied. A police officer was redeployed and then suspended because of your lies. And I know about the damage you caused to that officer's car. You passed on your lies to a reporter who published them in a newspaper.

TQ: (Interrupting) She's the one who told me about all the

childminders who abuse the children. Then, when I found out that Beverley was related to a copper, she said that the police were corrupt and, by working together, we could prove you were all closing ranks to protect her. She said that if we got the story into the paper, it would make our case stronger.

JR: Do you know why stories of abusive childminders or corrupt police make the papers? It's because it is so rare. Most are good people. If it was happening every day, as you are implying, it wouldn't be newsworthy.

MT: Most tragic of all this is, Jonathan died…

I didn't need to read more than that. Tracey had finally admitted that Beverley was not responsible. I didn't care if she was charged with anything, and I didn't care whether her sister ever spoke to her again or not. Jonathan was gone and nothing would ever change that. I had to have a think about Anne Leigh's part in this, though. With that interview and the information Irene got about Anne's sacking, I might have the basis of a claim against her. The brass wouldn't like it, but they hadn't had their reputations dragged through the mud. I'd take advice on it.

Chapter Twenty-Six

I drove around to Ma Thompson's for a cup of tea, as per her invitation all those weeks ago. The added bonus was that I'd see Bev too, now she was staying there. Ma Thompson showed me into the back room which now doubled as Terry and Bev's living room, and brought in tea and biscuits while Bev and I chatted.

'Come and join us, Ma,' Bev said.

'Oh no, I'll let you two youngsters chatter in peace. I need to make a start on dinner.' Ma Thompson walked towards the door then paused. 'Did you tell Samantha about that social worker?'

'No, thanks for reminding me,' Beverley said.

Ma Thompson left and I turned to Bev. 'What happened?'

'It was Alma. She turned up to tell me that they had had a meeting and had decided that they were going to reinstate me, but I would be subjected to six-monthly checks instead of annual for a couple of years, as well as the spot visits. She spoke to me as if they were doing me a big favour. She was quite taken aback when I told her to get lost.'

'I can see your reluctance, but it is a way to earn a living whilst still being there for your own kids,' I said.

'Never again. There will always be sidelong looks and suspicion, and that's just from the social services. I've got an interview lined up next Thursday as a medical secretary at the general hospital. 9:30am until 3pm, four days a week. Ma said she'd take the kids during school holidays so I can continue working.'

I didn't doubt that Bev would get the job; she'd been a top-notch secretary before she married Terry and had the kids.

'Do you think you'll miss working from home?' I asked.

She thought for a moment. 'At first, but I don't have any regrets about leaving childminding. The only thing I do regret is that I wasn't able to go to Jonathan's funeral.'

'Judith was amenable to you visiting the grave,' I reminded her.

'Yeah. Do you have time to go now?'

'I don't have to be anywhere. Let's do it. We can stop at the supermarket on the way to buy flowers or something.'

Half an hour later, I drove my car through ornate gates and slowly up the long, straight avenue that led to the chapels at the cemetery.

'Which way at the top?' I asked.

Beverley consulted the sheet she held. 'Right. Then it's on the right, almost opposite the garden of remembrance.'

I turned right and then I could see flashes of colour and sparkles.

'I see it.' I pulled over and, each carrying a little offering in a bag, Beverley and I walked across the grass to the area that had been set aside for children. I had never been to this part of the cemetery and I was moved almost to tears by the terrible dichotomy of sparkling wind chimes, colourful toys, little windmills and balloons resting against headstones.

I stopped by a small, bare, unmarked grave. This was the resting place of baby Rose. I had made enquiries after her father's arrest. Since she had no family to visit her, I had it in mind to bring flowers. From my bag, I fished out a posy of plastic flowers I had spotted at the supermarket and laid it on the ground. It was a little breezy, so I pushed the wire stem into the ground to keep it in place.

'Roses for Rose.' I murmured.

I closed my eyes and recalled her tiny, peaceful face as she lay lifeless in my arms. Eric had found time to arrange a quiet funeral for his daughter. I wished he had told me when it was; I would have attended. Now, the only care this grave would get would be the occasional grass cutting by the cemetery staff. There would be no headstone. Nobody would be visiting to leave little tokens or to remember Rose. Eventually, Cathy would, maybe, but that wouldn't be for a long time. She had gone far beyond the baby blues and was still very unwell. At least now the grave looked less bare and the flowers would not fade for a very long time. I might call back to replace them sometime.

'Over here,' Bev called.

I joined her at a grave on the other side of the plot flanked by similar graves, one with a teddy and the other with a toy fire engine resting on it. There was no headstone on Jonathan's grave but I expected that one would appear in the near future.

'What were you doing?' she asked.

'Another goodbye. You don't know her.' I pointed at the grave in front of us. 'Is this it?'

Bev nodded. She was visibly upset. We stared at the grave for a minute, listening to the windchimes and fluttering of paper windmills, then Bev placed a small box of blocks on the grave.

'It seemed a fitting thing to bring. He always loved building things,' she said.

'And knocking them down,' I added. I swallowed the lump in my throat, knelt beside the grave and added my own small package: more blocks.

'Great minds, eh?' Bev said, kneeling beside me.

I tipped out the contents of both boxes, then built them into a tower.

'The last time I saw him I promised him that I would build another tower.'

We stood up and silently regarded the grave again. I put my arm around Bev who was weeping into her handkerchief.

'Let's go back now.'

We took a few steps towards the car when a noise made us turn around. The blocks had fallen across the top of the grave.

For a moment I was back in Bev's house listening to Jonathan's delighted giggle as he demolished my tower.

'Wind's getting high,' I said.

We walked back to the car arm in arm.

*

Saturday mornings were always busy with shoplifters. When the town was heaving with shoppers, it was easy for them to slip away with odd items. I got to know the regulars.

Many people assume that one shoplifter is like any other, but there were several different types. The first was the younger kids who would try to get away with sweets. Usually a stern talking-to and a word with the parents put them right. The next were older kids who would go into the larger stores. Girls would be caught taking makeup. We always brought those in and contacted their parents. If it was a first offence and the property had been recovered, the bridewell sergeant would sometimes issue a caution then send them away with a flea in their ear.

Then there were the adults. Some would steal for the thrill. They might not need the item they had taken, and they might have enough money to pay for it, but they would try to get away without paying. Strangely, some menopausal women would fall into this group. Often they would be ashamed and unable to explain why they had shoplifted. I knew of at least one who had collected a long record of theft after a blameless life.

Others would steal to fund their addiction. They would take anything that could be sold on to raise money for drugs or alcohol. Personally, I would rather they shoplifted than rob someone, but, that didn't mean I wasn't going to arrest them. Shoplifting was not a victimless crime.

Then there were the career shoplifters. They might have no reason to steal other than they saw no reason to pay if they could get it for free. They regarded arrest as an occupational hazard. They were compliant and there were no hard feelings on either side. These were also the hardest to deal with.

Usually, I tried to help my prisoners make better choices in the future. I would speak to parents; I would contact social services if I thought someone needed support. I would recommend someone make an appointment with their doctor in case medication would help them. The latter group just didn't care. They didn't want help; they simply didn't want to pay.

The last category of shoplifter was the saddest. The person who would be stopped with a few essentials. I hated attending a shoplifter call and finding a skinny pensioner with a tin of corned beef, or a worn-out mother with baby milk. These weren't natural thieves, they acted from desperation. In these cases, I would ascertain how much money the offender had, then try to persuade the store manager to accept payment for the goods. Once or twice, I paid for the items myself. Most managers were happy to go along with this. Usually, they were following their head office's policy by phoning the police, and they didn't care how we chose to deal with it. Their box had been ticked. I always followed one of these jobs with a phone call to an aid agency. It was amazing how many people were not claiming what they were entitled to.

This particular Saturday, several of us were in the bridewell dealing with our prisoners. I was taking fingerprints when I heard a car horn announce the arrival of another prisoner. That was the cue to open the gate to the cage and allow the Panda car to enter. The gate would then be closed and then the prisoner would be transferred into the bridewell. It was a well-practised, slick procedure. I thought no more of it.

Fingerprinting completed, I escorted my prisoner to the waiting area and took the fingerprint sheet to the charge office to be added to the charge sheet. The outside door from the cage opened and in walked Anne Leigh, escorted by Charlotte, who was carrying a plastic bag.

Anne spotted me immediately but chose to look away. I couldn't resist it.

'Anne Leigh! What are you doing here?'

She scowled but didn't answer me.

'Is this an exposé of bridewell practices?' I asked.

'What the hell are you talking about?' Charlotte asked. 'This is a shoplifter from the supermarket.'

'This is Anne Leigh, she's a journalist. She thinks all police are corrupt and has dedicated herself to uncovering the truth, not that she would recognise it, so hide the electrodes and cat o' nine tails.'

'You what?' Charlotte eyed her prisoner. 'Are you an undercover journalist?'

'She is a journalist,' I confirmed. 'Not a good one. She got sacked from her paper for misconduct.' I addressed Anne. 'So, are you undercover or are you just a common shoplifter?'

'I could complain about you for that,' Anne snarled.

'Go ahead,' I invited her. With her history, I knew I didn't have anything to worry about. 'Speak to Irene about her,' I told Charlotte. 'And when you search her, make sure you keep a look out for recording devices.'

'Next!' called the bridewell sergeant.

Charlotte put the bag on the charge desk and said, 'I have arrested this woman for shoplifting. She attempted to leave the store without making any attempt to pay for the items in this bag. She was detained by store security…'

As she spoke, the bridewell sergeant emptied the bag. A tin of tomato soup, a tin of peas, a pack of spaghetti, a loaf. Basics. Had it been anyone else, I would have felt deeply sorry for them, but too much had happened. Anne's face burned red. She knew I was watching. When she turned my way, I gave a small, fake sympathetic smile and slowly shook my head.

I recalled Eric talking about fate. Anne had been a bitch and I loved that fate was doing its thing and had allowed me to witness her humiliation. I gathered my papers and went to the report writing room.

I quickly finished the paperwork for my prisoner's file and was about to fill in the holiday dates form when I became aware of a presence behind me. I turned around and saw Webby standing in the door.

'So you do know where the writing room is,' he said.

'Sir?'

He whisked a form from behind his back and plonked it in front of me. It was an application for a CID aide's course.

'Fill that in.'

'Now?'

'No, next bloody Christmas. Yes, now!'

'Yes, sir.'

He didn't move. 'Well, go on then.'

Feeling more than self-conscious, I pushed aside my file and filled in the form under DI Webb's gaze. When I had finished, he picked it up, scanned it, grunted once and left the room. It looked like I had finally submitted my application for my CID aide's course.

THE END

Did You Enjoy This Book?

If so, you can make a HUGE difference.

For any author, the single most important way we have of getting our books noticed is a really simple one—and one which you can help with.

Yes, you.

Us indie authors and publishers don't have the financial muscle of the big guys to take out full-page ads in the newspaper or put posters on the subway.

But we do have something much more powerful and effective than that, and it's something that those big publishers would kill to get their hands on.

A committed and loyal bunch of readers.

Honest reviews of our books help bring them to the attention of other readers.

If you've enjoyed this book I would be really grateful if you could spend just a couple of minutes leaving a review (it can be as short as you like) on this book's page on your favourite store and website.

Acknowledgements

This is a work of fiction. I feel the need to say this out loud because a couple of people have come to me with suggestions as to who some of the characters are in real life. They are not based on any particular person. The locations are based on real places, although I have put them in different areas and given them different names.

Anyway, now that's out of the way, there are some people I'd like to thank.

Thanks to those nice people at Burning Chair publishing. I'm so grateful that they saw promise in my submission and helped me make it better.

Thanks to the beta readers. Their observations and feedback is invaluable.

Thanks to hubby, Paul, for his willingness to spend evenings in our local chatting with me about murder scenes and how easy it would be to move a body. (Apologies to the people on the next table for alarming them, but Clatterbridge Roundabout would be a great place to dump a corpse.)

Thanks to the late Jenny O'Brien. It was through her and my friend, Christine, that I found Burning Chair. I will always be grateful.

Thanks to my lovely mum, Jean, who always said I could be a "proper writer". I miss you xx.

About The Author

Trish Finnegan has spent her whole life living on the Wirral, a small peninsula that sticks out into the Irish Sea between North Wales and Liverpool. She has always had an overactive imagination and enjoyed writing and reading, sometimes to the detriment of her schoolwork.

She first met her husband, Paul, in the charge office of a police station: where they both were serving as police officers. She has three grown up children and currently spends her time wrangling grandchildren and writing.

More From Burning Chair Publishing

Your next favourite new read is waiting for you…!

The Blue Bird Series, by Trish Finnegan
    Blue Bird
    Blue Sky

The Tom Novak series, by Neil Lancaster
    Going Dark
    Going Rogue
    Going Back

Killer in the Crowd, by P N Johnson

Run to the Blue, by P N Johnson

Burning Bridges, by Matthew Ross

Push Back, by James Marx

The Casebook of Johnson & Boswell, by Andrew Neil Macleod
    The Fall of the House of Thomas Weir
    The Stone of Destiny

By Richard Ayre:
Shadow of the Knife
Point of Contact
A Life Eternal

The Curse of Becton Manor, by Patricia Ayling

Near Death, by Richard Wall

The Haven Chronicles, by Fi Phillips
Haven Wakes
Magic Bound

Love Is Dead(ly), by Gene Kendall

Beyond, by Georgia Springate

10:59, by N R Baker

The Other Side of Trust, by Neil Robinson

The Sarah Black Series, by Lucy Hooft
The King's Pawn
The Head of the Snake

The Brodick Cold War Series, by John Fullerton
Spy Game
Spy Dragon

The Great Big Demon Hunting Agency, by Peter Oxley

The Infernal Aether series, by Peter Oxley
The Infernal Aether
A Christmas Aether
The Demon Inside

Beyond the Aether
The Old Lady of the Skies: 1: Plague

The Wedding Speech Manual, by Peter Oxley

www.burningchairpublishing.com

About Burning Chair

Burning Chair is an independent publishing company based in the UK, but covering readers and authors around the globe. We are passionate about both writing and reading books and, at our core, we just want to get great books out to the world.

Our aim is to offer something exciting; something innovative; something that puts the author and their book first. From first class editing to cutting edge marketing and promotion, we provide the care and attention that makes sure every book fulfils its potential.

We are:
- Different
- Passionate
- Nimble and cutting edge
- Invested in our authors' success

If you are interested in hearing more about our books, being the first to hear about our new releases or great offers, or becoming a beta reader for us, please visit:

www.burningchairpublishing.com

BABY BLUES

BV - #0044 - 190623 - C0 - 203/127/16 - PB - 9781912946389 - Gloss Lamination